AUTUMN KING

CAMILLA OCHLAN
CAROL E. LEEVER
OF CATS AND DRAGONS BOOK 5

Copyright

Autumn King

Cover illustration: Samantha Key

Visit our website at OfCatsAndDragons.com

Like us on Facebook @OfCatsAndDragons

ISBN: 978-1-7932490-0-5

Dedication

Für meine Mama.
-Camilla

For my Mother, T.O.Q.
-Carol

CONTENTS

Timeline of Books

Counted from the year of the last Covenant, 14,000 years ago.

❖

14,021 *Autumn:* Night's Gift (Book 1)
14,021 *Winter:* Winter Tithe (Novella)

❖

14,022 *Spring:* Radiation (Book 2)
14,022 *Summer:* Summer's Fall (Book 3)
14,022 *Summer:* Hollow Season (Book 4)
14,022 *Summer:* Autumn King (Book 5)
14,022 *Summer:* Solstice Thyme (short story)

❖

You can get Night's Gift (Book 1 e-book) for free when you sign up for the Of Cats And Dragons Newsletter.

Radiation (Book 2 e-book) is also available for free when you sign up for the Of Cats And Dragons Newsletter.

We offer Winter Tithe as a seasonal gift for our newsletter subscribers.

Solstice Thyme will soon be available on our website at OfCatsAndDragons.com

Chapter 1: Wyverns

OMEN

Unable to see at first, Omen oriented himself toward the roars. A slight change in temperature and a rush of foul breath hit him. His nostrils flinched at the stink of rotten eggs and dusty decay.

Smells like someone needs a mint.

Omen's eyesight swam back into focus, and he quickly scanned his surroundings.

The wild portal had deposited the companions at the bottom of a shale pit that looked to be half the length of a galleon and at least twenty feet deep. In the center rested a carved stone platform very much like the rune-covered square in Kadana's forest. The sides of the pit rose at a shallow angle to firmer ground, which in turn sloped upward to the enormous mountain towering above them. Its craggy peaks sparkled in the harsh morning sun.

Too close to Omen, three grey dragon-like creatures thrashed around, flapping leathery wings furiously and belching out guttural gnarls in a dissonant chorus. Each was easily large enough to bring down a warhorse.

Long scaly bodies . . . lizard heads . . . oversized bat wings . . . two legs . . . nasty teeth. And they stink. Omen scrutinized his opponents. *Sure enough, wyverns.*

"Get behind me," he hissed at Kyr and positioned himself in front of the boy. Then he tossed his backpack on the ground, freeing his movements.

Kyr, Tyrin swaying on his shoulder, grabbed the discarded pack and moved a safe distance away, but Tormy stalked

1

forward and stood at Omen's side. Orange coat on end, sticking out from beneath his saddle, Tormy looked three times his actual size. He snarled, baring fierce teeth and wrinkling his nose.

Omen saw that the others had spread out, taking up the far corners. They faced several more large lizard beasts who had wasted no time advancing on them. His companions had all drawn their weapons, and Dev and Liethan were already firing at the beasts — employing bow and crossbow respectively.

Just beyond them, a cluster of several more wyverns wriggled through the opening of a rounded cave. Foul-tempered, the creatures pushed and snapped at each other with great annoyance.

Like dinner's been served. Alarming.

Curiously, the creatures all swung a respectful distance around the portal stone, avoiding it as they advanced.

Omen took in the three beasts advancing on him and noted how their powerful legs tapered into long thick feet and ended in filthy clawed toes.

Talons long as swords. At least wyverns don't typically breathe fire, he thought, hoping he remembered his lessons on minor dragon kind correctly.

The wyverns' maws thrust forth, the creatures angrily displaying rows of sharp teeth formidable as jagged daggers.

"What by Night's pants are those things?" Nikki shouted from across the length of the pit. Protected by the armor Kadana had given him, he held the mace he'd been using against the orclets in one hand and a Deldano shield in the other.

"Wyverns! Hit their heads!" Templar hollered, bone

swords drawn. He too had dropped his backpack, leaving him free to move swiftly. "They're vicious!"

Nikki and Templar stood back-to-back; a wyvern faced each of the men.

Shale crumbled under Omen's feet, and he had to steady himself. "Keep your balance!" he shouted. "If you fall down, they'll eat you."

But Omen had hesitated too long.

The nearest wyvern dove for Tormy. Fortunately, its only middling wings carried it with the same lack of precision and grace Omen had observed in chickens. Unfortunately, the wyvern was several times heavier than Tormy. Omen's blood ran cold as the creature crashed down on top of the cat.

But Tormy wriggled out of danger, compressing his body concertina-like, and then thrust himself forward, scratching and biting the vulnerable skin under the wyvern's extended wing.

The wyvern howled a pained shriek. Its large taloned feet shuffled backward a few steps, and it bumped the body of a fellow creature.

They're about as smart as chickens too.

Two wyverns launched for him, their black eyes like polished onyx, while the injured creature swung its head around and flapped its bloodied underwing.

Sword ready, Omen mumbled the words of a common domestic cantrip used by his mother's cook to steam vegetables quickly. A jaunty tune springing to mind as he formed the required pattern in his head, he directed the spell at the moisture of his opponents' eyes. It wouldn't blind them for long, but drawing water from their shiny eyes and boiling it even for a moment would buy Omen time.

The wyverns hesitated as the searing pain flicked across their corneas.

Omen swung his great sword at one pulsing throat, drew back fluidly, and stabbed through the other's chest. He'd wounded both beasts enough for them to pull away and backward crawl toward the large cavern they'd emerged from. Black blood dripped from their wounds, coating the ground and sending more creatures scrambling toward the smell.

"Shalonie's in trouble," Kyr shouted from behind him.

Across the pit, Shalonie and Liethan faced a single wyvern, while Dev — now in the center next to the portal square — shot arrows into the mess of wyverns emerging from the cave on the far side. Liethan had tossed aside his crossbow and drawn his sword as the creatures had closed in. Shalonie held her golden dragonscale sword in her left hand, her sword arm hanging limply at her side. Bright blood welled from her right shoulder, and her face was pale as if she were going into shock.

Sword arm wounded!

Liethan hacked at the beast with his own blade, but it kept its distance, weaving its head to take sneaky bites at both Shalonie and Liethan.

Omen wanted to rush to their side, but the two wyverns he had injured and the one clawed by Tormy blocked him from storming ahead.

Templar and Nikki battled two creatures in relative unison near the pit's other corner. What Nikki lacked in training, he made up in strength and courage. He soundly walloped the side of a wyvern's head with the heavy mace, years of hard labor making him as strong as any trained warrior. But one of the beast's clawed feet angled up with enough reach to rake across Nikki's thigh.

Templar, bone blades in both hands, had woven a web of blue lightning around his body. He moved with deadly speed and accuracy, striking his own opponent with the one blade — lightning surrounded the creature's head and sent it to the ground — while driving his other blade through the beast's eye socket. Immediately, Templar rushed another creature, blades whirling as he shouted Terizkandian challenges, drawing attention to himself and away from the others.

But even given all of Templar's skill, Omen realized in a sickening flash that they were facing too many of the creatures. *The sides of the pit are too steep. They'll get us if we try to make it to the forest. We're trapped!* Even more wyverns poured out of their cavern. *There has to be another way.*

"I is seeing a tiny cave!" he heard Tyrin cry. Omen snapped his head around to see the little cat sprinting toward another round cave opening directly behind them. Kyr bolted after Tyrin without hesitation.

Starless Night!

"Protect Kyr!" Omen screamed after Tormy, who'd already leaped in the direction Kyr and Tyrin were running.

From across the pit, Dev glanced after the boy and the cats even as he fired off several more arrows. "He's right! The cave is too small for the wyverns!" he shouted toward Omen.

Templar downed his second wyvern with a whoop, leaving Nikki free to run to Shalonie's aid. The young man moved in front of the woman, shield held before him as he caught a heavy blow from the wyvern attacking Shalonie.

5

The wyvern's claws screeched across the shield's surface as Nikki pushed it back.

"Let's go!" Nikki yelled at Shalonie and Liethan. He bashed at the wyvern's flank with his mace, hitting it soundly. The creature briefly shifted its attention from Shalonie and Liethan in snapping pursuit of Nikki.

As if they'd rehearsed the maneuver, Nikki, Shalonie, and Liethan simultaneously started running in different directions, leaving the wyvern confused and frustrated. It howled and flapped its wings, kicking up dust and dirt.

Out of arrows, Dev drew his sword and sprinted toward the wyverns closing in on Omen. He brought his sword down on one tail, lopping the appendage off with one clean stroke.

Omen lashed out with his psionics, pushing all the creatures back with one hard shove and sending them scrambling to regain their footing — allowing the others to move in his direction. He and Templar took up forward positions, standing side by side as they faced down the attacking mob. Omen's only thought was to follow Kyr. Panic for what horrors could meet Kyr and the cats in the tunnel drove him forward, caution giving way to battle rage.

Long teeth grazed his side, but Omen twisted through the pain. The dearly won close proximity allowed him access to the biting wyvern's exposed neck. He hauled his blade back and drove it down into the wyvern's pulsing artery. Hot, dark blood shot out from between its grey scales and drenched Omen's face.

"Urgh, their blood stinks!" Templar hissed in disgust. He'd killed another of the advancing wyverns with his bone blades — striking yet another with the shimmering bolts of electricity that sparked around him.

"Get Shalonie into the cave!" Dev shouted to Liethan and Nikki as he pulled off his backpack and tossed it to Liethan. "We'll hold them off!" He then leaped onto the back of one of the creatures and sank his blade into its spine, bringing it crashing to the ground, while Nikki grabbed Templar's pack and Liethan's crossbow and retreated with Liethan and Shalonie toward the cave.

Dev rolled off the creature as it hit the ground and jumped to his feet a moment later, joining Omen and Templar in guarding the retreat.

The wave of wyverns rose before them, dozens now crawling over the bodies of their fallen nestmates as they rushed forward to strike. Their flapping black wings raised a screen of dust all around them, and their roars were deafening. Omen, Dev, and Templar backed away slowly, allowing the rest of the companions to make it into the small cave opening Tyrin had seen. Then, nearly as one, all three turned and ran for safety.

Chapter 2: Darkness

OMEN

Omen motioned Dev and Templar into the small cave opening the others had disappeared through while he raised a pounding song in his mind, forming a familiar pattern. He released it all in one violent burst, pushing back the horde of wyverns bearing down on them, giving them all another hard shove with his psionics. The creatures stumbled back and into each other. They roared and beat their wings, biting at one another in rage — giving Omen enough time to dive after Templar and follow him into the cave.

As Tyrin had announced, the cave itself was small — Omen had to hunch over to clear the entrance, and only a few feet in, he found himself crouching down, head ducked to avoid the roof. There was a faint light up ahead — the tiny blue glow of a candlelight cantrip most likely cast by Shalonie.

Templar quickly snapped a brighter ball of light into the air, lighting up the darkened cave and lengthening shadows all around them — the light bounced against the top of the cave as it strove unsuccessfully to rise higher in the air.

Omen glanced behind him. The wyverns had recovered from his psionic push and were now crowding around the cavern entrance. Several stuck their heads into the cave's opening, their long necks allowing them to reach several feet in — but even the smallest beast was too large to enter beyond its head and neck. They clawed angrily at the cavern opening, flying at the rock wall and digging their talons into the shale as they attempted to widen it more.

Shale is soft! Omen thought, alarmed. The rock in the main pit outside had all been broken sediment. The wyverns would be able to dig through easily enough. Indeed the opening was already crumbling as they pulled at it.

"They're digging through!" he called ahead to the others. With Templar in front of him, he couldn't see anything more than the dancing shadows cast by the magical light.

"Come in farther!" Liethan called back. "There's a carved tunnel here — it's solid stone. They won't be able to dig through that."

Awkwardly, Dev, Templar, and Omen crouch-walked deeper into the cave — the tight fit made it difficult to maneuver while wearing armor and carrying weapons.

How did Tormy squeeze through here?

"Is everyone all right?" Omen called out again, his fear for Kyr and the cats growing. Kyr had no means of casting light. *The kid followed Tyrin into total darkness without thought.* Granted the cats could probably see far better than any of them in the dim light — though it occurred to him that Kyr was also half-elvin. *His eyesight might be better than I think.* What the elvin races lacked in size and the brute strength of their human cousins, they more than made up for with their superior senses.

"Kyr and the cats are fine!" Liethan called back to him, no doubt guessing Omen's first concern. "Shalonie's hurt. Keep coming — the tunnel widens out in a few more feet."

Tormy must have belly-crawled through here! Dragon spit! Alarm flared through Omen's mind as he pictured the large cat chasing after his two small companions. *He was still wearing his saddle — how did he follow Tyrin and Kyr? I'm going to have figure out a way for him to get the saddle off himself in an emergency. Wonder if Tormy is capable of learning some minor cantrips.*

As Liethan had promised, the small cave led into a smooth cut tunnel, though it too was no larger than the cave had been. Omen placed his hand against the wall: smooth stone, granite perhaps, carved with precision. *Dwarfkin, most likely,* he thought. It would certainly explain the diminutive size — dwarfkin tunnels were not built for men.

They moved in farther, at least another fifty feet into the tunnel and far enough away that the wyvern screams were muted behind them. Then, as Liethan had promised, the tunnel widened out into a larger room. As Templar's magical light flew into the room and bounced against the low ceiling, Omen could clearly see all the others sitting in a circle, waiting for them. The room was much wider, but it wasn't much taller, and none of them could stand upright.

Tormy was belly down on the far side of the room, front paws stretched out with Kyr sitting between them practically buried in the cat's fur. Omen noticed the way one of Tormy's paws curved around the boy — no doubt holding him firmly in place. Kyr, his face set with fear, clutched Tyrin to his chest. The boy's eyes widened when he saw Omen, a grin lighting up his features as he smiled in relief. Omen smiled back, silently thanking Tormy for doing as he'd asked and watching the boy.

Shalonie was sitting nearby, her coat removed as she examined the long bleeding gash in her right arm — it extended from her shoulder all the way down to her elbow — two jagged openings that Omen guessed were caused by a wyvern's claws. Beside her, Nikki was attempting to stop the bleeding by pressing the length of a rolled up shirt to the wound — his opened backpack beside him suggested he'd simply grabbed the first thing he could find.

"Were you bitten?" Templar asked the girl quickly as he moved toward her. He snatched up his backpack from the pile in the center of the room and started rooting through it. Dev moved to pull one of the packs from Tormy's saddle, no doubt seeking out the medical supplies Kadana's servants had packed.

Despite the wound, Shalonie was calm; her face was pale from pain, but she made no other sign of her injury. Omen suspected she was using a psionic pain-blocking technique to dampen the effects of the injury. "No," she told them. "When I came through the portal I landed right on top of one of the wyverns — it snagged me with its claws as it was trying to get away."

"I can probably seal the edges together," Omen told Templar, "but it could get infected." Omen knew a bit about dealing with minor injuries, but Templar had a great deal more experience with battle wounds. He'd repeatedly claimed his Nightblood heritage made him ill-suited for healing, but that didn't change the fact that he'd studied in an Elder Temple and had spent a number of years being tutored by a healer in his father's service.

"I can clean the wound and stop the bleeding," Templar assured him.

"Use this as well," Dev told them, tossing Templar a small vial of ointment. Omen recognized the ointment his mother had made for Kyr's hex-burn. It would insure the wound would not become infected.

Templar turned his attention back to Shalonie, his hands raised and glowing with a golden light that reminded Omen of the sunlight spell he'd cast at Kadana's keep. Warmth radiated from the light, striking all of them, and washing over Omen with a calming sensation that eased his heart from the frantic pounding kindled by the wyvern attack. Bemused, he watched as Templar focused that light on Shalonie's wound, the blood seeping from the torn flesh slowing immediately. Beside him, he saw Dev shaking his head in silent disbelief.

He doesn't understand how a Nightblood can even use such magic. Mother says it's highly unusual as well — even Templar's human side should not be able to compensate for the inverse nature of his blood and magic.

When Templar was done, he smeared the sweet-smelling ointment onto the opening and then inclined his head to Omen, who reached out to place one hand on Shalonie's shoulder and another on her forearm near the bottom of the wound. "You're using a pain-blocking pattern?" he asked her. "Which one?"

"Zelgan's ninth," she replied, and Omen was guiltily reminded that his father had been attempting to teach him the patterns for years, but he'd only ever bothered to learn up to the third pattern. His body healed so quickly, he rarely had any use for the more powerful pain-blocking patterns.

I have got to start studying more!

He searched through his repertoire of psionic patterns for a suitable weaving pattern. To properly harmonize with Zelgan's ninth, he'd need to use Breckan's fifth at least and he'd only learned up to the fourth.

Shalonie second-guessed him, and despite the wound, he saw a faint flicker of amusement in her blue eyes. "I can stop — or switch," she told him.

Omen scratched at his chin. "Zelgan's second would be

better," he told her. "And remember, don't try to aid me with the mending." As long as she didn't try to actively join her psionics to his, he should be able to do what was necessary.

Shalonie nodded and closed her eyes, focusing on the shift in the pattern. He heard the intake of breath from the girl even as he felt the shift in the magic around her. Zelgan's second wasn't nearly as effective as the ninth.

He quickly focused his own mind, the music of the pattern rising within him, harmonizing against the vibration he could feel coming from Shalonie. He pushed his power down through his hands and into Shalonie's body. He felt his power vibrate briefly against the staccato rhythm of Shalonie's psionic shield, but in moments the two energies harmonized, and he was able to focus his attention on weaving the edges of her flesh back together.

It took several minutes, but when he was done he opened his eyes and saw the results. Her arm had raw-looking dark lines running down the length of it, but the edges of the torn skin had mended, sealing off the wound from the air around it. The flesh beneath wasn't entirely healed — it would take a few more weeks at least — but the wound was closed and would not worsen.

"It's going to be sore," Omen warned her.

"I'll be fine," she assured him. "Not my first injury."

"You two are healers?" Nikki sounded somewhat awed. But both Templar and Omen just laughed at the suggestion.

"No," Templar denied as he carefully bound Shalonie's wound with the bandages he'd retrieved from his pack. "We can both manage in a pinch — but this isn't much of anything. Her wound wasn't that serious. What about you? One of the wyverns caught your leg."

Nikki shifted aside the folds of his coat-hem so that they could see that both of his legs were bound in pieces of leather armor coated in thin black metal scales similar to the coat he was wearing. "Lady Kadana . . . Grandmother . . . insisted I wear these. I thought she was being overprotective, but they turned the claws easily. I'm a bit bruised — but they didn't break the skin."

"What about the rest of you?" Templar asked, turning to look at all the others.

Omen had felt the claws of one of the wyverns scraping his side, and he took a moment to pull open his coat to see the damage. The silverleaf scales of his jerkin were scratched, but still whole — and the painful bruising he'd felt earlier was already gone, faded as his body healed itself.

Satisfied they were all whole, Omen glanced around the small room they were in — only now realizing that while the room was certainly an improvement over the tiny tunnel they'd been in earlier, it was actually a dead end. Beyond the tunnel, there were no other passageways. The walls were all cut from the same smooth stone, and only the far wall looked different — made of hundreds of tiny interlocking rectangles of stone like some sort of granite tartan.

"How are we getting out of here?" he asked out loud. "Those wyverns aren't going to leave. And what is this place anyway? I'm guessing it's dwarfkin made."

"It is," Shalonie agreed. "And the only way out is through there — that's a dwarfkin puzzle door." She pointed toward the interlocking stones in the far wall.

"I thought it looked familiar!" Liethan exclaimed, excitement in his voice. "My father has several dwarfkin puzzle boxes. The pieces all slide — you have to put them in

14

the correct configuration and then the box opens." He moved toward the wall, kneeling in front of it as he put his hands on the stone pieces. A low, grating sound echoed through the room as he slid several of the small stone rectangles to one side. He threw a grin over his shoulder to the others. "We just have to figure out the correct pattern."

"Any idea what that might be?" Omen asked, staring at the wall in fascination.

"No." Liethan slid several more pieces around — entire rows of blocks would move when they were lined up correctly — the rest locked in place. "But give me some time and I'll get it — I was always good with these puzzles. Got all the boxes opened eventually."

"So we're going deeper into the tunnels then?" Nikki asked.

"Don't really have much choice," Dev replied. "Only way out of here is back through those wyverns."

"I is wondering what wyvern is tasting like?" Tormy asked, causing Omen to grin despite everything.

"Taste just like chicken," Dev replied without hesitation. "Bit tough, but edible."

Both cats turned to look back down the tunnel toward the distant wyvern cries.

Omen moved to block their view of the tunnel. "No, we are not going back to eat the wyverns," he told both of them as he winked at Kyr who looked relieved. Omen reached for the straps of Tormy's saddle, unfastening them so that the cat could move more easily through the narrow passageway.

Liethan continued to push and press against the stones of the puzzle wall, sliding the rows and columns around one way after another. The others watched, all equally absorbed by the ingenious creation. Several times they all heard distinctive clicks as if something had locked in place back behind the wall, and Liethan's grin widened each time.

Omen guessed the click was a good sign. "Well, I suppose this is one way of getting into the Mountain," he commented. "But not quite what I was expecting. I figured we'd have to climb it first — find a tunnel up at the peak. My mother always referenced going 'down into' the Mountain."

"There are many ways into the Mountain," Shalonie replied.

"I think I've got it!" Liethan exclaimed after several more minutes of sliding the panels around. He pushed another row of blocks, and they all heard another distinctive click — this time however several more rows moved on their own, sliding about until their edges all lined up, showing the clear outline of a door in the wall. Liethan pushed against it, and the door swung inward, grating against the ground with a low rasping hum. A long dark tunnel much like the one behind them showed beyond — the light from Templar's spell only reached a few feet in before fading to total blackness.

"This is likely to be a one-way passage," Shalonie warned the others as they gathered around the opening to peer in. Like the passageway they'd just come from, this one was built for much smaller creatures. Tormy would have to crawl to get through.

"One-way?" Omen asked.

"There's likely a pressure plate farther in that will close the puzzle door behind us," Shalonie explained. "I doubt it can be opened from the other side."

"Well, with those wyverns we can't go back anyway, so it's a moot point. We have to go forward," Omen decided.

"I'll go first. If there's anything blocking the way, I can probably clear it psionically. Tormy, you take up the rear."

The large cat nodded, staring down the tunnel curiously. His nose was twitching, his ears perked forward as he tried to catch sounds in the darkness.

At Omen's prompting, Templar sent his magical light into the tunnel ahead of them. Omen picked up his back-pack from where Kyr had dragged it. He adjusted the straps of the pack, lengthening them so that he could wear it much lower on his back. There wasn't enough room in the tunnel for anything else. He'd have to carry his sword in his hands — along with Tormy's saddle.

The others set about adjusting their own gear. Nikki insisted on taking Shalonie's pack as well, even though she assured him she could manage. They also distributed the saddle bags attached to Tormy's saddle among themselves, giving both Dev's bow and Liethan's crossbow to Kyr to carry. Once done, they followed Omen one by one into the dark tunnel.

Led by the magical light, Omen half-crouched. "Will you be all right, Tormy?" Omen called back over his shoulder as he moved ahead slowly. The light showed a long passageway ahead of him that disappeared into lurking blackness.

"I is good, Omy!" Tormy called out. With Tormy blocking the opening behind them, they could no longer see the doorway. But they all heard the distinctive sound of stone sliding against stone when the door behind them slid shut as Shalonie had predicted.

Omen glanced down at his feet. The floor beneath him hadn't felt any different, but he thought he detected a faint depression in the stone he was standing on, as if it had sunk some tiny distance. *Pressure plates!* They had nowhere else to go but forward.

Omen pressed on, a slow deep burn developing in his legs as he walked hunched over. Despite the natural coolness of the underground, he found himself sweating, the progress forward difficult. There was a sense of heavy weight all around him — as if the mountain itself were pressing down on them, and he found himself more than once deliberately forcing his thoughts away from images of the tunnel collapsing.

Don't think about it! he told himself, pushing forward after the magical light. Despite the brightness of the glowing ball of magic, he could only see about ten feet ahead of him. He suspected it was probably worse for those behind him — he blocked a great deal of light from reaching the others. And the tunnel seemed endless — each step just showing more tunnel beyond the sphere of light.

He couldn't really tell if they were going up or down. There were times when he thought the slope of the tunnel changed, but after a while he wasn't sure which direction that might be. For all he knew, they were descending down deeper into the bowels of the earth.

"Omen, we should rest," Liethan called up to him after about an hour of walking. Omen turned quickly to look behind him — he could hear the heavy breathing of his companions, and in the glowing light he could see the look of concern on Templar's face.

Shalonie, Omen thought, worried. *She's probably exhausted — wounded as she is.* He motioned briefly to Templar, and they all paused where they were, sitting down in the narrow passageway.

"Shalonie? Everything all right?" Omen called down.

Kyr was just behind Templar, Dev behind him — but he couldn't see much beyond them save shadows and darkness.

"Yes," she called up to him, her voice muted, but loud enough that Omen could hear the exhaustion in her tone. "I'll be fine," she assured them all. "I've gone on archaeological digs worse than this with my father."

They passed canteens of water around, all of them drinking deeply. Omen retrieved a wooden bowl from one of the packs and passed it back to the others, instructing Liethan who was just in front of Tormy to give the large cat some water. Tyrin, who'd been sitting calmly in Kyr's coat pocket, hopped out and ran back down the tunnel toward Tormy — no doubt to drink some of the water from the bowl himself. Omen heard the muffled voices of the two cats coming from the darkness — they were discussing mice and tiny mice holes.

"You all right, Kyr?" Omen asked his brother. The boy had been unusually quiet the entire time they'd been inside the tunnels. He was also much smaller than the rest of them. While he couldn't walk completely upright in the tunnels, he didn't have to duck down nearly as far as the rest to move freely.

"The forest will be better," Kyr told him, the glint of amber in his violet eyes glowing in the magical light.

"I'm sure," Omen agreed.

They didn't rest for long — all of them anxious to get moving once they'd caught their breaths. They started up again — Omen leading the way as they continued down into the darkness, footfalls muted in the stifling depths.

Nearly an hour later, on the verge of calling for another break, Omen noticed a change in the light up ahead. The magical glowing ball he'd been following suddenly vanished from sight, shooting upward toward some unseen height before him. It flared brightly, illuminating an area beyond. "There's a room up ahead!" he called back with excitement and pushed forward quickly.

The tunnel exited into a very large, wide room: cut stones and pillars lining the walls, an arched ceiling overhead not unlike the inside of a castle ballroom. The glowing ball of light had moved upward into the open space. Omen stood with ease, gratefully stretching his back as he stared into the room before him.

The room was exceptionally huge. On the far side, Omen spotted a large archway — a soft blue glowing light emanating from the cold rock. *Almost looks like moonlight shining on the surface,* he thought, perplexed, despite there being no light source other than Templar's magical illumination. And though the stone arch was solid, Omen thought he could scent fresh air breezing in.

But between him and the archway lay a wide grid of broad paving stones with large numbers carved into the center of each. Before he could take a step onto the pavers toward the strangely illuminated wall, Shalonie's sharp voice stopped him — stopped all of them. "Don't move!" she shouted with alarm, freezing them where they stood — even Tormy who'd pushed through the tunnel and was arching his back, stretching his front paws, tail raised high in the air as if getting ready to pounce forward.

The girl's gaze was fixed on the numbered stones — her arms outstretched as if to hold everyone in place. "No one step on the grid!" she commanded with authority. "It's another puzzle. If you step on the wrong one. . ." When nothing more was forthcoming, they all exchanged baffled looks.

"If we step on the wrong one . . ." Omen prompted.

Shalonie's face had drained of all color. "Most likely the floor will collapse — there's probably a deadly drop below it. We have to step on the stones in the correct pattern to cross." She moved carefully forward, crouching down to study the edge of the grid where the first row started. She ran her fingers along the seam where the regular tiles of the cavern floor met the edge of the grid. Omen noticed the sand she brushed into the crack disappear from sight, indicating that the girl was right. There was nothing beneath it.

She moved toward the far edge of the grid — studying the seam along the side wall, then she moved back to study the other wall as well. When she returned, they could all see the concern in her eyes.

"If we trigger the wrong stone," she said, "the tiles all slide beneath the side walls, leaving a deep pit between this side and the other. Assuming you didn't fall to your death, there's no way to reset it from here. Probably another pressure plate on the far side that resets the grid if it opens."

"How do we get across?" Templar asked — they spread out along the back wall, keeping well away from the numbered tiles.

"It's a number puzzle," she stated, pointing to the numbers carved in each of the squares. The grid was made up of a row of five stones across, with seven rows in total spanning the length of the room. The first number on the first stone was the number *1*. The last number on the last stone in the far row was *400*. The numbers in between seemed random to Omen. "We just have to figure out the correct sequence of numbers — one tile per row."

"And you know what the sequence is?" Templar pressed.

Shalonie fixed her eyes on the numbers before her. "No, but I'll figure it out — just give me a minute."

"I is flying over it?" Tormy asked excitedly. He raised his left front paw, then placed it down, lifted his right front paw then placed it down, dancing back and forth between the paws as he wiggled his tail. His face was fixed in excited concentration, his ears flattened against his head.

Omen placed one hand against the cat's ruff, worried Tormy might hurt himself if he concentrated much harder. On the few occasions that Tormy had "flown" he'd done it in a panic, without thinking, acting solely on instinct. His attempt in the forest a few days ago had been nearly disastrous. If this was indeed going to be a skill he developed, Omen knew it would take the cat a lot of practicing before he could manage it at will. "Can you carry all of us and all our gear too, Tormy?" he asked the cat gently.

Tormy's whiskers twitched, and his head turned slowly as his eyes swept over the group. He let his breath out in a soft *humph* and sat down on his haunches as he wilted. "No, Omy." He flicked his ears back. "I is sorry."

Omen patted the cat's head. "That's all right, Tormy. Shalonie will figure it out. Don't worry."

Satisfied that the cat was going to stay put, Omen joined Shalonie at the edge of the stone grid. As he hopelessly studied the numbers, it occurred to him that they had a couple of lengths of rope. *Might be able to swing across the grid. But getting our gear and Tormy across . . . And once we get across, what then? The archway looks like a door, but it obviously isn't opened.*

"So this pattern," he asked Shalonie. "Is it a pattern in the numbers in each row, and you have to find the one number that doesn't fit? Or is a pattern in the columns of numbers?"

"I don't know," she admitted. "Could be either."

He looked at the first row: *1, 3, 4, 9, 13.* "Four is the only even number in the first row," he pointed out.

"There are two even numbers in the second row," she told him. The second row consisted of *20, 23, 30, 31* and *53.*

"Does it have to be the exact same pattern in each row? Maybe each row is a different pattern or sequence entirely," he suggested.

She paused, thinking over his guess. "That's possible — but then we'd need to figure out what is unique about each row. Do you see anything in the second row?"

Omen frowned. Math wasn't really his strong suit, though he suspected he had a more extensive understanding of it than the rest of his companions due to his father's teaching. He knew, however, that his skills were no match for Shalonie's. "Prime numbers," he suggested, trying to remember what he knew about prime numbers. "There are three in the first row . . . which still leaves two numbers . . ."

"There are only two in the first row," Shalonie corrected. "One isn't technically a prime number, but there are three in the second row, two in the third row, but only one in the fourth row." She tugged at her hair in frustration.

"Hey! Look what I is finding!" Tyrin's voice caught their attention, and Omen turned to see the little cat digging at the back wall near the edge of the room. Hidden in the shadows along the wall was a tiny stone door — the seams of the doorframe nearly invisible against the rock wall. The door itself was only large enough for a small creature to fit through — no more than a few inches in height.

Curious, they all gathered around, and Omen pressed against the tiny door; instantly it slid inward, revealing a carved tunnel much like the one they'd just emerged from, only smaller.

Tyrin pushed his head into the tunnel, his tiny body nearly disappearing from sight until Kyr caught hold of him and pulled him back.

"Just exactly how small are these dwarves of Kharakhan?" Templar asked in amazement.

"Dwarfkin," Nikki corrected him. "They aren't a single race. It's a term for the old ones from the time of the giants. If they weren't giants, they were dwarfkin, beasties, boggets, or faykin. The dwarfkin were the ones that looked the most human."

Templar looked surprised at that. "Kharakhan had a giant problem as well?"

"Different giants," Omen told his friend, knowing he was thinking of the giants of Terizkand, ugly beasts who'd enslaved his people. "Not the same species at all from the ones you're thinking of. These giants were immortal and lived in Kharakhan long before humans even existed."

"This is probably a sprite tunnel." Shalonie examined the doorway. "Maybe a pixie door."

"I bet it is mouses!" Tormy exclaimed eagerly. The two cats, Tyrin still clutched tightly in Kyr's hands, were staring at the door in fascination.

"I is checking?" Tyrin purred. "I is finding it — I is betting there is being dinner inside there!"

Kyr looked warily at Omen, and Omen knew his brother was loath to let the little kitten go. He glanced at Shalonie.

The girl stared hard at the tunnel opening. "There might be a clue in there," she reasoned. "Or maybe a lever or button that solves the puzzle automatically — like a fail-safe for the dwarfkin to cross."

Omen placed a comforting hand on his brother's shoulder as he looked at the little cat. "Maybe you could just go in a few feet and look around, Tyrin," Omen suggested. "If there's anything in there, back out immediately."

Reluctantly, Kyr placed Tyrin on the ground.

"Hold on a second, Tyrin," Templar urged, reaching out and touching the small kitten on the left front paw. Immediately, the white fur on top of the cat's paw started to glow as a tiny ball of light appeared there. Startled, the cat shook his paw violently to flick away the light, his ears flattening back against his head.

"Don't shake it off!" Templar warned as the ball of light floated away from the cat and started to head up toward the ceiling. It was just a tiny candlelight cantrip — a dim glowing ball only the size of a coin, but it would be bright enough to allow the cat to see clearly in the darkened tunnel. Templar caught the tiny light in his hand and set it back down on the cat's paw — warily Tyrin watched, holding himself still this time as he did so. The ball settled just on top of the cat's paw, staying in place when Tyrin took a tentative step forward.

"Tyrin doesn't need that," protested Omen. "Cats can see in the dark."

"That's actually a myth," Shalonie corrected. "They can't see in complete darkness, they need some small amount of light. And they can't make out minute details in low light."

"Don't want him missing anything," Templar said, "if he's going in."

Hastily, the kitten pushed himself through the tiny opening and disappeared down the small tunnel. The faint glowing light emanating from the opening was the only sign the cat was there.

Kyr leaned over, bending his neck so he could peer after his kitten.

But Tyrin was only gone for a few short moments before they heard his disappointed voice calling back. "It's a &@#! dead end!" he snarled. "Who is putting a dead end at the end of my mouses tunnel? Where is being dinner?"

"There's nothing there?" Shalonie called after the little cat. "No button? No lever? No door?"

"No!" the kitten yowled back angrily. "No mouses neither! Just some &!#@*! words written on the wall!"

The look of astonishment on all their faces spoke volumes. "Tyrin! What do the words say?" Omen called to the cat, only to realize a second later what a foolish request that was. *The cats can't read!*

"Hold your pants on!" Tyrin called back, obviously annoyed. "I is still reading them! They is being a lot of words!"

Despite everything, Templar, Dev, and Liethan started to snicker.

Tormy wrinkled his nose in their direction, and the three of them made an effort not to laugh out loud.

Omen rolled his eyes with growing annoyance. *Trapped in a dwarfkin tunnel and the only hope we have is the potty mouth kitten's ability to read.*

"They is saying, 'the trell is in the soup appetizer!'" Tyrin called back after a few moments.

"That is being a great clue!" Tormy exclaimed, looking impressed. "Tyrin is such a bestest reader! All we is having to do is finding the trell and then we is having dinner soup!"

"What does fish and soup have to do with a number puzzle?" Nikki asked, as if not aware of the ludicrousness of their predicament. He looked over at the three snickering men, trying to figure out the joke. Then he looked to Omen and Shalonie for an explanation.

Shalonie pinched the bridge of her nose in frustration, closing her eyes briefly.

Omen tugged at his hair, trying to figure out a way to solve their dilemma.

"Tyrin!" Omen called back down the tunnel. "Maybe it's written in code. Could you read the individual letters to us instead?" Relief flashed through Shalonie's eyes. "In order!" he clarified last minute.

"Oh! Good idea!" Tyrin called back. "I bet it is being a code! It is saying it is being about soup, but it is really being about mouses!" He started reading off the letters to them, occasionally describing their shape instead of giving their actual name. But after a few moments, they gathered the real message: THE TRICK IS IN THE SECOND AN-TIPODE.

Tyrin's little head poked out through the doorway a moment later, his white and orange fur coated in dust as he stared up at them, the tiny ball of light still attached to his front paw.

"Is I solving it?" the kitten asked, amber eyes glowing.

Kyr gently picked up the little cat, placing him once again on his shoulder and brushing dust from his ears. "You did good, Tyrin," the boy praised the kitten, scratching him under the chin.

Omen gently patted Tyrin on the head.

"The trick is in the second antipode," Shalonie repeated to herself, rising to return to the edge of the puzzle.

27

Omen joined her.

"The second what?" Omen asked. "The second row, the second number, the second sequence? And does antipode mean we have to do it backward?"

Shalonie stared hard at the numbers, her eyes fixed in deep concentration. She murmured a few Melian words Omen hadn't heard before. A moment later her entire face lit up. "I got it!" she shouted. She pointed to several squares in succession. "Thirteen, thirty-one, seventy-one, yes, the pattern fits all the way across."

"What pattern?" Omen frowned, trying to see what she had seen.

"You were right about it being prime numbers," she told him happily.

"But there's too many prime numbers," he reminded her.

"But only one prime number per row that is still prime if you reverse the order," she announced. "The trick is in the second row — thirty-one is the reverse of thirteen, both prime numbers. There is a number in each row that's still a prime number if you reverse it: thirteen, thirty-one, seventy-one, ninety-seven, one hundred and seven, three hundred and eleven, and in the last row three hundred and eighty-nine."

Omen tried to do the math in his head; beyond the first few numbers, he wasn't really certain which numbers were still prime. "Are you sure nine hundred and eighty-three is still a prime number?" he asked the girl.

"Yes," Shalonie's eyes shone with certainty. "It has no other factors. I'll go first—" she started to step toward the first stone only to be stopped immediately by both Omen and Dev grabbing her shoulders.

"No!" Dev told her sharply. "I think somebody who is

less likely to die if you're wrong should go first. Not that I think you're wrong, of course."

Shalonie looked affronted. "But if I'm wrong, it's my fault! I'm the one who should take the risk!"

"No, Dev's right," Omen told her. "I'll go. It's safer that way."

"Actually, I think Templar should go," Dev amended, surprising Omen.

Templar laughed. "Not that I mind going," he told all of them. "But, thanks for making me the expendable one in the group."

Seeming deeply annoyed, Dev threw him a dark glare. "That's not what I meant — you and Omen are the least likely to get hurt if the floor collapses. But if you go, Omen can psionically catch you if you fall. It's much harder to levitate yourself."

Omen conceded to the logic in the statement, raising one eyebrow inquisitively toward Templar. His friend smirked and stepped up to the edge of the platform. "Just tell me which ones to step on," he told Shalonie, and they all braced themselves as Shalonie pointed.

"Thirteen first," she instructed. He stepped firmly onto the tile. They all waited in silence. Nothing happened, the floor holding in place.

"Hurrah! I is solving the puzzle!" Tyrin exclaimed joyfully.

One by one Shalonie called out the numbers in the sequence she'd determined.

Templar moved his way from step to step until he'd crossed all the way to the far side. He stepped off the grid and onto the solid ground near the glowing archway. "Well done!" he called back to Shalonie, and she smiled in relief, accepting the congratulations of the others.

Satisfied now that they knew the correct sequence to cross, they all began making their way over the grid — each going one by one as Omen watched intently, ready to catch any of them should the floor give way. He held Kyr and Tormy back for last.

When Kyr's turn came, Omen lifted Tyrin from his shoulder and put the kitten back into the boy's pocket. "Stay there," he cautioned the little creature, and Tyrin flicked his ears in understanding. It occurred to Omen with a start that while they had been teaching Kyr how to speak several languages in the last six months, and had made some headway in teaching him to read — they hadn't spent a great deal of time on numbers or math. *Kyr doesn't know his numbers!*

"You have to stay on the right tiles," he told the boy, trying to hide his sudden nervousness.

Kyr flashed Omen a smile. "I saw which ones," he assured his brother. "I remember numbers." He turned toward the grid and recited the numbers in sequence, speaking not in the Common tongue but in Kahdess.

The dead use numbers? Omen sighed a breath of relief as his brother began moving cautiously across the platform. On the far side of the grid, Omen saw Nikki making the warding sign against evil as he turned to the others in alarm. *That's the first time he's heard Kyr speak Kahdess,* Omen realized, his gut twisting as he awaited Nikki's reaction.

He saw both Liethan and Templar murmuring quietly to Nikki, likely explaining something of Kyr's past to him. Nikki nodded tightly in quiet acceptance, sending Omen a sharp look. But when Kyr reached the other side, Nikki patted the boy on the back as if welcoming him. Kyr smiled and then turned back toward Omen and Tormy.

"That's it, Tormy," Omen urged. "Your turn." He stared uncertainly at the floor as Tormy lifted one of his paws and held it over the tile that had the number thirteen written on it. Tormy's fluffy white paw was nearly the entire size of the stone tile. "Tormy, you have to be very careful. You can't step on the wrong tile — do you understand? And you have to watch your back paws — they have to stay on the right tiles too."

"Back paws and front paws." Tormy cocked his ears forward as he stared in consternation at the floor. "You is telling me which squares, Omy? I is counting all the way to nine but I is not knowing the big numbers."

"We'll go really slow," Omen told his cat. "Just stay calm and keep your balance."

"I is a cat, Omy!" Tormy protested. "I is always keeping my balanceses on account of the fact that I is cat-like . . . like a cat!"

"Exactednessly like a cat!" Tyrin called across to them.

"Exactednessnessly like a cat," Tormy agreed.

Considering that some of the clumsiest behavior he'd ever seen had also come from the two cats, Omen just grimaced and motioned Tormy forward. "Start with your right paw first on the square right in front of you — no, your other right paw!"

Tormy corrected himself and placed his right paw cautiously against the tile. Omen then directed him to reach out with his left front paw to step onto the correct tile in the second row. Slowly tile by tile, directing the cat one paw at a time, he talked Tormy across the grid — the others calling out helpful directions when the cat seemed to get confused about which back paw to move when. More than once

Omen reached out with his psionics to prod the correct foot forward, giving the cat gentle nudges here and there until he had at last cleared the squares.

Kyr threw his arms around the large cat as he made it to the other side.

Omen let out a heavy sigh of relief. Grabbing his own packs and Tormy's saddle, he quickly made his way across the tiles. Kyr hugged him as well, and he smiled sheepishly at the others. "If I'd known there was going to be math homework on this trip, I might have actually studied first," he joked, everyone laughing as the tension eased.

"Now what?" Liethan asked. "We crossed the puzzle, but there is no actual opening over here. Just this glowing archway."

They all turned toward the archway, each studying it to suss out the next puzzle.

Chapter 3: Summer

OMEN

Tall and ornamented with an imposing lion's head at its keystone, the archway was surrounded by a gilded edge etched with writing. *Not a language I recognize,* Omen noted.

"It's written in the language of the Aelaedrine," Shalonie announced and Omen had to smile.

Of course Shalonie would recognize it. I wonder if there's any language she doesn't know?

"Lords of the Summer Lands," Liethan responded to Shalonie's announcement. At the looks of surprise from the others, he just shrugged. "My grandmother is from the faerie realm. I grew up hearing stories about all the different clans of faerie."

"How do we get through?" Templar pressed. They all looked to Shalonie for the answer.

"Well, if we had the password — which I don't," she amended quickly. "We could open it right up. As it is, we're going to have to rely on Omen — use your lute."

"Another made up song?" he asked, feeling pained at the thought. He crouched down to retrieve the lute from his pack. He'd wrapped it carefully in thick leathers to protect it.

"No, it's an inanimate object," Shalonie assured him. "The words won't matter. Just play music and think about what you want to happen. If we're lucky it will open up a doorway directly into one of the faerie realms."

"Hopefully," Omen said, realizing there was an element of risk in this option. If it didn't work they'd have no choice but to go back through the tunnels and face the wyverns. Assuming he could open the puzzle door with his psionics. "No pressure."

"Tons of pressure," Templar jokingly told him. "If you don't get it opened, we're hip deep in wyvern droppings. Not a winning proposition."

He threw his friend a dark glare as he carefully un- wrapped the lute, revealing the metallic strings. Luckily the instrument had sustained no damage in the journey.

He looped the instrument's strap over one shoulder and placed his fingers on the strings, pausing a moment to think of what he wanted to play. He had numerous original compositions to choose from, and he decided to pick one he'd recently finished. It was set in a minor key and had some complicated fingering that he hoped would impress whatever governed the power of this archway.

He started playing — the music filled the room with a gentle melody and haunting harmonies. He felt the power of the instrument awakening once again, flooding him with a vibrating hum of magic. *It's like it wants to act on its own but doesn't have any direction.* Omen focused his mind on the end goal. *Open the gate, open the gate!* He hoped thought alone would be enough. *What was it Kadana said — it amplifies magic. If I just push it toward the archway maybe that will be enough.*

He saw the bluish light shining from the surface of the archway beginning to pulse. He slowed the song, timing it to the pulsing light. *Open!* he thought again, pushing outward with his thoughts. It wasn't exactly a psionic push — there was no pattern behind it beyond the notes of the music — but it was close enough that he could feel energy flowing through him and outward toward the gate. *Open!* he commanded again.

The archway pulsed brightly and the stone behind it seemed to melt away. A tunnel wide enough for even Tormy to pass through appeared before them. Intricately crafted pillars lined the tunnel on either side. Faint bluish moonlight radiated from the far end of the tunnel, and beyond it they could see the craggy shapes of shadowed trees.

Templar clapped Omen on the back. "You did it!" he grinned and Omen stilled his fingers on the lute.

"Let's get through before it decides to close," Shalonie suggested.

Omen grabbed up the thick leather hides, wrapping his lute once more as the others began moving forward. Placing the lute once again in his pack, and double checking that his sword was secured, Omen slid it onto his back once again. Omen grabbed Tormy's saddle and then urged Kyr and the cats to go ahead of him. The beautiful vine carvings embedded in the thick stone had caught Kyr's eye, and more than once Omen had to steer the boy away from studying the workmanship. Gently, he encouraged his brother to keep to the path.

"It can't possibly be night already," Templar considered as they moved closer to the moonlit forest. "We left at dawn. It's afternoon at best."

"It is being lunchtime!" Tyrin and Tormy purred out in unison, their stomachs most accurate in assessing how much time had passed since their breakfast at Kadana's castle.

"Doesn't look like lunch time."

Omen had guessed that the tunnel was leading them

deeper into the Mountain, but there was no mistaking the fresh air ahead. They seemed to be emerging into a forest. He suspected that, as Shalonie had predicted, they had crossed over some barrier and into another realm. *Brilliant.* Despite the excitement that would have typically engendered in him, a strange unease came over him. A chill wind blew down the tunnel, catching at his hair like icy fingers. He shivered.

"The Summer Lands?" he asked Shalonie, doubt coloring his words. *I expected them to be warm.*

"That's the most likely possibility," she agreed, cautiously. She pulled her cloak around her shoulders as if also chilled. "Tonight's the eve of the solstice. The Summer Gate should be open."

One by one, they cautiously stepped out from the shelter of the arched tunnel and into a clearing. Broken moonlight beamed through a heavily overcast night sky. A dense mist clung low to the ground and spread out around them. The forest ahead glowed with an eerie light.

Omen had not known what to expect of the Summer Lands — or any of the Gated Lands. But he hadn't imagined this darkness. This ugliness. *Hideous.* The grass was dead and black, more bog than meadow. A mildewy, putrid smell drifted through the air. Omen wrinkled his nose.

The trees around them were dead as well, hollow — only paltry bits of creeping moss and spider webs hanging from gnarled, decaying branches. The dank meadow itself was choked with weeds, and grey moths swarmed through the air. *Bugs.* Omen immediately felt itchy.

Farther ahead, the trees were charred and sloe-black. Shadows swallowed up pieces of them, the only relief coming from the eerie blue moonlight streaking through the shrouded sky.

"Isn't it beautiful!" Kyr exclaimed with excitement, and Omen turned in bewilderment toward his brother.

"What—" Omen's words choked off.

Kyr was gone.

So was Tormy.

Omen turned swiftly. The others were gone as well.

He stood alone at the edge of the dark meadow, heavy silence around him. Mist swirled through the empty places his companions had all stood.

"Kyr!" he shouted in alarm, his heart clenching in his chest. "Tormy! Templar!"

There were no replies — only the cold, moving mist and growing shadows.

He took a step forward, reaching out toward where Tormy and his brother had stood, hoping this was just a trick of the light and that they were all still there beside him. His hand met no resistance; a pale moth fluttered by, and Omen instinctively flinched away from it.

He turned again, spinning completely around, his eyes seeking out the tunnel they'd just emerged from, thinking that perhaps his companions had only retreated. But there was no sign of the tunnel either — behind him the blackened forest stretched away into shadows.

"Kyr! Tormy!" he called again. "Templar! Liethan! Can anyone hear me?" Despite shouting, his voice sounded muffled, muted by the heavy mist.

They can't be gone — they have to be nearby. It's just a trick — some sort of illusion preventing me from seeing them.

He took several deep breaths, trying to force his now racing heart to calm as he stilled the chaos churning in his mind. He reached out with his psionics, forming a simple pattern with a soft tune. *I'll be able to sense them psionically!* he assured himself. He pushed outward with his senses — one foot, two, then three.

Nothing! No minds, no thoughts, no warm bodies. He pushed out farther — ten feet, then twenty. He could feel the trees now — their shapes twisted and empty. *Dead wood — no life at all. Old.*

Fear gripped his heart, and he dropped the heavy saddle he was carrying along with his backpack. The silver glint of his sword strapped to the pack caught his attention, and he closed his hand around the sheath, releasing the straps that held it in place. He didn't draw the blade, but holding the familiar weight in his hands calmed him briefly.

Have to try again — have to reach out farther. I can sense what's around me better with my eyes closed. Every instinct told him not to close his eyes — not to look away from the swirling mist and the flickering shadows. He turned again, spinning fully around once more as if to assure himself there was nothing behind him.

Shivering, he breathed deeply and forced his eyes to shut, forming the pattern again, stronger this time, the music that triggered his psionic patterns shifting as he added in a line of harmony and the cold tones of a high-pitched melody. He pushed outward with his senses again. He could feel the dead sensation of the trees, the ground at his feet, rocks, tangled weeds. *There are lichens, moss, spiderwebs — the weeds themselves. I should be able to feel all that.* But while he could sense their shapes, their outlines, there was no sense of life. *Not even the spiders who made the webs.*

Something fluttered past his face, like ghostly fingers

38

trailing over his skin and moving through his hair. Omen flinched away sharply, his eyes shooting open.

Another moth fluttered nearby, caught up in a swirl of mist before alighting upon a twisted blackened root. *The moths! I should be able to sense the moths!* They, alone, were the only signs of life around him.

Eyes open this time, he pushed out with his senses once more, focusing on the moth. *There!* He could feel its shape — gossamer thin wings coated in white dust, skittering legs, spindly antennae — but all just shapes and nothing more. *No life!* He might as well have been touching the mist instead of a living creature.

Despair washed through Omen, followed by growing horror. Nothing about this was right — nothing felt normal. His psionics had never failed him before. *Which either means this isn't real, or that the moth isn't actually alive.* He wasn't certain which option he preferred.

Gripping his sword firmly in his left hand, ready to draw it at a moment's notice, he took several more steps toward the dank meadow where the majority of the moths were silently flitting about in the moonlight. "Can anyone hear me!" he shouted again.

Movement off to one side caught the corner of Omen's eyes — he turned sharply. There among the shadowed silhouettes of the dead trees, he saw shapes in the mist — a swift swirling of the air and the flickering of large shadows moving amid the bluish moonlight. He took several steps toward it.

The back of his neck prickled as if someone were standing directly behind him. Alarmed, Omen spun, right hand grasping his sword hilt. There was no one there.

More movement caught his eye — another shadow on

the far side of the meadow among the trees. He could feel eyes watching him — something old, something menacing, angry.

He turned again — there were even more shadows now — movement all around him. *Too many to be my companions,* he realized. And even without extending his psionics further, he could tell that these forms were not his friends — they felt cold, dead.

Oppressive weight pressed at his chest as if something were squeezing the air from his lungs. His heart raced, his skin growing clammy and cold, and Omen drew his sword, tossing the scabbard down amid the weed-choked ground as he gripped the hilt of the blade with both hands.

The shadows grew, gathering, twisting, surrounding him. *Men,* he thought. *Or wraiths perhaps.* They seemed one moment solid and black as night, and then the next moment became nothing but mist swirling away into the sky. But from all of them, he could feel a sense of rage — a sense of deadly anger as if something old and powerful had turned its eyes on him with hatred.

Whispers reached his ears. He thought at first it was just the fluttering of the moths dancing around him, their powder wings brushing past his face and hair no matter how often he shook them away. But the sound rose above those fluttering wings, hissing and cold, and he could just barely make out words amid the noise. The language, however, eluded him — words he had never heard before.

He braced himself; something was approaching, something ancient and filled with rage, something deadly. He could sense it all around him. His knuckles turned white around the hilt of his sword. Trembling with a terror he couldn't recall ever feeling before, Omen turned again, looking behind him, again to the right, to the left — he couldn't tell where it was coming from. The presence was all around him — the shadows were moving faster, the mist swirling.

"Are you awake, Omen?"

Kyr's voice was like a clear bell, sharp and pure, and Omen gasped in shock, a jolt of bright energy flashing through his entire body. He felt a small hand upon his own and found himself staring down at his brother.

Kyr was standing before him with a curious expression on his face, head tilted to one side as if puzzled. Tyrin, perched upon the boy's shoulder, looked equally perplexed. Tormy stood just behind both of them, peering over Kyr's head at Omen, ears perked forward, whiskers flared.

"Kyr!" Omen shouted, reaching out with both hands to grip the boy's shoulders. A loud thud at his feet caught his attention — the saddle he'd been carrying rocked on the ground as it settled where he dropped it.

I dropped that already! I was holding my sword! He could feel a heavy weight on his back — he was still wearing his backpack. A glance over his shoulder showed his sword strapped to the pack where it had been earlier. He caught sight of the others then — all standing just where they had been before they had vanished. They looked as confused as he felt.

"Is you all rightness, Omy?" Tormy asked worriedly. "You is just standing there. You is all just standing there. Kyr is saying you is all falling asleep."

"What was that?" Templar hissed. "You were all gone!"

"There were shadows in the trees!" Nikki added with a thin voice.

"You is not gone!" Tyrin protested, standing up on his

41

hind legs and bracing his front paws on top of Kyr's head as he faced all of them determinedly. "You is right here. You is standing here and you is not moving, and we is talking to you and you is all falling asleep."

"Asleep?" Omen shook his head. "Are you saying we never moved?"

Tormy flicked his tail back and forth. "You is not going anywheres, Omy. Kyr is saying you is asleep."

Omen looked to the others. Liethan and Templar were both watching the woods distrustfully. Nikki was shivering and had moved closer toward Shalonie, who was staring down at her hands in confusion. Dev alone seemed calm, the expression on his face one of annoyance rather than alarm.

"I had drawn my sword," Shalonie stated definitively as she stared at her empty hands. "I had dropped my backpack and drawn my sword." Her backpack was still on her back.

"I shot a bolt at the shadows in the mist," Liethan agreed. His crossbow was still attached to the back of his pack as well.

"I heard voices," Omen told them all. "Whispers, words — I couldn't make out the language." There was no sign among the dark trees of the moving shadows now; all Omen could see was the slowly swirling mist.

"Kyr is saying sometimes they speak and they're not even there," Tormy exclaimed. "'Member, 'member, Omy! He is saying that in Melia."

Omen felt a chill move down his spine. "I remember," he agreed. He looked at Kyr intently. "You didn't fall asleep? You didn't see the shadows in the mist?"

Kyr solemnly shook his head from side to side.

"Maybe it's our human blood?" Shalonie suggested.

"What?" They all looked at her expectantly.

"There are countless stories about people falling asleep in the faerie lands and never waking up," she explained. "But those stories are always about humans. With the exception of Kyr and the cats, all the rest of us have human blood in our veins. You may all have other races in your bloodlines but all of you have at least one human parent. And I'm just Melian — entirely human. Kyr, on the other hand, doesn't have any human blood — nor the cats, obviously."

"Whatever it was, it was just a trick," Dev proclaimed. "An illusion designed to keep us here, designed to frighten us."

"It's hard to fool my psionics with an illusion," Omen argued.

"If we truly were asleep, I doubt you used your psionics any more than I actually drew my sword," Shalonie replied. She took a step toward Kyr and the cats. "How long were we asleep, Kyr?"

"Just a moment," the boy explained. "I stopped as soon as I realized you weren't following. I called your names, and a moment later you all woke up."

It sure felt longer than that! Omen exchanged worried glances with the others — the same unease clear in their eyes. "Wait!" Something jolted Omen's mind. "You stopped?" He looked at Kyr intently. "Stopped what? What were you doing?"

Kyr grinned then, his eyes lighting up as he turned his attention back to the dead, moth-filled meadow. "I was going to go pick flowers!" he exclaimed and then ran forward into the blanket of weeds and tangled dead grass.

"Kyr!" Omen hurried after his brother.

But Kyr did not go far. He dropped down in the muck of the clearing and began picking thorny weeds while grey moths landed on his pale hair. He hummed happily to himself.

Omen slid to a stop and stared at his brother with consternation. *What do I do?*

The others moved up alongside him, watching Kyr suspiciously, but making no move to stop him. Tormy scooted close and crouched down beside the humming boy while Tyrin hopped from Kyr's shoulder to Tormy's head.

"I think there's a chance that we're still not seeing the same things," Shalonie murmured beside Omen as they all watched the happy boy plucking weeds from the ground.

"Have I mentioned to you that your brother is a bit . . ." Templar began.

Omen glared at him. "Repeatedly!" He tugged at his tangled hair in frustration. "He does have this thing about weeds though, so maybe . . ."

"If we can't see what's really here, how are we supposed to find our way through this land?" Dev asked. No one answered.

Omen shivered, unease rising within him again. He turned his attention back to Kyr. *Nothing about this feels normal.* He moved forward and crouched down next to Kyr and the cats. He felt torn. The boy looked utterly carefree, which was rare, and the cats did not seem unduly concerned.

Grey moths had settled upon Kyr's golden hair like a crown of dead leaves, and Omen had to resist the urge to shoo the pests away. He feared the motion might startle his brother. "Kyr, what are you doing?"

Kyr looked up at him and smiled, showing him the

44

weeds he had gathered. "I'm picking flowers for the lady. We cannot greet her without a gift."

Omen scanned the dead land, his gaze resting briefly on Shalonie. As far as he knew, she was the only lady around, and he doubted very much Kyr felt a need to greet her. "Which lady, Kyr?" he asked hesitantly.

"The sister," Kyr explained, and a sharp memory pierced through Omen.

"Dawn's light! This is still part of that same conversation," he heard Templar mutter, knowing his friend also remembered the conversation about flowers back in Melia. At the time, he'd thought Kyr had been talking about his sister Lilyth.

"Which sister?" he asked, not entirely certain he wanted to know the answer.

Kyr settled the pile of weeds he'd collected into the crook of his left arm, and then rose to his feet, reaching out to take hold of Omen's hand. "Come on, I'll show you." He smiled sweetly and tugged Omen after him as he headed off across the meadow toward the dead woods. Sharp fear gripped Omen's heart — he didn't want to enter the woods. But neither Kyr nor the cats looked worried, and the helpless look Shalonie gave him reminded him that if none of them could truly see what Kyr and the cats were seeing, they had little choice but to follow them.

Templar snatched up Tormy's saddle as he and the others fell into step behind them.

The wind blew away the debris before them, revealing a cobblestone path winding through dead leaves and blackened moss.

That wasn't there before.

The inherent malevolence of the place — the near-dark,

the decay, the creeping mist, the tangled vines, and thorny overgrowth — raised the hair on the back of Omen's neck. "We need to proceed cautiously," he warned. But Kyr hurried them along as if he hadn't a care in the world.

The path widened out into an open clearing; a stone gazebo perched in its center. Dark green vines snaked around the structure's pickets and up to its corner braces.

Upon seeing the gazebo, Kyr released Omen's hand. With a happy laugh, the boy skipped forward and climbed the stone steps. He knelt down before a stone chair, which rested at its heart.

Omen took in a sharp breath as he realized that seated in that chair was a figure: a woman wrapped in shadows, unmoving as if stone herself. *Is she the presence I sensed earlier?*

He felt nothing now — no menace, no threat — but the cold dread inside him didn't fade.

Kyr placed the weeds down at her feet with extreme care. His smile had grown even larger.

Hesitantly, Omen moved forward, trying to get a better look at the woman in the shadows. She looked harmless — nothing more than a statue seated upon the throne. *Is she asleep too — is that what happened to us?*

His companions might as well have been turned to stone themselves. They neither moved nor talked.

"Kyr," Omen said softly. He worried about startling either of them, so he moved forward very slowly and very cautiously.

But the moment his foot touched the first stone step of the gazebo, the woods around them exploded with movement and noise.

Tall, fierce warriors burst from the trees, all wielding

white blades that burned with light. They surrounded the companions and barred their way forward, shielding the lady and Kyr in a protective ring.

Fair-skinned, dark-eyed, the warriors had sharp, angular faces that were filled with a cold rage. The very air around them seemed hard and menacing. Shadows whipped around them like smoke.

Faerie lords! Omen surmised, despite having never crossed their paths before. *There was something watching us! There was something in the shadows!*

Cold and unyielding, the warriors reminded him immediately of Indee and the dark menacing magic she'd used to hex Kyr. These men might not be her kin, but they were of a similar bloodline as the sorceress queen.

Instinctively all of his companions reached for their weapons. Omen held his hands up in warning. "Stop." *Whatever magic they have, it was able to put us all to sleep — able to overpower all of us except Kyr and the cats. We don't want to start anything here.*

One of the warriors stepped forward, eyes blazing with anger, his fair face both beautiful and terrifying as he glared down at all them from the top of the steps. "You dare approach my sister!"

"We mean no harm," Omen assured him, holding up his hands in a gesture of peace.

"You reek of harm!" the faerie lord shouted, brandishing his burning sword; the blade illuminated the darkness around him like a torch.

"So pretty!" Kyr laughed from behind him and several of the dark-eyed warriors cried out in alarm, flinching away from the center of the gazebo.

The warrior confronting Omen turned swiftly toward the

boy, outrage in his eyes as he stared at Kyr still kneeling before the unmoving woman.

"We did not see him!" one of the other warriors cried out.

"How could he approach without our noticing?" another protested.

The warrior in front of Omen snarled and tightened his grip on his sword hilt, taking a step toward the kneeling boy.

"No!" Omen shouted and hastened forward, hands outstretched to grab the man. Before he could pivot aside, the faerie lord pressed the white blade against Omen's throat. It felt like a sliver of ice against this skin.

A voice rang out, stopping the blade's bloody intent, freezing the faerie warriors surrounding Kyr in their tracks. "No!" The word echoed through the woods like a bell.

A look of profound shock crossed the face of the cold warrior threatening him. The man backed swiftly away, his blade dropping from his hand to clatter upon the stone ground. He turned to stare in utter amazement at the woman in the center of the gazebo.

The woman had risen to her feet. She was tall and slender, clad in a simple gown of white silk, her unbound, red-gold hair falling to her waist, her face so fair she looked like something from a dream. And though the gaze of everyone in the clearing was turned toward her, she stared upward at the sky, her ocean blue eyes seeing something they could not. She tilted her face upward, as if toward sunlight that wasn't there, and closed her eyes. "The sun is shining," she declared, and all at once the world around them melted away.

Where there had been shadows and decaying woodlands

black with death, a new beauty bloomed, complete with warm sunshine and green, flowering life. The sentinel trees around them rose tall and stately, pale golden bark, emerald green leaves. Growing among them, flowering trees filled the air with the scent of honey. The vines upon the white stones of the gazebo were ablaze with red roses, and the air was alive with floating blossoms and gem-colored butterflies. The meager weeds Kyr had rested at the lady's feet were now vibrant flowers, red and amber and gold. And while Omen and his companions were stunned by the overwhelming beauty of the world around them, it seemed that the faerie warriors were more stunned by the woman herself.

The dark-eyed lord stepped closer to her, his left hand outstretched as he raised it to the woman's face. He touched her white skin with such care Omen found himself moved in spite of the threat still facing them.

"Airmeethe?" the lord whispered. "You spoke."

"She cannot hear you," Kyr told him, still kneeling on the ground amid the colorful flowers and blossoms. The ring of moths around his head had transformed into delicate butterflies and looked like a crown of precious stones. "She is too far away. But the sun is shining."

The lord looked down at Kyr, his face filled with confusion and wonder. "Did you do this?"

Kyr's eyes flashed in the sunlight. "I cannot make the sun shine or the green grow. I tried." He placed both his hands against the white flagstones on the ground. "But I can make the stones dance!" he laughed.

The lord backed away then, looking down at Kyr for a long moment before turning toward Omen. "What manner of creature is this?" he demanded, though it would seem that some of the anger had left his eyes.

"He's not a creature." Omen frowned. "He's my brother. He's just . . . different."

As poor an explanation as it was, it nonetheless appeared to satisfy the man, for he did not press his question. Instead, he turned to one of the warriors closest to the woman. "Take my sister home," he commanded, and the warrior inclined his head in respect, before stepping forward and taking hold of the woman's pale hand. He led her away, vanishing with her into the woods in utter silence.

The lord turned toward Omen, his initial rage seemingly passed, replaced with cold reserve. "Who are you, and why have you entered our lands uninvited?"

"My name is Omen," he replied cautiously. "We're here looking for someone who was taken into the Autumn Lands against his will. We did not mean to trespass. We're merely passing through." He was hesitant to say too much about his quest for fear of triggering the hex mark on Kyr's arm.

"These are the Summer Lands. None may pass through our lands without the Queen's permission," the warrior informed him. He glanced back at Kyr, still seeming confused by the boy. "The company you keep is too strange for me to decipher. You will speak directly to her and she will pass judgment upon you. But first, you will rid yourself of the poison you bring with you."

"Poison?" Omen asked in surprise. "What poison?"

"The metal that burns," Kyr supplied helpfully.

The warrior stared down at Kyr. "What do you know of such things?" he demanded.

Kyr looked up at him, his gaze suddenly fierce. "I know burning!" he whispered with such intensity that all the faerie lords stepped away. "I know fire and ash and dust

50

and wind that screams!" With each word, his voice grew louder and more alarmed as panic filled his eyes.

When Omen moved toward him, none of the warriors tried to stop him. He dropped to one knee before the boy, gripping his arms.

"Kyr!" he shouted, stopping the flow of words from the boy. "We're here, in the sunshine. Remember?"

All at once Kyr smiled and looked up at Omen in amazement. "The flowers can fly, Omen!" he laughed as he shook his head, sending the ring of butterflies dancing through the air.

"They're butterflies," Omen explained, bemused.

Tormy and Tyrin padded forward to stare in fascination at the fluttering insects. Oddly enough, it seemed to Omen as if the cats had hardly even noticed the faerie lords around them, and in turn the warriors gave the cats little attention — as if giant cats were a common sight to them.

Kyr laughed again, and he and the two cats raced after the swirl of butterflies into the green meadow beyond. Previously weed-choked, the field was now ablaze with a kaleidoscope of flowers that defied the imagination.

Two of the warriors had disappeared momentarily into the woods. They returned carrying a large wooden chest between them. They set it on the ground just below the steps of the gazebo.

"Remove your iron and place it in the chest. You may collect it if you leave here."

Not liking the word *if* in the statement, Omen glanced at his companions. None of them looked pleased.

"You would have us all disarmed?" Omen started to argue.

But the faerie lord glared at him with acute displeasure.

"We do not fear your weapons; it is the iron that offends us," he informed them. "The Nightspawn's swords are made of bone, he may keep those. And the lady's sword is made of dragon gold. She may keep that. But all iron must go into the chest."

That's what Kyr meant. The metal that burns. Omen glanced uncomfortably toward Shalonie. "Iron?" he asked her.

She looked fascinated. "I had heard there were faerie races who would not tolerate the presence of iron."

"You have little choice," the faerie lord cut in. "Remove your iron or we will leave you in the drifting fog."

Uneasy, Omen motioned the others to comply, pulling the dagger from his belt first and tossing it into the chest. *These warriors don't consider us a threat even if we are armed. Lovely.*

His companions followed his lead, slowly and methodically removing their iron.

While most of Omen's armor was made of Lydonian silverleaf, iron was embedded in key pieces — particularly in his belt, which was lined with iron studs. *This is going to take a while.* He whipped off his belt and crammed it into the chest.

The others grumbled and began combing through their packs and clothing to seek out stray pieces of iron. Nikki's armored coat of elemental steel and most of their belts had to be removed. Shalonie alone had nearly no iron on her except for the metal pen nib that was part of her quill and ink set. By her expression, she looked more vexed at giving up her pen than the others did their weapons.

Kyr's sword was also made of Lydonian silverleaf. Nikki, who'd been carrying the weapon along with a large number of the packs that had been attached to Tormy's saddle, handed the blade to Omen with a pointed nod. "I've no training," Nikki murmured.

Grateful, Omen strapped the sword belt around his waist. *Twiggy blade is better than no blade.* He knew Kyr wouldn't spare the weapon a second thought.

Tormy's saddle, fastened with iron rivets, and Liethan's crossbow also had to be placed in the chest.

No matter how much we put in there, the chest isn't getting crowded. Figures.

But it was Dev who caused the longest delay, for though he initially tossed in his empty quiver and removed a sword and four daggers from various hidden locations in his clothing, the continued glare from the faerie lord made him remove several more concealed daggers.

"I can smell it on you, wolf!" the faerie lord snarled. His words brought forward several flat throwing blades from the back of Dev's coat; further glares produced a metal garrote from his collar, and then a few moments later several thin needles from hidden pockets in his sleeves. When the glare still didn't stop, he finally just sighed, and took off his coat entirely and tossed it into the trunk, then sat on the ground and pulled off both his boots, tossing them into the chest for good measure. Considering that he'd already removed the daggers from the knife sheaths in both boots, which appeared to be made entirely of leather, Omen couldn't fathom where else he might have hidden iron, but the faerie lord seemed finally appeased.

Once free of the offending iron, Omen called to Kyr and the cats to return from the field — oddly the faerie lords backed away from the three of them, leaving them free to roam as they pleased.

Looks like even the faerie don't know what to make of the cats or Kyr.

A quick search of Kyr assured Omen that his brother had no iron on him. The fastenings on his coat were all silver. And the dagger Templar had given him in Khreté was made of dwarfkin blackstone.

No iron to be found.

Once ready, they set out at a brisk pace through the honey-scented woodlands, surrounded by the faerie on all sides.

"He called her Airmeethe," Shalonie said softly, walking alongside Omen. She kept her voice down, and Omen tilted his head toward her to hear better. "Airmeethe is the granddaughter of Queen Illythia, ruler of the Aelaedrine. They're one of the eldest of the faerie races. If that warrior is Airmeethe's brother, then he is Prince Cuillian, a great warrior. We don't want to cross any of them."

"That powerful?" he asked in a whisper.

Shalonie shot him a look. "Queen Illythia is said to have ruled the world tens of thousands of years before the Covenant was even formed."

Tens of thousands! Omen shuddered at the thought. *That's a long life. A long time to rule.* He thought of Kadana's warnings about immortality.

"Are they . . . malevolent?" he asked softly. He knew some of the creatures of faerie were the very stuff of nightmares, evil beyond imagining. *They don't seem evil, just temperamental and intense.* Certainly, neither Kyr nor the cats had shied away from them. *The cats have good instincts,* he pondered, and yet he could not help but remember the way the land had looked until Airmeethe had spoken. *What is real? The wasteland or the dreamland?*

"People who have crossed them have not fared well," Shalonie told him. "But I have not heard of anything awful about them. They are not one of the clans that interacts with the mortal world anymore. To be honest, I'm surprised we found ourselves here. If we passed through the Summer Gate to get here, we should be on the borders of the Summer Lands where the young Summer races live. If this is Illythia's kingdom, then we are in the heart of the Summer Lands."

Dragon droppings! We aren't close to the Autumn Lands? Omen remembered that Indee's people, the Teyledrine, were one of the younger races of faerie. They lived closest to the borders of the mortal realm and interacted with humans from time to time. *How are we going to get there from here?*

Chapter 4: Heritage

DEV

*N*ow we're in for it, Dev thought, and not for the first time, as he followed the others through the woodlands. The woods had turned into something out of a dream — verdant, rich with flowers and trees of a thousand different types. Warm air caressed his skin, and the sweet smells of summer flowers enveloped him. Songbirds warbled and cooed unseen in branches and thickets. And though twilight had fallen, momentary patches of golden sunlight slipped through the canopy overhead and illuminated the world in dappled light.

Ignore the flowers, ignore the sunshine and tweeting birds! You know better than that! Dev silently scolded himself every time he felt his attention slip, and he forced his senses back on the faerie lords walking alongside them. *Can't trust anything they say. They'll bring back that blasted mist from earlier. Stay alert. Faeries breathe deceit.*

Filtered among the warm shadows of the trees, archers held weapons trained on the group. The warriors nearest them never sheathed their glowing white swords. They remained ever vigilant as they moved silently through the woods, unwavering in their quick stride. All were well armored, though at first glance their armor looked more decorative than functional; it was designed to flatter form and frame, the shining metal colored in jeweled hues that were not naturally found in steel. Dev, however, recognized its make.

56

Dragon bone mixed with spiderweave. He'd heard legends of how faerie smiths had learned to mix ground dragon bone with the silk of giant spiders. The material could be fashioned into any form, dyed any color, yet it was stronger than any steel known to man.

Dev was sure the faeries' appearance was the greatest deception of all — unearthly beauty haloed by a glow of light. But he knew they were predators. *Like snakes and scorpions.* Though Dev had not had many dealings with the faerie races before, he knew their type — manipulative, powerful, deadly, capable of trapping mortals with little more than words and minor spells. *And they're the kind of enemy that will hunt you to the ends of the earth. Obsessive. Uncompromising.*

Agitation swelled inside him as he followed after the others — not because he'd been disarmed. He hadn't — not really. Even now, he still had several weapons, just none made of iron. The thin wooden blowgun up his left sleeve and the deadly poison tip darts carefully sewn into the inner lining of his leather bracers were deadly enough to kill a man in seconds. *Not sure what they'd do to these creatures, but I doubt they could just shrug off the effects either.* He just hated not being able to predict what would happen.

He also hadn't missed how accurately their leader, Cuillian, had identified them — noting immediately Shalonie's Melian heritage, Templar's Nightblood, and his own Shilvagi ties. *Wish there was some truth to the stories that the Shilvagi can transform into wolves. That would certainly come in handy.*

Soft murmuring reached his ears. Some of the warriors were talking quietly among themselves, speaking in a language he'd never heard before, their voices whisper-like

57

and musical. *Sounds a bit like Melian.*

Walking just steps ahead of him, Shalonie stared blatantly at the ones speaking, turning her head swiftly each time someone else joined in the conversation. More than once she reached for her notebook at her belt, only to stop as she realized she had nothing to write with.

Omen moved to her side. "You know what they're saying, Shalonie?" Omen asked, keeping his voice low. It didn't matter, Dev knew; the Aelaedrines' hearing was far superior to any of theirs, human or otherwise.

"I've studied the language," Shalonie admitted. She reached again for her notebook, only to catch herself once more. Her lips twisted in frustration. "It's been dead in our world for thousands of years — only ever seen it written — I've never heard it spoken. It's exquisite."

"But do you know what they're saying?" Omen pressed.

Dev noted that the girl hadn't actually answered the initial question.

"Oh." She frowned as if realizing that she should be paying more attention to the content of the conversation than the sound of the words. "Right — well, the younger warriors think we should all be killed and dumped back into the mortal world. But Prince Cuillian and the older warriors insist we be taken to their queen instead."

Knew it. Dev ground his teeth together. He noted that while the Aelaedrine must have surely heard Shalonie's translation, they showed no sign of being perturbed that their discussion about killing all of them had been found out.

"Wait a minute, Shalonie," Omen cut in, curiosity lacing his tone instead of the alarm warranted. "How do you know who is younger? They all look the same age — and by that

I mean ageless."

Dev looked to the girl.

"Their accents are different," she explained. "There's been a vowel shift in their language — probably happened after the forming of the Covenant. The younger ones are using a pronunciation that is similar to Naracheian which is what Merchant's Common is derived from."

While the Aelaedrine still made no sign of noticing their discussion, they'd fallen silent — their whispered chatter ended.

Dev smiled in spite of himself. *That had to sting — to be told that they sound like humans!* Cuillian might have been able to guess much about the companions, but it had to alarm the faerie lords that Shalonie was able to discern something as indistinguishable as their age just from their accents alone. *Wonder when that last happened? They probably aren't used to surprises.*

Dev wasn't really certain how long they'd walked through the woods — the time of day was impossible to pin down. The sights all around him were distracting in the extreme. The constant barrage of visual stimuli caused his mind to drift. He'd catch himself from time to time, unable to remember the last few moments. It alarmed him, enough so that he found himself nervously lifting his left hand to his neck and touching the pulse point there — an old habit, one begun in his youth and now a marker of unease or nervousness. Counting the beats of his heart calmed him, settled his mind.

Eventually they arrived at a hall — not one made of brick or stone, but rather a great room formed of impossibly large and twisted trees that had grown together to create a living bower draped with flowering vines and an abundance of leaves. The dense canopy overhead arched into a protective domed roof.

The living hall was lit with magical lights that flitted and weaved among the bright flowers curling all around them. Long ornate tables had been arranged along the outer edges of the great room — all surfaces laden down with mouth-watering food and vibrant drink. In the center of the hall on a floor made of paving stones and moss, countless lords and ladies of the Aelaedrine danced a solstice revel amid the magical lights. The Aelaedrine, tall and fair, were bedecked in radiant, multicolored cloth which flowed and twirled around them as if alive. The lords and ladies glided and spun to the lilting music that came from a host of tiny sprite musicians who drifted through the air with glittering pipes made of silver reeds.

At the far end of the hall, seated regally upon a throne made of glowing pale-colored wood was an imposing woman clad in white silk, a crown of burning stars set upon her brow. The bright gemstones' glow was so dazzling Dev could not distinguish her features — all he could make out was golden hair woven together with strands of white pearls.

The music stopped as Cuillian and his warriors entered the hall. The dancers drew back and cleared a path toward the throne. Murmurs of curiosity and alarm spread like a rising wind through the host of faerie as they were led forward.

At the sight of all the scrumptious food, Dev placed a restraining hand on Kyr's shoulder. He needn't have bothered — Omen had done the same, also grabbing hold of Tormy's fur and whispering quietly to the large cat and to Tyrin seated on Kyr's shoulder. Both cats eyed the long tables piled high with treats greedily. "We haven't been invited," he overheard Omen say. "It wouldn't be polite."

Invited to dinner? We'll be lucky if we're not beheaded and dumped on the border.

As they crossed the long hall to the throne, Dev apprehensively scanned the room, seeking exits. The crowd of Aelaedrine and strange twisting vines amid the overarching trees made it impossible to see much beyond the main area however.

Dev redirected his gaze to the woman on the throne. As they approached, the light from the jewels in her crown dimmed, revealing her features. Like the rest of her court, she appeared ageless. She was as beautiful as any woman he'd ever seen. Her hair was white gold — nearly the same color as Kyr's. Her face had the same strong features as Cuillian's — cold, stern brow, high cheekbones, hauntingly alluring eyes. But unlike Cuillian, she had eyes as blue as the summer sky, clear and powerful. Superfluously, a shimmering light surrounded her, one that made it both difficult to stare at her for too long and impossible to look away.

I imagine men have ruined themselves over that face, Dev thought, glancing warily at his companions to see if they would become beguiled by her beauty, but their expressions showed more apprehension than charm. Regardless, he suspected all of them were responding to the lull of comfort radiating from the light that shone from the queen. Obstinately, Dev would not be beguiled. He knew better than to trust in such ephemeral things. Dawn's Children were just as dangerous and manipulative as those of Night.

He caught hold of Omen's wrist as they walked forward, pulling him briefly closer so that he could speak directly in his ear, though he doubted that would prevent the faeries

61

from hearing. "Promise nothing," he advised, not hopeful his words had any impact. Omen was still too young to truly understand the danger of oaths and promises, despite the oath-binding hex his brother currently suffered.

They stopped at the foot of the dais, where Cuillian paused to bow low to his queen. "We found these trespassers in the gazebo, my queen."

Dev did not think the word *trespassers* boded well for any of them. A sharp intake of breath from Shalonie confirmed his fear.

Cuillian spoke to his queen in Common instead of their own tongue. *He wants all of us to understand his words.*

"Is this not the start of the solstice?" asked the queen. Her voice was soft, but power coursed through it. The sound moved through the room like a bellowing wind. As if in response, the great trees rustled.

All the Aelaedrine faced her and bowed low, many looking startled as if the occasion of hearing the queen speak was highly unusual. Cuillian's face paled when the queen rose from her throne and took a step toward him. For a moment, the white light all around her flared, bathing everything in a radiant glow that sank deep into Dev's bones, warming him clear through. He thought he heard deep bells sounding far off in the woods.

The warriors who surround them all looked to Cuillian.

If they didn't expect the queen to speak to any of us, why would they bring us here to meet with her?

"Yes. It is, my queen," Cuillian answered after the long pause. "It is the eve of the solstice. Dawn will soon break on the longest day."

"Does not the Covenant say that on this day *we* may walk out into the world of old and look upon the bleeding

62

lands?" she continued.

Dev shivered, fighting the instinct to make the warding sign against evil. He'd never been religious — had no use for the gods — yet he was familiar enough with the words of the Covenant as they were read in temples around the world. Nowhere had he ever heard the mortal world called the *bleeding lands,* and he did not care for the implications.

"It does, my queen," Cuillian agreed. "That is what the Covenant states."

"We may move freely. But I recall no words that say the cursed children may enter our lands and walk amongst us," said the queen.

Dev tensed, understanding the breadth of the trouble they had walked into. Of the group, only Kyr and the cats seemed unperturbed — Tormy's and Tyrin's attention on the tables filled with foodstuffs, and Kyr's attention captured entirely by the great trees that made up the walls of the hall. The boy stared in rapt fascination, his mouth hanging open.

"There are no words, my queen, that grant the cursed children that freedom," Cuillian replied. His dark gaze swept over the group, his expression unreadable.

"But perhaps, they are not what they appear to be." The faerie queen took another step forward; immediately her people took one step back as if it were necessary to maintain a certain distance from their ruler. Only Cuillian held his place.

Are they afraid of her — or afraid of the situation?

The crown of jewels on the queen's brow flared again briefly before dimming to a soft glow. The queen tilted her head downward, her attention fixed on those before her. Her blue gaze moved slowly over each of them before coming to rest on Shalonie.

"A child of the Sundragons, our kin," she announced. "How astonished we were when the sun singers left our land to take up human form and dwell amongst mortals. Do they fare well?"

An astonished murmur rose all around them, the crowd shifting as they sought each other's counsel. Even Cuillian looked surprised, his focus flicking from the queen to Shalonie and back again. *He didn't expect her to speak,* Dev realized. *And certainly didn't expect her to address any of us directly. Bringing us here was just a formality to him — and now he doesn't know what to do.*

Shalonie lowered her head humbly, cognizant of the unusual honor. "The Sundragons fare well, my lady," the girl replied. "They are the gods of my land, the guardians of my countrymen, and we their devoted people."

A faint smile touched the queen's lips as if pleased by the girl's response. Her attention shifted toward Nikki and Liethan. One pale eyebrow arched up in astonishment. The crown of stars flashed briefly. "But you two are not human at all," she exclaimed. She turned first to Liethan. "You are of the lost line of Firodala!" Murmurs followed her words.

Liethan nervously cleared his throat. "My grandmother is Fion Firodala."

"Such a tragedy what befell her. We still weep for her loss and quake at the tales of her fate," the queen replied.

Liethan brushed his tangled golden hair back from his face, bafflement in his eyes. "Tragedy?" he asked uncertainly. "My grandmother is fine, and quite happy. She lives on the Corsair Isles with my grandfather."

"If you think a Firodala is 'fine' living amongst humans, you know nothing of your own history," she admonished curtly. Her words rang clear and sharp through the hall, the light of her crown turning briefly cold and hard.

"And you, Greeneyes," she addressed Nikki, the light still harsh and frosty. "You are of the line of Rillian, descendant of Straakhan." Loud, almost rude, gasps of shock and unkind titters burst forth from the Aelaedrine. "Are you of their ilk — bringers of chaos and disorder, defiant of the gods?"

Nikki looked flummoxed by her accusations. "I only just found out who my father's family is, your ladyship. I've met my grandmother . . . she seemed to be good people. And I have never defied the gods." If nothing else, Nikki's Kharakhian accent marked him as a common man, low born.

Unimpressed, the queen shifted her attention away from him and toward Dev.

The light from the crown seemed to soften briefly, grow warmer, but Dev took no comfort in it. The queen's head tilted upward, her delicate nose wrinkling as if she were scenting the air. "But you reek of the mortal world . . . and wolf!" she scoffed. "Shilvagi! Not human at all."

Dev said nothing, holding her stare despite the desire to flinch away. He hated the way her blue eyes shifted and changed into different hues.

"But there is something else too — you are not at all what you appear to be," she remarked, less mocking and more curious. "You have a very strange soul — I have never seen its like."

For a brief moment, Dev felt fingers combing through his thoughts. While the very notion that someone could look into his mind sickened him, he found himself growing still and calm at her touch. It was not the first time his mind had been attacked. He had learned many secrets in his lifetime, secrets that could not be unlearned, secrets that left him with the unshakable knowledge that he would endure — no matter what.

"So I've been told before, my lady," Dev remarked, a cold smile plastered on his face.

He felt her touch withdraw from him, and a genuine smile crossed her lips as if she were satisfied with something she'd learned, some secret she'd stolen from his mind. Dev could hear his blood coursing in his ears, the instinct for flight rising in his chest. Steel determination alone held him in place.

The pearls in her hair shimmered softly as she turned her head toward Kyr, her gaze moving rapidly over the boy's features. Kyr, however, still seemed captivated by the trees all around them and made no sign he'd even noticed the attention he was garnering.

"A Venedrine if I am not mistaken." The faerie queen glanced briefly at Cuillian who took several sudden steps forward and bowed his head to whisper quietly in her ear. She looked intrigued at his words and turned her gaze back toward Kyr. "But it is very unusual for our young elvin cousins to mix their blood with others," she remarked.

Dev shot Omen a warning look, hoping he wouldn't become angry at the queen's insult. All the elvin clans held themselves superior to humans, prejudiced against anyone considered beneath them. And while the elvin kin were generally thought to be a lesser offshoot of the faerie races, inferior perhaps if he understood the term *young cousin,* few were more looked down upon than those among the elvin races who mixed their blood with humans. Half-elvin offspring often found themselves without claim to either race. *Despised by the elvin kin. Feared by the humans.*

Omen placed a hand upon one of Kyr's thin shoulders. "My brother is the son of a Venedrine princess and Cerioth, The Dark Heart." His voice hard, Omen was in complete control.

There's the arrogance I expected.

The whisper of alarm that moved through the room was far louder and faster than the previous disturbances. The trees around them once again shook and trembled, and the distant bells sounded low and mournful, echoing all around them.

"Brother? Then you are both the sons of Cerioth!" the queen shrilled. "The Autumn Gate stands open out of season and now children of The Dark Heart have entered my realm. Does this not seem preordained! Does this not reek of fate! Have you come here to break the Covenant! Our anger has not abated!"

"No!" Omen called out, switching from arrogant to conciliatory. "We're here to try and fix things! We're not going to break the Covenant!"

"I know who you are now!" The queen's eyes flashed, and she seemed to grow taller. "You were born when Lord Cerioth escaped his imprisonment. But you are kin to more than just this boy here. You have the blood of Straakhan in you, and the Shilvagi. But there is something else, something foreign, something I cannot name." She met him head-on, but her stance had grown tense, wary, like a hunted deer. *As if she might flee at any moment. Wonder if Omen sees it.*

"I have Cerioth's and Straakhan's blood in me, it is true," Omen said slowly. "But my parents are Avarice Machelli and S'van Daenoth."

Must burn his butt to have to talk about his birth. Dev

67

bit back an inappropriate snicker.

"S'van Daenoth, son of Queen Wraiteea of Lydon," the queen murmured as if puzzling something out. "But who is your father's father?"

"Oh . . ." Omen hesitated.

Dev waited, curiosity gnawing at him too. He knew nothing of the history of the Daenoth line beyond what he knew of Avarice and 7. No one had ever told him anything about 7's past, save that he was the son of the Queen of Lydon. He could not recall ever hearing of a King of Lydon.

"A little hard to explain," Omen replied awkwardly. "Even harder than the rest of it, if you can imagine." He visibly gave up. "My grandfather was from far away — really far away."

"What strange company your family keeps," the queen remarked, and though Omen's answer was a poor explanation she seemed content to let it be. "But certainly no stranger than this creature beside you." She assessed Templar, her brows furrowed as if genuinely puzzled. "Equal parts Night and Dawn — unnatural by any judgment. Not possible by any law."

Dev's startled at that and felt Shalonie shift beside him as if trying to see what the queen saw. *He's Nightblood — what's the connection to Dawn? Can't be both. Obviously.*

Templar placed one bejeweled hand against his heart and inclined his head to the queen respectfully. "It's true, I possess Nightblood from my father's line, but I assure you my mother was entirely human. She was a princess of Windheim, a province in my land. Entirely human many generations back. No doubt about it."

The faerie queen's blue eyes turned glacial. "Your face seems familiar," she muttered as if to herself. "Your voice is familiar — I have heard it before . . . somewhere. Are you a bard, perhaps?"

Templar laughed. "Me? No, my lady," he assured her. "I can carry a tune well enough, but I've never studied music. I have no skill in it."

"And yet I recognize you," insisted the queen. "Who is your father?"

"King Antares of Terizkand," Templar replied.

Her frown deepened. "I have never met him." She tossed her head back as if still deeply bothered. "And who is his father?"

"His name is Shauntares of the city of Revival," Templar answered. "I doubt you've ever—"

An anguished wail went up, spreading throughout the room as all the Aelaedrine cried out denial and dissent.

The queen drew back toward her throne. The crown of stars blazed upon her brow, burning now like flames. Rage hardened her face, and she fixed her gaze upon Templar as if he'd done something unforgivable. "You are the grand-child of Caradzun the Destroyer!" Her words a condemnation.

Dev cautiously reached for the blowgun in his sleeve. *Something just went horribly wrong.*

Cuillian drew his white blade from its scabbard.

Omen and Templar both held their hands up in alarm, as if trying to hold back the rise of the ocean. "No!" both men shouted.

Templar took a half step forward. "That can't be! My grandfather is a peaceful man, a pacifist, devoted to the gods! I've never heard of anyone named Caradzun. You have the wrong man! My grandfather's name is Shauntares."

69

"He's right!" Omen added zealously. "I've met the man — he's a good man. He won't even eat meat he's so opposed to violence. He could never destroy anything. You're wrong about him!"

Dev flinched. *Don't tell a queen that she's wrong, you fools.* He wasn't certain which was going to doom them first — Templar's supposed heritage or the insult Omen had just inadvertently blurted out.

"Wrong?" The queen's voice rose over the furor. "How old are you!" she demanded of them both.

"I'm fifteen," Omen replied, cooperating hesitantly as he'd realized his misstep. "And Templar is seventeen."

"And in all your many long years of life you have come to learn the entire history of your parents and their parents before them?" Her voice dripped with sarcasm. "You have learned all of their secrets, know of all the lives they have lived, all the people they have met, all the deeds they have done! You think I'm wrong when you and your companions know nothing of your own bloodlines!"

"Well, no . . ." Omen stammered. "I guess . . . we . . . "

"Omy, when is we going to have lunch?" Tormy broke in, interrupting the tense conversation as if utterly unaware of the danger.

Dead silence settled over the room.

The faerie queen looked at the giant cat. She blinked twice and worked her jaw, but no words escaped her perfect rose petal lips.

Did she not see him before? Dev wondered. *How do you miss a giant orange cat?* Until he'd spoken, none of them — not even Cuillian — had taken more than a passing glance at the creature, as if a giant cat were nothing particularly unusual. *In this land that might be true.*

70

"Tormy . . ." Omen began quietly. His shoulders sagged as if a heavy weight had been placed upon it.

Is he embarrassed, or worried they'll hurt the cat?

"I is sorry, Omy," Tormy insisted blithely, tail lashing from side to side. "I is listening really good to all the talkings and carryings on about all of the peoples. But my tummy is rumbling something fierce, and there is being lunch just over there. Do you see it, Omy? It is being just right over there on the tables!"

"I is hungry too!" Tyrin proclaimed. He'd squirmed his way out of Kyr's pocket and had climbed onto the boy's head, draping himself like an orange cap, white paws dangling over the boy's brow.

Kyr still seemed oblivious, his attention on the trees and the lights moving among the flowers.

"Mrow," Tyin cleared his tiny throat. "I is counting numbers to be patientnessness, but I is running out of paws and is having to count my tail, so I is counting all the way to five. I is thinking that is too many numbers for all the talkings and carryings on."

"Way too many numbers!" Tormy agreed vehemently.

"You have brought the Tau el Faigntha into my realm," the queen uttered so quietly that Dev could barely hear her. Then she sank into a low curtsy. Around them, all her people did the same, the men going so far as to drop to one knee and bow their heads.

On his knees, Cuillian hung his head.

Chapter 5: Lies

OMEN

*T*hey're bowing to my cat! Omen thought in astonishment as he stared at the lowered head of Queen Illythia and the kneeling form of Cuillian beside her. Around them, all the other Aelaedrine were bowing as well, dead silence settling over the woodland hall. Omen suspected the flabbergasted look on Shalonie's face mirrored the one on his own.

He quickly tried to translate the words the faerie queen had used. She'd spoken in Sul'eldrine, which he'd become quite fluent in since the cats' arrival. But she'd used terms he wasn't familiar with. *Tau el is a high honorific. Faigntha . . . blessing, bless . . .*

"The ones who bless?" he whispered to Shalonie for confirmation.

But she shook her head, her eyes gleaming with curiosity. "The ones who are blessed, the ones who are sacred — a state of being rather than an action."

"And what has brought the Tau el Faigntha into the Gated Lands?" asked the queen, rising slowly. Her court followed suit, Cuillian going so far as to leave his drawn sword lying untouched on the ground at his feet. All their attention was on the two cats now, Omen and the others having been dismissed from notice.

Tormy's ears perked forward as if realizing the queen was addressing him directly. "We is on a noblenessness quest," he exclaimed proudly. "Exceptedness I is not being supposed to be talking about some of it — which I is not 'member, 'membering, on account of the fact that Kyr is being hexed."

"That is why we is bringing Shalonie!" Tyrin explained from his draped position on Kyr's head. "On account of the fact that she is being good with the words and the talkings."

"A quest?" The queen directed her question to Omen and Shalonie. Her expression, though rage-filled only moments ago, was now the picture of solicitation.

Thrown by the fact that his cat had managed to derail the tense situation, Omen placed a hand against Tormy's white ruff. "We were trying to get into the Autumn Lands." He prompted Shalonie with a tilt of his chin. *Someone else better explain or I'll say the wrong thing and hurt Kyr!*

Luckily Shalonie caught on immediately, taking up the narrative for him. "We're here to rescue King Khylar of Kharakhan who has been kidnapped by the Autumn Dwellers. We hope that when we find out what happened to him, we can also figure out what went wrong with the Autumn Gate — find a way to close it."

The queen exchanged a long look with Cuillian, both of their expressions unreadable.

Omen's legs twitched with frustration. He didn't dare use his psionics to try and read them — when the queen had questioned him earlier he'd felt the full force of her powerful mind pressing around him. Her mind was unlike anything he'd ever sensed before — not truly psionic in nature, but something more elemental and raw. He suspected reading her mind would be like reading the mind of a lightning storm.

"King Khylar of Kharakhan has not been kidnapped," replied the queen.

Omen found himself shaking his head involuntarily. *Mother was right all along. Indee lied.*

"Khylar Set-Manasan is the Gatekeeper of the Autumn Lands," the queen continued. "He is the one who has opened the Gate out of season."

"The Gatekeeper!" Omen exclaimed, shock overcoming any sense of decorum. That was the last thing he'd expected to hear. "Since when?"

"It is a recent thing," the queen replied. "Anyone can find themselves tasked with being a Gatekeeper — it is a duty that changes hands without notice. What governs the choice is something only the gods themselves know. The current Gatekeeper of our lands is a human woman named Roe Traveen."

Recognition flashed through Omen at the name. "Contessa Roe Traveen of Lydon?" Omen asked.

"Even so," the queen agreed.

"But she's a friend of my grandmother! Are you saying I could have just asked her to open the Summer Gate for us?" Omen demanded. *We have a Cypher Portal directly into Lydon! It would have taken two days at the most to reach the Contessa's home!*

"Perhaps," the queen replied. "Though I do not know if she would have done so. She, like most Gatekeepers, holds her duty sacred and would not flagrantly defy the words of the Covenant for the sake of your convenience."

"But when did—" Omen broke off in frustration, worried about Kyr. The boy made no sign that any of this had triggered the hex mark on his hand, but Omen feared saying too much. The hex mark had grown so large — triggering it now would be unspeakable.

"When did Khylar become the Gatekeeper?" Dev spoke

74

up, asking the question most on Omen's mind. One look at the Machelli confirmed that Dev was not surprised by the turn of events.

He knew this was all some horrible lie to begin with — just like my mother did.

"The previous Gatekeeper was King Galseric, ruler of the Teyledrine," said the faerie queen. "It is whispered that he wandered deep into his lands to seek the answer to a riddle he had found. And instead of finding answers, something found him. Something happened to him; it changed him. He awoke something old and ancient — a power that even I have never heard of. A power that predates the Aelaedrine. It twisted him, and now he destroys everything that stands in his path. The duty of Gatekeeper immediately fell from him and passed to another — to Khylar Set-Manasan of Kharakhan. It is he who threatens the Covenant by holding open the Autumn Gate. If you wish to learn why and set right what has gone wrong, you must go into the Autumn Lands and seek him out."

"Before lunch!" Tormy protested in horror. "But it is being right there on the table!"

The queen's blue eyes lit up with amusement. "No, certainly not," she agreed. "Let it not be said that the Aelaedrine denied hospitality to the Tau el Faigntha or their companions however questionable their pedigrees."

So now we're the cats' companions, Omen thought, imagining that his parents were not going to believe any of it. *And we have all been judged to rank beneath the fuzz faces.*

"All right, we is not saying no words about hospitalitinessness," Tyrin agreed. "As long as we is getting lunch."

"We is getting lunch, right Omy?" Tormy pleaded.

Omen wavered. *Considering the Aelaedrine were ready to kill us before they noticed the cats, I doubt they'd react well if I denied their request now. Not to mention Tormy and Tyrin would never let me hear the end of it.* "Well, I suppose we could stay for a few hours," Omen conceded, hoping he wasn't making a mistake.

"Excellent!" The faerie queen clapped her hands. The deep bell sounded once more, and for a moment it seemed to Omen as if the room was filled with a blinding light. He thought he had drifted away again — from one moment to the next the room had changed. The tables that had been lining the walls were now set in the center of the hall, the Aelaedrine seated, already participating in the great feast set before them. And while Omen could not remember moving, he was being led to an empty seat at one of the tables along with the rest of them. Cuillian himself escorted them to their chairs, his movements formal and sharp as a knife's edge.

Omen glanced back over his shoulder at the dais. The queen had retaken her seat on the throne and sat utterly unmoving, the glowing light of the crown of stars on her head burning once again so that he could not make out her features. He thought she seemed more stone than flesh, and he shuddered. *Unnatural — like a living dream.* To his frustration, he could not truly discern what was real and what was not.

At the table with the others, he watched in astonishment as dish after dish was placed before him by small men with fur-covered bodies and cloven hooves instead of feet. *Fauns!* Omen realized. He'd seen their kind before in the wild woods of Scaalia, but he had never heard of them acting as servants, had thought them too savage and feral to be tamed.

He glanced down at the full plate of food before him. While he'd been quite hungry a moment ago, he did not feel so now. *Did I eat already?* His companions were all seated on either side of the table, partaking of numerous dishes filled with sweets. The two cats happily devoured the delicacies placed before them while Aelaedrine women gathered around, entertaining the felines with stories about dancing fish and chasing sprites and spriggans in the woodlands. *The faeries are flattering the cats. How strange.*

Seated next to them, Kyr intently studied a strange, glowing glass object one of the Aelaedrine had placed before him. The device was made up of sliding pieces that fit together in various patterns to create different shapes — a puzzle of some sort. His brother looked enthralled with the object.

Omen found his eyes drifting over the others. Save Kyr and the cats, all of them looked deeply disturbed — picking at their food, pushing around utensils, checking the exits, flinching away from the Aelaedrine. *Faeries . . . I knew they were dangerous, but they've upset everyone with nothing more substantial than vague secrets. We don't even know if any of it's true.*

He guessed at his companions' thoughts. Shalonie, thrilled by the new knowledge she'd gained, was nonetheless offended and disturbed that the Aelaedrine believed her beloved Sundragons had humbled themselves by living among the Melians.

Liethan and Nikki were both working out what they'd learned of their families. The Corsairs were a tight-knit bunch, devoted to one another. The idea that the matriarch of his family was hiding some tragic secret did not sit well with Liethan. And no doubt, Nikki was now wondering if the new family he'd discovered was somehow not what they seemed, and if the monstrous stories his mother had told him about his father were true after all. *I've never heard much about Straakhan or Rillian — neither Beren nor Kadana ever wanted to talk about them, saying some things were best left forgotten.*

And Templar . . . Omen shot him a worried look. His friend's face was fixed in anger, his eyes burning with an unnatural light. *He doesn't like what they said about his grandfather.* Omen could sympathize — while Templar spoke blithely about the contentious relationship he had with his family, Omen knew he was devoted to them. And while Omen didn't know Templar's grandfather Shauntares well, he'd also never heard anyone speak ill of him. Certainly he'd never heard of anyone named Caradzun the Destroyer. *Caradzun is also not a Terizkandian name. Sounds more Ezthedian.*

And should we believe any of this — Indee lied. Why not Illythia too? But then what is the deal about the cats?

A thought struck him, and Omen shivered. *Indee sent us here to rescue Khylar . . . but if Khylar has not been kidnapped . . . This isn't a rescue mission. If he's here willingly, there's nothing to rescue him from. But I have to force him to go back in order to save Kyr.* Omen's heart stirred with trepidation. *Am I supposed to kidnap him back?*

"Indee lied," he stated out loud, trying to wrap his mind around what that might mean for all of them.

"Didn't we know that already?" Templar asked, his anger still clear in his voice. "I thought it was sort of implied."

Omen's hands tightened into fists. "Yes, we knew she was lying about something, but all this time I thought this

was a rescue mission. It never even occurred to me that—"
he broke off and glanced at Kyr.

"It never occurred to you that Khylar might not want to
be rescued," Dev finished for him. "You do realize that to
save your brother, we may have to force him to return
against his will."

Omen glared. "You knew this was a possibility all
along?"

"I knew that things were going to go horribly wrong,"
Dev corrected. "The world is filled with people you can't
trust. Your mother knew that too. I always expect the worst
from people, and I'm rarely disappointed."

That sounds like a horrible way to live. Omen chafed at
the thought.

"Khylar is an honorable man," Omen stated firmly,
glancing at Liethan for confirmation. "Right?" Truth was,
Omen knew Caythla far better than he'd ever known Khylar.

But Liethan was frowning. "Something else has to be
going on here," the Corsair insisted. "My cousin Tara
would never go along with this — would never do anything
to endanger the Covenant. She's devoted to the gods, and a
priestess to The Lady. And I can't imagine Khylar would do
anything to damage the Covenant either."

"Really?" Dev asked. "This is the son of Indee, the person who hexed Kyr in the first place. And let's not forget
that his father is a man who sold out his own people and
made a deal with a Night Lord in exchange for immortality.
I'd say he certainly has it in him to cause chaos."

"This does put Indee's motivation in a new light however," Shalonie chimed in, sounding oddly hopeful. They all
looked at her as if she'd suddenly sprouted wings.

Still doesn't want to think ill of a Sundragon's wife. "What do you mean?" Omen asked. "She still hexed Kyr."

"But if she knew Khylar didn't want to be rescued, she'd have no choice but to force him to come home to protect the Covenant," Shalonie explained.

"She still didn't need to hex anyone," Omen grumped. "Does anyone here think I would ever refuse a quest to protect the Covenant? And now she's tied my hands — I have to bring him home to protect Kyr."

"Not to mention that it may not solve the problem," Dev pointed out. "Bringing him home may end the hex. But just because we bring him back to Kharakhan doesn't mean he'll close the Autumn Gate. We also have to figure out why he's defying the Covenant and solve that problem as well."

"Which means figuring out what happened to the Teyledrine king," Templar considered.

Omen glanced to Cuillian seated nearby and conversing with several other Aelaedrine in his native language; it was obvious to him that these faerie knew a great deal more than they'd let on. *Let's see how badly they want to please the cats!* "Lord Cuillian?" he called out. "Do any of you know exactly what happened in the Autumn Lands?"

The man turned, inclining his head stiffly. Cuillian's eyes were unreadable. "We have little interest in the other lands, and little contact with the younger races like the Teyledrine. All we know is that some time ago Autumn Dwellers began appearing on our borders, fleeing from the Teyledrine King. They spoke of some dark shadow that was spreading over their lands. The younger Autumn Dwellers sought refuge in the mortal world, but there are many in the Autumn Lands who will not find the mortal world hospitable. If the Gate remains open, there will be war, the

Covenant will be broken, and mortals will die." He spoke calmly as if imparting trivial information.

Cold bastard! Omen thought in shock. "And this doesn't concern you?" he demanded incredulously.

Cuillian tilted his head, amusement lighting his eyes. "Why should it? The Aelaedrine are strong enough to protect themselves. We have been to war many times — we do not fear it."

"And what about all the races that can't protect themselves?" Omen pressed on.

"I imagine they will die," Cuillian said simply. "It is what the mortal races do."

"You is being mean," Tormy proclaimed. He looked up from cleaning cream off his front paws. There was a half eaten trell on his plate and a large bowl of cream beside him.

Cuillian and the Aelaedrine nearest him looked startled by the cat's pronouncement. Omen nearly laughed out loud at the looks upon their faces. *Good for you, Tormy! Maybe Tyrin will curse them!*

"You is supposed to be helping peoples on account of the fact that you is great heroes," Tormy continued firmly. "That is what it is saying in all the story books. Tyrin, 'member 'member the storybooks?"

Tyrin, who lay stretched out next to Tormy's plate, raised his fuzzy head, ears twitching. "I is 'member 'membering," the little cat agreed. "Heroes is always helping with the questings and carryings on."

"Exactednessly!" Tormy thwacked his tail hard against the ground. "So, you is helping."

Cuillian opened his mouth to protest and then promptly shut it again, staring at the cats in bewilderment. It occurred to Omen that the man had no idea what to say to the cats. *He actually cares what the cats think — they all do. They don't know how to respond to this.*

"What was that term you used earlier — Tau el Faigntha?" Omen asked, looking from Cuillian to Tormy. "Tormy, do you know what it means — is that what your race is called?"

"I think we is being called cats, Omy," Tormy replied.

Omen chuckled. "No, I mean — do you know what Tau el Faigntha means?"

"It is meaning that we is being special," Tormy purred.

"But why are you special?" Omen pressed, realizing too late what he said. The look of astonishment on Tormy's face almost made him choke. *Didn't mean that the way it sounded!* He could hear Templar and Liethan biting back laughter.

Tormy's eyes widened, ears perked forward, whiskers flared. "I is having freckles on my nose!" the cat exclaimed as if the answer to Omen's question was painfully obvious.

"And I is being good at maths!" Tyrin added for good measure, also staring at Omen as if he were ready to pounce on his face. The little cat's tail was lashing violently from side to side.

Omen cringed "Oh . . . right . . . of course! I knew that!" he sputtered. "You're brilliant of course — and freckles! They're . . . really frecklish."

"Omen, how many is a few?" Kyr broke in, looking up from his puzzle suddenly.

Distracted, Omen frowned. "What?"

"A few? How many is that?" Kyr asked again, seeming quite serious.

Omen's attention was still on the cats. "I don't know —

three perhaps."

"Then it's time to go," Kyr announced.

That caught all their attention. The boy had set aside his puzzle and risen to his feet, looking ready to leave.

"What do you mean?" Omen asked, reaching out to grab his wrist in case he walked off.

Kyr just stared at him guilelessly. "You said we would stay for a few hours," he explained. "We have been here three hours. It's time to go."

"Kyr, we just sat down," Omen reminded him. "Just a few moments ago."

But Kyr gave a sharp shake of his head. "No, that was three hours ago. I looked at the clock. Lilyth taught me how to tell time."

They all looked around the great hall, seeking some sign of a clock. As far as Omen could see, there was nothing of the sort anywhere.

"What clock?" Omen asked.

"The one in our front hall," Kyr explained.

"In our house in Melia?" Omen clarified, perturbed. There was a large chiming clock in their front foyer at home; every morning at dawn one of the servants wound the gears that made it work. When Kyr had first come to live with them, he'd been fascinated by the object.

Kyr's eyes were clear and unwavering. "I looked at it before we started eating. It's been three hours."

Omen grimaced. "Kyr, it doesn't actually work like that," he started to explain.

"Actually it might," Shalonie interrupted him before he could continue. The girl looked as if something had just occurred to her. She was staring ponderously down at her plate of food.

"What?" Omen asked warily.

"Time doesn't pass the same way in the Gated Lands," she began. "There are hundreds of stories about people who enter the faerie lands for one night only to return to the mortal world a hundred years later. Or the opposite sometimes. It's entirely possible that we've been here for three hours. Are any of you still hungry?"

Omen glanced down at his plate. He couldn't recall actually eating anything, but she was right. He was no longer hungry. He looked toward the cats — if anyone would still be hungry it would be them. But both Tormy and Tyrin were now contently cleaning their whiskers. While there was still food on their plates, both seemed disinterested in it. *And that never happens — not unless they'd eaten a great deal already.*

Omen took in a sharp breath and looked at Cuillian. "How long have we been here?"

Cuillian, still subdued by Tormy's scolding, waved one hand dismissively. "We have no interest in time here," he explained. "Clocks are an invention of the mortal world and have no meaning to us."

"Do you mention that to the mortals who come here?" Omen asked.

"Mortals do not belong here," Cuillian reminded him. "They come here at their own peril."

Omen stood up. "If Kyr says it's been three hours, then I'm guessing it has been," he announced. "We should go."

Dev stood as well. "What about our belongings?" he asked. "And how do we get to the Autumn Lands from here?"

Cuillian glanced briefly at the other Aelaedrine sitting around the table, his gaze turning then toward the queen.

She remained unmoving. He stood and inclined his head to them, his eyes resting briefly on the two cats. "Very well," he agreed. "If you wish to enter the Autumn Lands, you must go through the Shadows Between — it is a passage-way of sorts. You might perceive it as a tunnel. I will show you where to enter, and your belongings will be returned to you."

"The Shadows Between," Tyrin mused out loud as if testing out the name of the passageway. "I is not liking that name. Is we having to do more maths to get out?"

Uncomprehending, Cuillian stared at the small cat. "I do not believe so," he replied. "You need only stick to the path I show you."

Omen exchanged a pointed look with Templar who just shook his head. He was right of course. They had little choice but to trust the Aelaedrine. *And when has blind trust ever gotten me in trouble?*

Chapter 6: Camp

OMEN

They followed the path Cuillian had shown them. Omen, leading the group, found himself looking back over his shoulder repeatedly to assure himself the others were all still there. Time dragged, and the path stretched endlessly forward.

The Shadows Between, well-named, he thought, for he had no other words to describe the area they traveled through. It was neither tunnel nor roadway. All he could see were dull grey shadows and a subtle eddying of black and white mist that parted in one direction as if showing them the way. Not even the glow from Templar's light spell helped, neither illuminating nor obscuring the dense shades. *Just mist — drab and swirling and damp.*

Omen tapped the fingers of his sword hand against his leg, increasing the beat from half notes to sixteenth notes against the tempo of the imaginary common time metronome in his head. He'd wanted some sense of time — some concept of how long they'd walked, but even the beat of music wasn't helping him. He wished suddenly he could see the clock in their front hallway the way Kyr apparently could.

What if the Aelaedrine betrayed us, and the tunnel leads nowhere? And we're trapped. Forever.

"Do not step off the path," Cuillian had warned them when he'd returned their belongings. But Omen was still unable to see what path the warrior had been referring to.

Just mist and more mist. *Guess we go in the direction that seems less misty . . . How is less misty a path?*

He could barely see his companions, but even obscured their faces showed grave concern — all save for Kyr, Tormy, and Tyrin who were blithely trotting after Omen. *They're following me . . . I have no idea where I'm going.* At one point, he'd even thought about suggesting they turn around and go back. But there was nothing behind them — just more mist. *There is no way back.*

Even his psionics felt dull and muted as if he were half asleep. *This is madness — I can't sense anything out here.* But just as Omen was ready to air his increasing misgivings, the haze in front of him swirled away, leaving only darkness. It took Omen a moment to realize that what he was seeing was a cave entrance. A moment later, he could make out the rock forming around it.

Not a cave entrance — a cave exit! We're inside a cave!

He stumbled to a stop and narrowed his eyes, trying to peer through the darkness — it cleared, solidified. The stone walls of the cave grew sharp; the glowing ball of light following just over Templar's left shoulder illuminated the yellow ocher stone walls of the cave. Past the blackness of the cave mouth, Omen spotted color variations — a dark sky cast into midnight blue, filled with pinprick stars.

He stepped forward carefully, testing the ground as he went — hard stone met his probing, and he breathed in fresh air. Vast sky and moonlit woodland stretched out before him.

The others followed hesitantly.

"Between earth and sky, we seemed to have landed halfway up the mountain," Dev gauged.

"Or halfway down, depending on your disposition,"

Templar quipped.

The night they had stepped into was dark and cold, not even the lingering scent of summer remaining. The sky was icy, lit with stars and a heavy harvest moon. And while the thick fog of the Shadows Between was gone, a dark brume still lingered in the air — cold and wet. It settled over Omen, icy fingers moving down his spine as it drenched his face and hair in a matter of moments.

They found themselves on the edge of a mountain path — vast rocks and trees below them, more above them. The path in front of the cave entrance curved upward around the mountain, leading toward the summit.

"I is being wet!" Tormy exclaimed, outraged, and shook his body violently. He was once again wearing his saddle. A light dusting of icy dew had settled upon the leather. The straps and buckles flapped wildly as Tormy shook out his coat.

"&$@*#!" Tyrin agreed, mimicking his brother's mighty shimmy in miniature from atop Kyr's shoulder.

"Quiet!" Omen urged. "We don't really know where we are. Let's just get the lay of the land."

The companions grouped closer together and formed a protective circle around Kyr and the cats.

"Something is moving in the dark," Kyr whispered. "It's all around us."

"Where Kyr?" Omen pressed, guessing his brother could sense something he could not. His eyes were still adjusting to the change in environment as he tried to take in the surroundings as quickly as possible. They were exposed on the mountainside — Templar had reclaimed his magical light and smothered it so that their eyes could better adjust to the darkness.

"There!" the boy whispered, pointing up toward the mountaintop. Omen could see now that another path led up from the floor of the valley below along a gentler rise toward a cresting peak, easier to reach than the cave they were standing before.

Tormy had pushed himself forward, ears pivoting in the direction Kyr was pointing, amber eyes focused on the distant shadows. As Omen followed the cat's eyeline, he could see eerie shapes moving up the mountainside, silhouettes scrambling in the darkness as they climbed upward toward the peak. Omen struggled to identify what he could see in the moonlight.

"There's a purple glow at the top of the mountain," Shalonie interrupted his intent focus. She motioned to where a disc of light radiated purple and gold beams. It was pulsing as if the light emanating from it was spinning, and Omen thought he could distantly hear the sound of a slow deep drum coming from the glow. There was something ancient and eternal about that pulsing light — like a beacon fixed in a permanent point in space and time. And though Omen had never before seen it, had little knowledge of such things, and had never thought overly long on the subject — he knew immediately what it was.

"The Autumn Gate," Dev breathed.

"Opening up a direct path to Kharakhan," Shalonie concluded.

"And that's where all the beasties are going," Templar said, resigned. "Like moths to a flame." The dark shadows moving upward from the valley floor were all marching in the direction of the pulsing light.

"What beasties?" Nikki and Liethan asked at the same time.

89

"There, in the shadows along the tree line," Omen pointed, his voice clipped. "There are critters climbing up toward the Gate."

Nikki hurriedly scrambled through his pack and fumbled out the brass tinderbox Kadana had included in his supplies.

"Hundreds," Templar added. "I can't tell what they are — but they're all sorts of different creatures judging by the shapes."

"The mountain is crawling with &$%#@* orclet & %^$#@!" Tyrin added and licked his tiny pink tongue across his teeth. "I is still wondering how they is tasting."

"Not now," Kyr tried to soothe the hungry feline, reaching up to scratch the kitten's chin.

"Kyr is being right. We is eating the orclets later," Tormy agreed. "They is being bestest for breakfasts."

Nikki lit his torch after several tries, the wet air making the simple process tricky.

"Fine," Omen whispered sharply. "Eat, later. Now, shush! We have to get past them if we want to find Khylar. Nikki, the torch will just draw attention to us — there's too many of them." He motioned to the young man to put out the flame.

But Nikki stubbornly glared, holding the torch away from Omen as if to protect the burning light. "We can't allow the Autumn Dwellers through the Gate into Kharakhan!" Nikki spoke up with unusual authority. "They'll kill every human they run across." Without waiting for a reply, he set off on the narrow path winding away from the cavern opening and toward the long line of shadows moving upward toward the Autumn Gate. He held the flaming torch aloft.

"Nikki, what are you doing?" Shalonie hurried after the young man, rushing to try to catch up to him. She held her right arm stiffly at her side, no doubt still in pain from the only partially healed wyvern wound.

"Nikki!" Omen hissed after them — of all the members of their group to act out of turn, he hadn't expected it from the normally amenable Deldano.

"Now what, oh great one?" Templar shoved Omen's shoulder in jest, looking amused by the sudden rebellion. "We can't exactly allow them to go up there alone."

"I know!" Omen growled, not entirely certain that he enjoyed taking someone else's lead but at a complete loss what to do instead. He pushed forward after the two figures, Tormy and the others swiftly following as they chased after Nikki's bobbing torch.

As his eyes adjusted further, the others also found their footing more confidently. Their path was narrow and led upward toward the glowing Gate along a separate approach from the one the dark creatures followed.

Tormy's giant foot slipped once or twice, but the cat brought himself back to balance before anyone had the chance to come to his aid. Walking beside him, Kyr clutched onto Tormy's saddle and kept the feline's pace with no complaint.

The glow of the purple and golden lights grew more vibrant as they neared the top of the mountain. The lights bounced off the wet surfaces of the surrounding rocks and trees as if they were reflecting off mirrors. The effect dazzled Omen's vision and distracted the cats, whose heads whipped from side to side as if they were watching a charm of hummingbirds in flight.

The Autumn Gate itself rose like an enormous spinning

91

wheel of colors and lights. Omen thought he heard a crack-le emanating from within, and the small hairs on his arms stood up.

An indiscriminate multitude of creatures, visible to all in the Gate's light, continued to rush upward along the sec-ondary path. Creatures as familiar as orclets and fire lizards wiggled between both the hideous and breathtaking Dwellers of the Autumn Lands: glorious faerie ladies on lit-ters borne by hedgehogs and giant mice, ludicrous toad fig-ures that spanned the colors of the rainbow and hopped over one another in a frantic game of leapfrog, skeletal horses, swine made of dripping honey, Treewalkers with their roots dragging behind them, creatures made of clay, creatures made of mist, creatures made of fire, creatures Omen had to turn from. All clambered toward the open Au-tumn Gate. And all did so in ominous silence, predator and prey walking alongside one another in harmony.

Something invisible pushed Omen aside. The force of the unexpected shove sent him bumbling into Templar.

"Watch it," Templar said, but caught him from falling to the ground nonetheless.

"Halt!" Nikki's voice boomed through the night, shatter-ing the silence. "No one else enters my home! You're defy-ing the gods!"

"Ah, great," Dev scorned. "Tavern boy is championing the gods now. They don't care."

The swelling tide of Dwellers paused briefly. Hundreds of eyes fastened on Nikki, who stood before the Gate, his mace in one hand, his torch in the other, both presented with purpose. The silence broke as the creatures roared out clamorous sounds that rushed toward Omen, streams of gnarls, chirps, squeals, croaks, growls, bleats, warbles, and roars swatting him as if they had mass and heft.

Omen heard a quick inhale from Shalonie, and for a brief instant even he had to admit that Nikki looked the part of the fierce hero. But reality set in all too soon.

The swath of Dwellers moved forward and flooded around Nikki who seemed like an islet in a maelstrom. None attacked, so the young man found himself unable to strike and unable to drive back any of them. They moved around him, ignoring his very presence as they continued to swarm toward the Gate.

Omen moved ahead of the cats and Templar to stand at Nikki's side, sword still sheathed. "We can't stop them like this, Nikki. There are too many," he said to his new-found brother. "Put your weapon away."

"Maybe I can close the Gate," Shalonie called from beside Dev. The Machelli had moved in front of her to protect her from the onrush of creatures. Her words, unlike Nikki's, however, had a profound effect. With a sudden shift, the onslaught of creatures turned their gleaming eyes on the girl.

"I mean . . ." Shalonie stammered.

Omen and Nikki pushed through the mewling mass to reach Shalonie, but Tormy protectively leaped in front of her first, right paw raised in warning. The cat let out a terrible gnarling hiss, ears flattening, nose scrunched up as he drew his muzzle upward, baring his long deadly teeth.

At that, the threatening mob made no further move toward the girl and the giant cat, but from between clawed toes, cloven hooves, wide-spread flippers, and every variety of shod and unshod foot, pieces of rock and segments of boulder began moving as if the ground itself had come to life. The rocks and gravel rolled and flew together, swirling upward into two enormous forms. In moments, two stony hulks took shape in front of them, great fists balled and raised to the sky.

"Stone guardians!" Templar warned. "Step back!"

The sea of creatures parted and dispersed, moving back toward the open Gate, the stone refining as if invisible sculptors were busily chiseling their lines and brutish features. The stone monstrosities took several steps forward.

Omen gaped for seconds before a rough shove from Templar brought him back to the urgency of the situation. Abruptly, Omen unslung his great sword and drew the blade from its sheath. Gripping it with both hands, he brought the blade down on the closest hulk's thigh with all his might. The great leg cracked, and Omen felt a cocky grin cross his face, but then the crevice mended as tiny pebbles seamlessly embedded themselves in the gash, filling in the cut. The stone guardian stood whole once more.

"Stoneskin!" Dev yelled, grabbing Tormy's fur, stopping him from chomping down on the guardian's arm. "Stay out of its way!" The young Machelli shrugged off his pack and reached for something inside it. *Another weapon,* Omen guessed.

The mountaintop teemed with the ebb and flow of escaping Dwellers, and Omen's group to a person and feline stood momentarily helpless in their wake, unable to move past the stone guardians.

"We guard the Gate," a hollow voice sounded all around them. "You will not interfere with the Gate." The sound was coming from the stone guardians' gaping mouths.

"We guard Kharakhan," Omen threw back. "You will not defy the Covenant and interfere with Kharakhan."

The bulky stone warriors halted, perhaps unable to formulate an answer or to respond.

"They are supernatural constructs," Shalonie whispered to Omen. "They can only respond in ways that their creator foresaw."

The hulks no longer moved on the group, but they placed themselves to either side of them, prohibiting any movement toward the Gate or toward the groups of strange beasts slipping through the light and disappearing into the hills and forests of Kharakhan on the other side.

What if the horde just appears in the middle of a village or a city? Omen shuddered at the thought. *They'll destroy everything.*

"Take us to your master!" Omen demanded loudly, filling his voice with as much authority as he could muster.

"Who speaks?" one of the stone guardians asked, turning its hollow eyes on Omen. The carved face shifted and moved as if trying to simulate the muscle movement of speech.

"I am Omen Daenoth!" Omen rose to his full height. "I will see Khylar Set-Manasan."

Omen hadn't finished pronouncing Khylar's name when the hulk nodded its giant head, stone swirling and moving around like a body of water as the creature turned and began a steady trudge down the mountain path. "Follow!" it commanded.

"Well, that works too," Dev said with a wry smile. He held a thick coil of rope in one hand. "Would have been more fun to lasso the critter though. They shatter when they fall." Reluctantly, he started stuffing the rope back into his pack.

The group followed behind the stone guardian, whose quick pace belied the enormity of its mass. With little to do but go along, Omen noted that the other stone warrior remained to guard the Gate, allowing droves of the large and small to enter the mountains and woodlands of Kharakhan.

If ever we get that Gate closed, we're going to have to catch all of them and throw them back into the Autumn Lands, he thought with chagrin. Like Dev, he had little faith that the gods would interfere to put things back where they belonged.

Following after the stone guardian, the group was ignored by the crush of creatures moving upward past them — all still perniciously silent and some so strange that Tormy was practically vibrating with excitement at the need to chase them.

Omen, for his part, felt disturbed — he'd never seen such creatures before — had never even imagined that such a wide variety of things could exist. To see them all together, all moving in unison with one purpose in mind, was extremely unsettling. *I thought humans were the most populous creatures in the world. But one look at this . . . a simple farmer can't face this horde. Without the Gated Lands, what must the world have been like?*

They entered the valley at the base of the mountain and made their way through a thickly wooded forest. Another gradual rise upward led them across a hilltop and onto a cliffside clearing where they could look outward across a wide expanse of land. The plump harvest moon had risen higher in the sky directly ahead of them, and they could see now the glimmering shine of a vast ocean, a trail of silver moonlight shining like a watery path from the horizon. A cool, salty breeze whipped over them.

The moonlight was bright enough to reveal a sight that took Omen's breath for several long seconds. The rolling

96

waves of the bay below were dotted with black, shadowy shapes — rigid wooden ships and undulating giant serpents. Closer to shore, smaller shapes moved inland, driving toward what looked like an already crowded beach.

The beach itself spread out in a crescent ringed by the very cliffs they stood upon. Omen could see a clear demarcation of two groups within the crescent bay.

Perched upon the wide stretch of the rocky outcropping was a cluster of campfires. The wide outcropping jutted toward the beach, which lay far beneath them. Omen and his group were descending into the middle of the great camp at the very center curve of the crescent. Beyond the rocky outcropping, the bay spread out below to their right and to their left — like two great horns of a creature pointing toward the vast ocean. Straight ahead, facing due west, a swath of empty sand stood between them and the water's edge where wave after wave crashed upon the shore.

A second group of shapes awaited just at the shoreline, spread out along the wet sand of the surf from one tip of the crescent horn to the other. It was an immense horde of unmoving shadows that simply stood motionless, heedless of the surf swirling around their feet as they waited, silent in the moonlight, no fires illuminating their numbers. This second force was swelling as the shadows coming from the great ships out at sea joined them, easing into their numbers before growing as still and unmoving as the rest.

High tide, Omen thought, guessing that when the tide went out there would be even more room upon the beach for the shadows to crowd the shore. *But why are they just standing there in the water — why aren't they advancing forward onto the sand, toward the mountain?*

"I'd say the shore to the pinch points is about six miles

long and at best two miles wide at the center," Dev spoke over their footfalls, assessing the shore below as Omen had been. Their stone guardian was leading them down a narrow path toward the closest group upon the rocky mountain base — those with the lit fires and moving shapes. But it was the far group along the shore, the ones just waiting in the rising night breeze, that most unnerved him.

"Can't really tell from here," Templar stated thoughtfully. "But I'd say we're looking at tens of thousands, between both groups."

"If all of them cram into Kharakhan—" Nikki didn't finish.

"Why aren't they moving?" Liethan voiced the thought that was most on Omen's mind. Despite the distance, they could all see that there was something extremely wrong with the group on the far side of the bay and those coming in from the water. They just sat or stood utterly still in the sand, watching, waiting, like statues spread out across the beach. What Omen knew about crowds, it was nearly impossible to get any group that large to remain still for any length of time. Unease settled over his heart.

The pathway down the cliffside began leveling off as they neared the rocky outcropping where the eastern mountain-side camp waited. Amid the moonlight and flaring campfires, Omen could make out trees sprinkled among the crags and gaps of the cliffs they descended — modest pines, cedars, and myrtle. Spiky shrubs with tiny white flowers grew in abundance and gave off a sugary perfume that reminded Omen of breakfast.

"I is wanting pancakes," Tormy exclaimed, as if attuned to Omen's stomach. "With maple syrup."

"I is smelling the syrup already," Tyrin concurred. "It

98

must be being a mystical sign of breakfasts yet to come."
The little cat looked at Kyr expectantly, but the half-elvin
mystic voiced no opinion regarding the future consumption
of syrup, pancakes, or any other delicacy associated with a
morning meal. Omen placed a hand on his brother's thin
shoulder — the boy was shivering, and Omen knew he felt
as uneasy as the rest of them did.

Treading carefully in the footsteps of their enormous
stone guide, the group rounded another wide curve, keeping
on the path close to the inner cliff wall and as far as possible from the sheer drop. But they were nearing the outcropping now, the steep slope of the cliff giving way to leveled
rock as they stepped into the sprawling encampment. There
were fires everywhere and shapes huddled tightly around
them as if desperate for the light, but the camp was strangely silent. Along the cliff walls were large limestone boulders that shielded off one section of this camp from the
cold wind blowing in from the ocean waters. It was to this
area that the stone guardian led them.

A group of five rabbit-headed warriors jumped out from
the shadows of one of the limestone boulders and circled
the stone guardian with quick, powerful hops. The rabbit
men stood perhaps five feet in height and wore dark
leathers over their undeniably fluffy cream fur. They carried long spears and had oval shields strapped to their fuzzy
backs, presumably protecting their spines and cottony tails.

"No!" Kyr hissed, stopping little Tyrin from letting loose
any words they would all have soon regretted.

"Ones have come to see the Keeper." The stone guardian
stood statue-still and let the words ring out without the
movement of its lips.

Maybe the big stone giant nitwit is tired from the walk.

99

"Get on with you, stone face," a rabbit man said and sniffed through the delicate slits of his triangular nose. "Wanting to see the Keeper, do you? Come along then with us," he told Omen. "The giant cat will be a welcome addition to our troops when the fighting starts."

"Omy?" Tormy dragged Omen's moniker out as a question that encompassed and reflected so many of Omen's own thoughts. "Is we fighting with the bunnies?" Tormy was practically vibrating with excitement, and Omen placed a hand against his furry shoulder to restrain him. His cat's instinctive desire to chase after the rabbit men had to be nearly overwhelming.

What is this? What is going on here? Does Khylar think we are here to help him? To fight for him? And who, by the deep ocean, is he fighting? What is happening here? And why are the bunnies so hostile?

"Don't worry, Tormy," Omen said, sounding more confident than he felt. "I've got this." He threw Templar a silent look that said most assuredly that he did not have this. Templar's expression tightened. He didn't like this any more than Omen did.

We're here to get Khylar and nothing else, Omen told himself. *Return Khylar to Kharakhan, close the Gate, and Indee will remove the hex from Kyr. That's it, that's all.* But despite the reassurance he gave himself, he doubted it was going to be that straightforward. He couldn't help remembering his mother's words about things going horrifically wrong.

100

Chapter 7: Manipulation

DEV

Dev trailed behind the group as they followed the warrior hares to the singular tent set against the sheer limestone mountain wall. The twenty-foot square tent had been draped with overlapping leather panels, which created a tall canopy but, being merely half-stitched, flapped in the wind to allow quick peeks inside at random intervals.

His companions all pretended not to look, but each in turn stretched their necks to see better what awaited them. A tall, armor-clad man stood in the center of the tent, alone. Dev couldn't be sure from the quick panel flicks, but the man's height and bearing seemed familiar.

"I think that's Khylar," he heard Omen whispered to Shalonie unnecessarily.

"That's the Set-Manasan brat all right," Templar scoffed and tipped his chin to the black unicorn coat of arms blazed across the blood-red banners on either side of the tent's entrance. One of the rabbit warriors hurried inside to speak with the tall man, while the others held them there, crossed spears preventing them from moving forward.

This should be fun, Dev thought as he chanced a quick glance at their surroundings. His companions were focused on the tent and the man inside, so they'd failed to notice the large group of Teyledrine warriors moving in. Like the Aelaedrine, these warriors were well-armed and armored — but rather than the disdain that had been present in the features of the Aelaedrine, these warriors appeared weary, exhausted. The plethora of less humanoid creatures among them seemed odd as well. Dev knew that within the faerie clans, old rivalries were strong — for so many diverse creatures to mingle without conflict, something extraordinary had to be occurring.

Like at the Gate — natural enemies and yet none of them attacked or fought each other.

The warriors eyed the newcomers with world-weary curiosity.

"Omen Daenoth," Khylar Set-Manasan greeted as he pushed aside the tent flaps, drawing Dev's attention back to the group.

Dev hadn't seen Khylar in several years, but he didn't remember the boy king of Kharakhan looking as formidable as the warrior standing before them. Khylar's black plate armor was faerie-made like that of the Aelaedrine warriors. He was nearly as tall as Omen, broad-shouldered, fair of face. His long black hair was wild and unkempt, held back by a thin band of silver. His eyes were the shocking black of his mother Indee'athra's, cold, hard, piercing. But while his features were familiar, his expression was not — this was not the boy Indee had crowned when she'd handed over Kharakhan all those years ago — the one with the quick smile and the uncertain gaze. This man's features were unyielding, his eyes stern.

"Shalonie, Liethan, Templar." Khylar inclined his head slightly. His gaze briefly skated over Nikki, Kyr, and Dev himself before turning to take in the figure of Tormy standing beside Omen. The cat's white ruff gleamed in the moonlight. "Your cat is rather large," Khylar observed humorlessly.

"I is being large," little Tyrin piped up from Kyr's shoulder. "And the hunger growing in my belly is being large too."

"Isn't that always the way," Khylar told the kitten without missing a beat.

Tyrin let out a tiny huff.

He knows about the cats — and has had some forewarning of our arrival. Dev noted with curiosity. *He's not surprised to see us.*

Khylar addressed Omen once more. "Did my mother send you?"

Omen look around uncomfortably. The entirety of Khylar's freakish horde listened. "Maybe we can discuss things in private, Khylar," Omen said with a grimace.

Not that the tent will provide much privacy, Dev thought, guessing that those enormous ears of the rabbit warriors were probably capable of hearing anything within the camp's confines. *But at least Omen knows enough to try to be diplomatic.*

"Very well," Khylar agreed and swept aside the tent flaps. "Welcome to my bower."

The tent was far more spacious than Dev would have believed. Furnishings had been carved, or had perhaps risen — if the stone guardians hinted at Khylar's elemental magic — from the rugged limestone beneath their feet. Rugs had been spread throughout the tent, cast upon the cold ground.

Tormy paused to sniff and paw at one tightly woven rug before settling himself down upon it, folding his front paws beneath him and curling his tail around his body.

Dev moved off to one side where he could clearly see the others and the shapes still milling outside beyond the tent's opening.

103

"Speak," Khylar said what could have sounded like an order with curious resignation.

"Your mother—" Omen cut himself off mid-statement and shot a worried look at Kyr who had pinched his eyes shut as if anticipating pain to blast through his hex.

And Kyr says nothing — just waits and accepts. Unease filled Dev's heart. That level of trust was foreign to him.

"Hex?" Khylar asked.

Omen nodded.

"How big has it grown?" Khylar addressed Kyr, who turned pomegranate red.

"All the way up his arm to his neck," Shalonie threw in quickly.

"He'll be fine . . . until it reaches his heart," Khylar said coolly.

"Indee promised to take it off when you return with us," Liethan spoke up.

"Say goodbye to the boy then," Khylar shot back. "Because I am never going back."

And there it is, Dev thought. *Defiance. Righteous defiance unless I miss my guess.* He could see the light of absolute certainty burning in Khylar's eyes — it was a look Dev was quite familiar with. *Omen has only three options — shatter his belief in his cause, destroy him, or join him.* He didn't need to work hard to figure out which path Omen was likely to take.

"The boy is my brother!" Omen's voice quavered with sharp anger, his back stiffening.

Dev saw the irritated look in Khylar's eyes as he took in the situation, sizing up those standing before them. While Khylar was the King of Kharakhan, and now apparently the erstwhile leader of the Autumn Lands and Keeper of the

Autumn Gate, he had to realize that these people, despite their youth, were not readily dismissed. Shalonie was a Melian Hold Lord's daughter and an ally of his mother's. Omen and Templar were both princes of their own lands — with powerful parents also allied with his mother. But more than that, Templar was a Nightblood, and Omen the son of the Elder God Cerioth, The Dark Heart.

Something shifted in Khylar's eyes, and he raised one eyebrow in a perfect arch. "That is different. My apologies. But, as you can see, I can't leave here even if I wanted to. Which I do not."

So, not stupid. Dev preferred blind righteousness over cleverness. That Khylar knew enough to be diplomatic meant he understood exactly what Omen's presence could potentially mean. *And he means to turn Omen to his cause — means to tug at his heartstrings and play on his compassion.*

"And why is that?" Omen asked, jaw still fixed in anger. He shot another wary look at Kyr as if worried he'd somehow triggered the hex.

Twist the dagger, little king, Dev thought as he waited for Khylar's answer.

"Too many innocents depend upon me to save them, Omen," Khylar said earnestly.

Unease crossed over Omen's features, and he turned toward Templar as if to confirm what he'd heard. It honestly surprised Dev how often the two men turned to each other in an effort to check themselves. Omen seemed to value Templar's brashness, and Templar saw Omen as a voice of conscience. But now Dev could practically see the same thought going through both of their minds. *Innocent Autumn Dwellers? Saving them at the cost of innocent hu-*

105

mans? Dev knew this group would hold up the mortals of Kharakhan as more deserving of their protections than the monsters and immortals of the Autumn Lands.

But you're going to change their minds, aren't you, little king? Turn their narrow world upside-down, Dev thought, guessing at the game Khylar was playing. *Make them see the other side. Broaden their horizons.*

"The Autumn Dwellers don't belong in the mortal lands," Omen started, searching.

"They are beset upon by the very Gate Keeper they once trusted, their beloved King Galseric, ruler of the Teyledrine for a thousand years, and of late turned mad and blood-thirsty. And thus far, unstoppable." Khylar's words hung in the air like an accusation.

Omen and Templar both threw questioning looks at Shalonie who looked equally pained.

She doesn't know how to respond either. Can't exactly argue morality when discussing who has more right to live.

"I am granting the Autumn Dwellers refuge in Kharakhan to save their very lives," Khylar went on. "To do otherwise would be unspeakable — they would be slaughtered."

Nikki's face had turned nearly purple with anger, but the young man heroically contained himself. Templar clamped a heavy hand down on Nikki's shoulder to hold him in place.

"You can't," Shalonie corrected him. "It is forbidden by the Covenant."

"It is not," Khylar stated back emphatically. "I am the king of Kharakhan. I can grant asylum to anyone I wish. And as the Gatekeeper of the Autumn Gate — it is mine to open."

106

"On the equinox only!" Shalonie insisted.

"I have opened the Gate out of turn into Kharakhan only," Khylar corrected. "There is no Covenant stating how I govern my own lands."

"It doesn't work that way!" Shalonie said. "The Gates touch all lands, in all worlds, in all dimensions. It affects everything — not just Kharakhan."

Khylar's jaw tightened, and he glared down at the young woman. "You claim more knowledge of the Gates than one who was appointed Gate Keeper by the very gods you claim I am defying?"

Impressed, Dev glanced at Shalonie, wondering if she'd respond. *Challenging her on an intellectual level at the same time as hinting at knowledge she does not possess. Doesn't matter if he's making it up — he's made her doubt.*

Liethan stepped forward suddenly, his normally friendly face fixed in an angry scowl. "Where is Tara?"

Dev almost applauded. Omen, Templar, and Shalonie had no choice but to think of the long-term consequences, but the Corsair remembered what was important. Khylar's words had been lost on both Nikki and Liethan — Nikki because he was too closely tied to Kharakhan to care about the Autumn Lands, and Liethan because despite everything else, the Corsairs held nothing above family.

"Tara?" Khylar said briskly, clearly caught off guard by the question. Dev's eyes narrowed slightly as he tried to discern if Khylar was truly surprised or playing out a reaction he thought would suit.

"Yes, Tara," Liethan nearly yelled her name. "Your wife-to-be. My cousin."

"We were never officially betrothed." Khylar's words came out so quickly they seemed rehearsed.

107

Also untrue, Dev thought. He'd seen the betrothal contract over a year ago when he'd procured a copy of it for Avarice.

"Where is she?" Liethan came up close upon Khylar and stood almost chin-to-chin with the young king. The golden-haired, blue-eyed Corsair was fearless in his defiance.

He knows Omen and Templar will back him, no matter what, Dev realized. The trust among the three friends was unshakable.

"I'd guess, in the capital. Where I left her." Khylar didn't move. "Why don't you go look for her there? But don't believe for a moment she can change my mind."

That was a deflection! Dev thought, vaguely amused.

"Why?" Shalonie jumped in, pulling Liethan's arm to step aside. "Did she try already?"

Good guess, Dev agreed. *Tara is priestess to The Lady. Of course she tried. She would have known more about the Covenant than any of us — and Shalonie's already figured that much out as well.*

Khylar inclined his head. "When I first learned of my new role, the guardianship of the Autumn Gate. The night I became the Keeper of the Autumn Gate, Tara told me to refuse the honor. She said it would bring me strife and that I was ill-suited to handle the position. As if I am incapable of managing challenges set before me!" Khylar's eyes gleamed.

Dev saw the uncomfortable air that settled over his companions. *Sharing a private argument with your bride-to-be — how devious of you.* Though Dev wasn't entirely certain if Khylar simply didn't see such a comment as uncouth — he was a Kharakhian after all — or if he'd done it purposefully, knowing Omen and Shalonie, both Melian raised, would find such private details embarrassing. Templar would likely find it nauseating. *The Corsair and the Deldano won't care of course — but it's really Omen he needs to convince in the end. Omen can rein in the Corsair.*

The young king didn't seem touched by embarrassment or even anger. He spoke as if the details were merely facts he needed to convey to make a point.

"Everyone," he said without bitterness, "including Tara, thinks I am not capable of leading. My mother coddled me during my upbringing. No one saw my training or how mercilessly and thoroughly my mother prepared me to be king. All anyone saw was Indee giving her baby boy a kingdom on a whim. And nothing I do will convince anyone in power to take me seriously. I know that. I've ruled Kharakhan with the threat of my mother's power as my greatest ally. The other rulers treaty with me only because they see me as her mouthpiece, her puppet." He strode past them to the tent opening. "But I am nothing like what people believe me to be."

Khylar left them standing in the tent, momentarily dumbfounded.

Poor little king, Dev thought in amusement. *Mommy was mean and no one would listen to you. And now you're going to break the world to pay them back.* He turned his gaze back to his companions, curious to see how they would react.

"That's a little more honesty than I expected," Templar said, a strange look on his face. Dev supposed in some ways both Omen and Templar could probably sympathize — they both would not respond well to being told they could not handle a challenge.

The difference is, these two are capable of laughing at

their own failings — they don't try to punish those around them. Unease stirred Dev's heart as he realized how that went against everything he'd come to believe about Night-bloods and godlings. *Now what are you going to do, son of Cerioth? It's all fallen apart — he's made you think, made you sympathize with him — and the Corsair and the Del-dano are not going to like it.*

"Did he just tell us that he's willing to sacrifice Kharakhan to prove that he can rule Kharakhan?" Nikki asked, making no effort to keep the bitterness out of his voice.

"And he's lying about Tara!" Liethan insisted. "Tara has always stood by him — always supported him. So has her sister Ty — she's Khylar's personal guard and his best friend. For them to have left Kharakhan, something else must have happened. Something more than what he's telling us."

"There is always a spider at the center of the web," Kyr spoke up, startling them all. "And now it is all lost, all gone, no more family."

Dev's eyes narrowed as he took in the boy — Kyr was staring down at the mark upon his hand. *Now what has he seen? Something else, some card yet unplayed. Khylar is definitely lying about Lady Tara, and there's something more he hasn't told us about his place here in the Autumn Lands. But what else is missing?*

"What spider, Kyr?" Omen asked, but his brother was silent, still focused on the hex mark. It did indeed look like an intricate spiderweb crawling over his skin, black and deadly. Omen closed his eyes for a moment and took a deep breath. Dev wondered what conclusions Omen had come to — or even how much of the situation he'd correctly under-

110

stood.

"All right," Omen said finally. "I came here to get Indee's blasted hex removed from Kyr's arm. And that's what I am going to do."

"We need more information," Shalonie cut in. "We need to know more about Galseric and the threat to the Autumn Dwellers."

Omen hurried after Khylar, the others trailing after them. Dev followed in silence.

The pale moonlight overhead illuminated the entirety of Khylar's waiting army. The surrounding Teyledrine warriors had closed ranks around the tent. At that moment, they all realized as one just how precarious their position was. Only the cats and Kyr seemed unconcerned. Tormy stretched out his front paws, arching his back as he swirled his tail back and forth — unconsciously warning those closing in to stay away.

"There is being so many beasties, boggets, and faykin," the cat said with palpable awe. "What is they all doing here?"

"These Autumn Dwellers," Khylar answered, "are here to fight the darkness that threatens to consume them."

"Galseric?" Shalonie prompted.

"The thing that King Galseric has become." Khylar let out a sharp whistle. Loping from nearby, a boyish shape dressed like one of the pages of the Kharakhian court skidded to Khylar's side. The page's face was that of a brown hunting dog, long-snouted, lop-eared, with a black nose and shiny amber eyes. Dev could only imagine how poorly he'd be received in Kharakhan.

"Puppy," Khylar addressed his servant. "Bring Reclare. I must speak to him."

The dog boy gave a short bark, startling Tyrin who had climbed onto Kyr's shoulder again. The little cat fluffed into a fuzzy ball and gave a venomous hiss.

"Reclare," Khylar explained, "was the first to sense the danger. He came to warn me, to bring me across to the Autumn Lands."

The page named Puppy returned shortly, a tall, spindly figure in tow. The figure — Reclare, Dev presumed — was undoubtedly a Child of Autumn. His skin was golden as the sunset, his hair ebony, and his eyes the polychromatic hues of autumn leaves. A web of tiny scars marred the otherwise perfect face and disappeared down his neck beneath the high collar of his dark shirt. Dev guessed he was one of the Teyledrine — younger than the Summer Lords of the Aelaedrine, but still the uncontested rulers of the Autumn Lands. There was the sharp scent of magic about him.

"Tell my friends what has happened," Khylar charged Reclare, who looked wary not only of the strangers but also of Khylar.

"My Keeper," the Dweller began haltingly, his voice hoarse and wispy. "To tell my tale once more will risk the hex rooting in my heart."

Shalonie gasped, and Omen shifted uneasily. Dev stilled. *Khylar has never been cruel — at least not from all I've heard of him. And yet Reclare is frightened — truly frightened.*

"The magic is similar, but not exactly the same as what my mother inflicted upon your brother, Omen," Khylar explained dispassionately. "A secret embedded in the skin that is fed by the telling and grows roots with the nourishment. Old magic. Unpredictable."

"You don't need—" Omen shot out.

112

"But yet, he does," Khylar declared. "Tell the tale, Reclare, so that there is no misunderstanding."

"A pernicious evil waited in a dark place," Reclare spoke firmly, keeping the slight shake in his voice under measured control. "Dark hatred. Unjustified, unstoppable. It waited and waited for centuries, hidden in the core of a precious ring. Its prison, but also a trap waiting to be sprung. There is no defeating that which is eternal. It cannot be dispelled. It will not lessen. It is pure. Hatred. A piece of the universe, unchangeable. Destruction reigns in the end. And so it waited.

"Great King Galseric, our Keeper for generations, our hero, our leader, found the ring among an ancient treasure. I, Reclare the Wise, was his sorcerer. Not so wise now. Not knowing. Not seeing. Useless Reclare."

The Dweller gave out a high howl of frustration and pain.

"Useless, foolish Reclare. I did not stop my king, my friend from sliding the ring onto his finger. I watched as the corruption flowed over him, took hold of the soul inside the body — destroy his essence. I saw his eyes change. Then I watched him rip apart our retinue. He slew friend and servant, even his sons. He tore to pieces the poor beasts who'd carried our burdens. He destroyed all with little effort and no reason given. All. All. Except Reclare. Reclare was made to watch. Reclare was made to run. To flee. To know the nightmare that moves in the darkness."

The man clutched his side and moaned. "It spreads . . . Please . . ." He sank to one knee and held out his other hand as if begging for alms.

"That's enough," Omen croaked out, repulsed by Khylar's cold cruelty. "Enough. Khylar. Tell him to stop."

"Is it enough?" Khylar asked. "Do you understand?"

"We understand," Shalonie said hurriedly. "Tell the poor man to stop before the hex kills him."

And now the knife has been twisted utterly — both Omen and Shalonie feel for this poor man. And that's all Khylar needed. Resignation washed over Dev. *And Avarice insists I allow it — let Omen make the decisions.* He shouldn't care — not really — and yet in the few weeks he'd been traveling with this group, he'd grown fond of them. *I should know better by now.*

"Reclare knows he is dead already," Khylar countered. "And you long for it, do you not Reclare?"

"I wish for a death that will never come," the Dweller gasped, leaning on Puppy's leg. "The dreams that come eat my head and bite at my body. Madness will be a blessing."

"Immortality certainly complicates matters," Templar said, and though he'd tried to speak with sarcasm, Dev could hear the despair, anger, and disgust in his tone.

Maybe they get it now — that there really are worse things than death. This is what will happen to Kyr if you don't follow through on your original mission.

"So, then why are you letting any of the Dwellers escape the Autumn Lands?" Nikki asked plainly. "If the threat is so big, why not throw everything you have at him. If they're at risk anyway, why not turn them against Galseric and his forces?"

"You have a heart of stone, Deldano," Khylar said, intrigued. "The gift of your human side, stone cold pragmatism. I am afraid, I am far less blessed."

Nikki shifted uncomfortably, working out what he was being accused of.

"Explain yourself," Shalonie demanded.

She is losing her temper, Dev thought, hoping that perhaps something more would come to light. *They're still thinking they can change his mind. Still hoping there's a way to win the argument.*

"There is no stopping Galseric and the dark allies he's gathered," Khylar said, sadness creeping into his voice. "I am merely providing the escaping Dwellers with a head start. Galseric will make his way through the Gate, and chase down every Autumn Dweller that has managed to flee."

How noble of him, Dev thought dispassionately. He spoke up this time, unable to hold his tongue any longer when he knew there was a great deal more Khylar was not telling them. "That's not all he'll do."

Khylar turned dark eyes on him. Dev noticed the moment Khylar took in his appearance — dark hair, silver eyes. He could almost see the flash of realization when he recognized the Machelli in him. A muscle in his jaw twitched, and he inclined his head briefly as if acknowledging that perhaps he'd not been quite convincing enough for all of them. And yet to Dev's consternation, he smiled. *Now we hear the truth,* Dev thought. *And he doesn't really care how the others will react — never did.*

"Correct," Khylar agreed. "While Galseric is contained in the Autumn Lands, no one from the other side will help to stop him. Once the monster crosses into the human realm . . . Well, you know how protective the powers that be can become when their favorites are threatened."

"You are trying to manipulate the gods?" Shalonie asked, sounding appalled.

"Not just the gods, Shalonie," Khylar answered with a sort of triumph in his voice. "Everyone."

"That's your plan?" Templar spat out. "Threaten all the mortal kingdoms so that we all rise up against this?"

"My plan," Khylar said wistfully, "and our best chance of stopping Galseric."

"You speak as if defeat is a foregone conclusion," Omen chanced a harsh reply.

"The battle is written in the stars," Khylar said. "Before midday, Galseric and the strength of his horde will storm the mountain. We will fight. We will lose, and he will take the Gate. The rest is out of my hands."

Break the world, and hope the gods step in to stop you. Dev had to hand it to him — he had all the classic traits of a true believer. *Except it doesn't work that way, little king. You cannot manipulate the gods. They don't play by your rules.*

"You're giving up without fighting?" Nikki blurted out. "You're giving up? Sacrificing everyone. What kind of leader are you?"

"The kind of leader who has spent a hundred years battling Galseric!" Khylar bit back. "Time passes in a hurry on the battlefields of the Autumn Lands. I have fought. I have been beaten, time and again. I have lost many, many good and true friends, immortals who were not meant to part from this world! My time is nearly up. And Galseric will reign."

"A hundred years in the blink of our eye," Kyr said thoughtfully, confirming to all of them the truth of Khylar's words. "His time has ticked away. All gone, all lost, while the dead swell and the shadows grow."

"A hundred years?" Dev breathed out, understanding now why Khylar was not the boy he should be. *He's not human at all anymore — he's Teyledrine, faerie, complete-*

116

ly. He doesn't care because he no longer sees the mortal world as his home. What was it the Aelaedrine called the mortal world — the bleeding lands. That's all he sees now too.

"And thousands of defeats," Khylar confessed. "This will be my last effort to stop Galseric. I have no more to give."

"What if we found a way?" Omen tried again. "You've lost a thousandfold, but you never had us at your side."

So, he chooses option number three — join his cause. Despite knowing that was the only possible outcome, Dev had held out hope that they might try something more ruthless.

Khylar communicated his skepticism with one slightly raised eyebrow.

"If Galseric can't be defeated . . ." Omen looked at Shalonie and the two of them suddenly lit up like the noonday sun.

Dev frowned. *Now what? They've actually thought of something — remembered something that can help them?*

The girl's eyes twinkled. "Good thought!" she exclaimed. "And of course it's the only logical solution. I just have to figure out how to replicate what they did."

Khylar made a disdainful sound.

"The power, the corruption you speak of, was trapped before," Shalonie continued as if thinking out loud. "Reclare said so. It resided in a ring. Now it resides in the body of King Galseric."

"You think we have not thought of this before?" a new voice interrupted her. A cold chill moved down Dev's spine.

They all turned and saw a Teyledrine woman approaching. She was clad in a long black gown with trailing

117

sleeves, her dark hair pulled back from a pale face with a circlet of silver. For a moment Dev thought it was Indee herself, so like in appearance was the woman to the sorceress queen, but as she drew closer Dev noticed the differences. Her eyes were crystalline blue like the deepest waters of the ocean, her features somewhat sharper, harder. And for a moment it seemed to Dev as if shadows swirled around her.

Here is the last card — the final piece of the puzzle, Dev thought. He knew this woman — not her name or her rank of course, but he knew her all the same. He'd known women like her before — creatures like her.

"Allow me to introduce my great aunt, Lady Morcades," Khylar informed them. "Her magic alone has kept us alive."

"Spinning her web," Kyr murmured beside Dev. Startled he glanced down at the boy, but both Kyr and the two cats were moving away as if uncomfortable in the woman's presence. *So this is our spider? Does Khylar know? Do the Teyledrine?* Puppy too flinched away as the woman approached, and Reclare turned his head and would not look at her. *They're afraid of her.*

"You think we have not already tried to remove the ring from his hand," Morcades demanded of Shalonie. "We have tried to slay him; he does not die. We have tried to destroy his army, they rise up again and grow in number. Our bravest warriors have tried to cut the ring from his hand — he slaughters them and then animates their corpses to march against us. We have fought him for a hundred years. Do you think we have not tried the obvious, girl?"

Despite the fact that the woman was intimidating, Dev saw Shalonie's spine stiffen as she stared the woman

118

straight in the eye, refusing to be cowed. "I had assumed you'd have tried that," Shalonie stated. "Logical steps would have been to try to remove the ring, or failing that, remove the entity or power inside King Galseric's body and trap it in another vessel."

The mere thought of doing such a thing made Dev shudder in alarm. *They would be mad to even consider it!*

"Of course we have tried to save our king," the woman agreed. "But nothing works. The ring cannot be removed, and the entity cannot be drawn out of his body!"

"After a hundred years I can't imagine there would be anything of Galseric left inside that body," Omen replied, glancing at Shalonie for confirmation.

Dev felt compelled to offer him a warning, knowing Avarice would never forgive him if he did not.

"He would be mad if anything of him remained," Dev stated bluntly. "And if you attempted to draw the entity out of him, you would risk it jumping into another, more tempting vessel . . . which this group presents in spades. You can't even think about attempting that!"

Shalonie paused for a moment, her lips pushed into a pout. "Exactly how long until the sun is directly overhead?" she asked finally. "I might have an idea."

Chapter 8: Battlefield

OMEN

O men stood at the top of the sandy slope and surveyed the entirety of Galseric's camp. The companions — Templar on his right, Khylar on the
left, both Nikki and Liethan just behind him along with
Kyr, Tormy, and Tyrin — shivered as a cold morning
breeze blew past them, whipping their hair and fur respectively into a frenzy. Omen wished he'd brought a helmet.

The enemy's ranks had swelled in number, the host having moved in from the ships anchored in the ocean shallows. The tide had gone out, leaving a large swath of wet,
hard-packed sand for Galseric's army to converge upon,
battle-ready. Most of the monstrous fighters had their backs
to the sea, facing the sunrise that gradually broke over the
mountaintop. They stood utterly still and silent as if waiting
for something else to control their actions. They had erect-
ed no tents against the elements, and Omen could see no
signs of cooking fires. *They're living creatures, most of
them anyway — they have to eat and drink. They must be
getting tired just standing there in the wet sand. What's the
point of that?*

In contrast, Khylar's camp was stippled with cooking
fires as creatures tall and squat dragged themselves around
at a sluggish, just-risen pace, vying for breakfast and struggling to outfit themselves. Omen caught random whiffs of
bacon and fermented herring.

Khylar held the high ground — his army could readily

flee back up the rocky outcropping, and then upward through the Gate. But they were there to hold the escape route as long as possible.

Galseric's forces, waiting along the shoreline, had nowhere to go but forward. The northern horn of the bay crescent was comprised of rocky outcroppings that would be too difficult for an army to navigate. The southern horn was swampland they couldn't pass for fear of getting bogged down. If they wanted the Autumn Gate, they had to march straight ahead into the sunrise and take the mountain.

They seemed to be waiting for some signal, remaining fixed and unmoving on the beach. Once they did move, marching toward Khylar's army to storm the heights, Khylar would have no choice but to fight or flee.

Omen squinted as he studied the groupings of guards along the front lines of Galseric's troops. They were square, muscular beasts, encased in heavy armor. *From this distance it almost looks like they're encased in stone,* Omen thought.

The strength of the enemy had been hard to determine during the dark of night, but now that early dawn painted the sky a rosy red Omen had to agree with Templar's guess as to their numbers.

"We're outnumbered two to one," Omen murmured in a rough voice, lack of sleep finally catching up to him. A nervous energy was keeping him going — either excitement or dread — he could no longer really tell the difference. This wouldn't be his first fight by a long shot — but it certainly was his first major battle. He'd never marched with an army before — never faced such overwhelming forces on such a scale. He'd grown up hearing stories of great battles with armies clashing against armies, and the thought that he was about to be in one curled like an icy snake in his brain.

"It's a little late to change your mind, Omen," Templar murmured back. "Not to mention your sister would never let you hear the end of it if you chickened out at the last minute. Come to think of it, neither would I. Would ruin our Nightball reputation."

Omen grinned at his friend's joke. Unlike him, Templar had been to war — as a young child, he'd seen his father lead the armies of Terizkand against the giants who had once enslaved his people. Templar had confessed to being only ten years old the first time he'd been forced to fight for his life, when the enemy had broken through their line, forcing even the non-combatants to fight or die. Templar at least knew what to expect from the day. His easy bravado was familiar enough to ease some of Omen's tension.

"No, I mean," Omen adjusted to an artificially jovial tone, "Galseric's army is in deep wyvern poop."

Puppy, who had started to whine nervously, tittered in excitement at the comment. The young page held Khylar's shield with great effort, standing as straight and still as his quivering arms and legs allowed.

Khylar gave the boy a quick nod. "Go on now, Puppy," he said, taking the black unicorn shield from the child. "Go sit on the big rock with Tormy and Kyr. Watch the battle closely. Lady Morcades will tell you if you have to retreat through the Gate." Khylar smiled broadly. "But I expect victory. Which means . . ."

"A triumphant victory march and a feast!" Puppy punctuated his excitement with a spontaneous bark.

Omen watched the youngling scamper off, the child's long floppy ears bouncing with every step. *Puppy is very obedient. I guess dog people have it easier.* Omen looked sideways at Tormy who had pushed himself to the front of the line and sat primly, tail curled around paws, next to Omen and Templar. The cat's orange fur swirled in all directions as the wind plucked at it, making him look twice as fluffy. *This is not going to go over well.*

"I is having a question," Tyrin piped up before Omen had a chance to open his mouth. He'd been sitting on Kyr's shoulder, as the boy leaned against Tormy's right flank, seeking some shelter from the wind. "How is Puppy dog boy sitting next to Tormy on the rock at the same time as Tormy is fighting the great battle alongside the hero peoples and things?" As the little cat spoke, he leaped from Kyr's shoulder to Tormy's head so that he could look down at Omen.

"It's—"

"Is it being a magicky thing — like eating two dinners at the same time?" Tormy guessed, barely able to contain his excitement. His giant tail began to swish, mercilessly brushing across the warriors lined up behind them.

"Bless the tail!" Kyr, who was nearly hidden in the blanket of Tormy's orange fur, called out with gusto. "Know your hearts and bless the tail!"

The warriors seemed annoyed, but Omen heard a few gruff mumbles of, "Bless the tail!" from a cloven-hoofed gladiator faun and a green-feathered frog creature with enormous teeth.

"Tormy." Omen steeled himself and bravely looked square into the cat's giant amber eyes. "I want you to stay up here on the mountain and guard Kyr."

Tormy's tail stopped swishing, and his ears drooped.

I feel like such a louse.

123

"It's safer up here, and you have Kyr and Tyrin for company—"

"What the &$#@!" Tyrin shouted with all the terrifying might of his tiny lungs. "I is not staying on the &$%^@* mountain. I is being a hero! Tormy is being a hero! We is not sitting and waiting on a &*$#@%^ rock."

"It is the right horn that is the true horn," Kyr answered Tyrin's rage with a calm, almost meditative voice. "The path of the right horn is the path of the cats and the boy. We must blow our battle horns upon the mountain."

"Oh," Tyrin said, instantly calm. "That is being fine then."

Without further complaint, the cats and the boy retreated to the back of the line near the mountain cliffside and climbed the giant boulder Puppy had already staked out.

"You know, that didn't just resolve smoothly," Templar pointed out. "Nothing Kyr says is ever what it seems — and like it or not, the cats seem to understand him better than we do."

"I know, but if they're safe up here, what harm can it do?" Omen said, uncertain even as the words left his mouth. *I think I've been had again.* The uncomfortable feeling growing into more than merely a sneaking suspicion.

They waited, the sun crawling slowly toward its zenith. *Noon,* Omen thought. *We have to hold until noon. But if Galseric attacks first. . .* He knew their plans could collapse if the enemy preempted the battle. *Waiting and waiting — hope Tormy doesn't get too restless.*

The wait was nearly unbearable, the tension in him rising with each crash of ocean wave against the shore.

"Battles are often made up of long waits," Templar murmured to him. "We once waited three days in a swamp before attacking a giant camp. We were nearly eaten alive by mosquitoes."

"I hate waiting," Omen murmured back.

The sun had nearly reached its noonday mark when Khylar stepped forward.

"Dwellers of the Land of Autumn," Khylar raised his voice to address his warriors. His words carried with unnatural volume.

Maybe magically amplified? Omen wondered, eying Morcades who stood not far away surrounded by her own retinue of Teyledrine warriors.

The faerie woman wore a billowy cloak that seemed to be made of shadows and smoke as it curled around her lithe form. Her ankle-length ebony hair shone, blue and purple lights glowing from underneath its thick mass.

I think those lights might be tiny sprites nesting in her hair.

Her eyes, blue as the sea, wandered over the gathered forces, wide and unfocused as if she were lost in concentration and had cast her mind elsewhere.

I wonder what her part in all this is, Omen considered the possibilities. *She sure as Nightfire isn't outfitted to go into battle. What did Khylar tell Puppy? She's been left to manage the retreat through the Gate should the battle not go to plan. Will she know to get Kyr and the cats to safety?* He glanced warily back over his shoulder at his little brother. *They'll be fine,* he tried to assure himself.

"Today we face the creeping darkness that corrupts our land and savages our peace," Khylar declared. "We have tried to reason; we have tried to run; we have tried to fight. Many of you have stood with me for a hundred years, confronting Galseric's every advance. We have battled him on

125

fields of blood, in our forests, in our cities, through the realms of ice and fire. We have stood against him with all our might, but we have not been able to stop him or drive him back.

"By the hundred-year law as laid down by The Dwellers of Old, this is our last battle. As we follow the decrees of those who founded and secured our world, we will lay down our arms against his greater force if we are beaten in this battle today. So the laws guide us into eternity. It is a covenant we made at birth."

Omen heard the rest of Khylar's speech — which went on to single-out and praise individual warriors — as if through a wall of water, the words he'd just heard resonating over and over again in his mind. *He plans on giving up after this battle because of some ancient Autumn Lands code of conduct? Why didn't he mention that earlier? Rat's teeth!* Omen's thoughts cantered through his head, stopping and starting in a driving syncopated rhythm.

"Has he already given up?" Templar hissed close to Omen's ear. Omen could see anger burning in Templar's yellow eyes — his Nightblooded nature rebelling against the thought of surrender.

"I don't care!" Omen bit out. "I won't give up. We are winning the day no matter what."

Dark Morcades threw her eerie gaze in Omen's direction, and she smiled at him with palpable superiority.

"What is her game?" Omen asked Templar quietly.

"Ignore the faerie woman," Templar replied. "If she's not actively getting in our way, she's just a distraction. Right now, this minute, we're on the same side."

"We will win this field, friends," Khylar finished off with a flourish, "for freedom, for honor, and for life eternal!"

The crowd of Autumn Dwellers cheered, waving weapons and their diverse appendages in the air. Drums began sounding along the back of their line. Over the top of the mountain, the sun's bright rays cast a golden glow across the opposing army.

Khylar turned toward the beach, lowered his arm and let out a war cry of ear-shattering proportion. The rousing cry set an overwhelming wave of adrenaline rushing through Omen's body. Impelled, he answered Khylar's call with a deep howl of his own, and — like the rest of Khylar's army — started running down the slope toward the beach.

Khylar's horde descended the mountain like a stampede but miraculously fell into formation once they reached the flat plain of the beach. Backs to the mountain, eyes toward the ocean and Galseric's shadowy, unmoving army, they paused for moments while the warriors on both sides of the line sprinted toward the farthest reaches of the crescent-shaped bay, onward to its farthest extremities where the rocky terrain stretched all the way to the water.

In the momentary pause, Omen's thoughts went to Shalonie and Dev. They had chosen to climb down the southern horn of the mountain under cover of darkness and were presumably close to reaching the ocean. *From there . . .* Omen shooed the distracting thought from his mind and looked to the field of battle ahead. They had to hold the line until noon. A quick glance at the sun showed its slow crawl across the sky.

Despite the advance of Khylar's army, Galseric's forces still did not move. They waited like shadows, watching, staring, as if unconcerned with the army advancing upon them. Omen had hoped Galseric's troops wouldn't attack them as they were getting into position, but he couldn't believe that the enemy army hardly seemed to take note of them at all. *Is this a spell of Morcades perhaps?* he wondered. *Can't be. If Morcades can make an army silent and invisible, Khylar would have won this thing a century ago . . . A* century *ago.* Omen had a hard time wrapping his head around the idea that Khylar had been fighting Galseric for a hundred years.

Maybe Khylar lied about that. Omen snuck a glance at the Kharakhian king who stood in the center of the line, just to the left of him, ready to give the command to engage.

The straight-on attack had been Omen's suggestion: "The outcome of this day is entirely up to you, Khylar," Omen had told the Keeper of the Autumn Gate bluntly. "Kharakhan can't sustain constant invasion, and the Autumn Dwellers can't keep fighting endlessly against unstoppable forces. Our plan will work — but you have to win on the field of battle. You have to hold the line. We have to stop Galseric or he'll ruin the world. We will win, but only if we hold together."

Omen hadn't liked the full smile on Morcades' lips as he'd counseled Khylar. He hadn't been able to tell if her smile meant she'd approved or disapproved of his advice.

He never did find out, but in the end Khylar had agreed to the straight on attack.

"Forward!" Khylar commanded, and the lines hit the beach at a dead run.

Omen's feet virtually flew across the sand. His sword drawn, he held the flat close to the silverleaf armor protecting his chest.

A race to the first strike — that was what Omen had told Khylar when he'd laid out his plan for the sudden attack, merging it with Shalonie's own idea.

"Reckless," Khylar had scoffed at first.

"Far less reckless than remaining inactive," Omen had told the king. "If they attack first, it's over. We have to time it correctly. We have to control the battlefield. If we relinquish that control, we can't succeed. We have to hold him on the beach."

The faerie sorceress had agreed with an almost imperceptible nod, which Omen had noted and after which Khylar had given his consent to the stratagem.

He deferred to Morcades, Omen had thought with some discomfort. *But not openly. I wonder who else knows.*

Now as Omen ran alongside Templar, his mind began focusing on the familiar battle song that triggered the psionic patterns he used in combat. He could feel his energy rising — his mind attuning itself to the power around him. When he engaged, his sword would be backed by the crushing force of his psionics.

Omen's first opponent rose up between the sand and the sea and blocked his view of the horizon. The beast was bulbous and dark purple like the rutabaga that also accurately described its body shape. Its upper half was comprised of rows and rows of tiny eyes and a wide mouth filled with what looked like saw blades on both the top and bottom of the opening. It ran swiftly on a multitude of spindly white legs.

"Root vegetable, huh?" Omen barked and pivoted his sword with one swift movement from across his body and pointed the tip at the rounded belly. The reach of his arms and sword kept him clear of the beast's snapping maw. Omen stabbed through its center, expecting a crisp crunch. Instead, his sword passed through the creature's body as if the globose belly were made of lard.

Pink goop splatted on the sand to either side of the puncture. A raw pungent smell hit Omen's nostrils.

Rows of tiny round eyes all focused on Omen's face.

Shuddering, Omen slid the sword into his opponent's wobbly frame nearly to the hilt. *Too close!* The thought screamed through Omen's head, and he pulled back just as the beast's saw blade mouth snapped shut a hair's breadth from Omen's cheek.

Omen felt the displacement of air and a scratch of metal against his skin, like the scrape of a shaving blade. He hauled his sword back, hands and hilt arching toward the blue sky, and then brought the blade down in a flurried zigzag of psionic-backed slashes that cut his enemy into four equal pieces and detached the root-like legs at the hip.

Immediately, Omen spun to take on the five wriggling warriors surrounding Khylar and taking shots at him with their whip-like barbed tails.

"Weasels!" Omen shouted at the creatures, for indeed their long cylindrical forms were topped by large pointy weasel heads. Cinched in padded leather, the scruffy brown weasels stood about five feet in height and had short arms that tapered into clawed fingers. They screeched and chittered with fury through their snaggy teeth and used their tails as distance weapons, slashing and hacking at Khylar and Omen with impressive speed.

"Shields!" Khylar called out in Kharakhian and rammed forward into two of the creatures. From Khylar's other side, Nikki appeared and smashed a third creature into the first two, making what briefly looked like a giant weasel sandwich.

More soldiers maneuvered alongside him, shields out as

they held fast in the sand. Teyledrine warriors with long pikes joined them, pushing their pointed weapons past the wall of shields, keeping the enemy at bay as long as possible.

Defense, not offense! Omen tried to remind himself over the battle thrum of music running through his head.

The weasel creatures were difficult to hold back with shields alone. They ran at the row of warriors and leaped, scaling up the shields and scampering over top of the soldiers barring them. Even the long pikes were little deterrent and, time and time again, Omen found himself having to beat back creatures who'd made it past the shield line.

He tried to pace himself — measuring his blows and his psionics so that he didn't exhaust himself too quickly. Templar had warned him that exhaustion would be his greatest challenge. Omen had a habit of throwing everything into the start of a fight — expecting immediate calm after the storm. But in this battle, he knew the enemy would just keep coming. There would be no break, no rest. And he had to keep fighting, had to keep swinging his sword.

Omen struck the closest weasel warrior in the snout with the hilt of his sword. The large rodent went down like a felled tree.

Another took its place, clawing at him until he bashed it back with a hard psionic shove. The creature turned on its five-toed back feet and sprinted away, long barbed tail flailing through the air.

Briefly, Omen regretted leaving Tormy behind. *He would love to chase giant weasels.*

But Omen's giddiness only lasted a short moment.

With a start, he realized that their far line was collapsing. Nearly the entire front left wing, which was comprised of mostly rhinoceros-like battle beasts, had gone down at first shock.

Slugs the size of wolverines covered the fallen from head to toe. There was a sizzle in the air as the hefty slugs' acidic slime burned through the warriors' thick protective skins, melting away the layers of flesh and fat in dark, stinking streaks.

Omen looked away. Through the chaos, he couldn't discern much, but the bodies rushing around were not wearing Khylar's colors. The wet sand beneath his feet was churned up and colored red and black, and even the crashing sound of the waves hitting relentlessly against the shore was drowned out by the sounds of screaming and shouting from the armies around him. But something else penetrated the steady song of his psionic pattern — breaking the rhythm. A strange energy filled the air — a growing cold as something unknown moved relentlessly forward. Omen's pulse beat loud in his ears, the screams around him surging as the dreadful power rushed over them all.

Fear gripped his heart as the permeating energy assailed the warriors nearest him. Some dropped to their knees, some struggled to remain upright. Omen's head was filled by whispering, a voice commanding him to fall. Instead, he raised his shield — using every pattern his father had ever shown him to block it. Screams echoed across the sand.

The noise was deafening, but through the clash of steel on steel he suddenly heard an all too familiar voice, "Omen!"

"Templar!" he shouted back and dodged past two of Khylar's rabbit warriors as he sought out his friend. Locked in a fierce match, Templar traded mighty blows with a large warrior bedecked in plate armor. Templar's bone blades danced up and down his opponent's form in a desperate search for a weakness that wasn't there.

"Galseric!" Khylar cried out, already running toward the scene.

Omen sprinted ahead. He could see Templar's burning tendrils of magic lashing all around him only to be repelled by a pounding energy pulsing out from his opponent. *Templar's magic isn't having any effect!*

Tall and broad-shouldered, Galseric wielded a mighty battle-axe with ease and remarkable dexterity, despite his full suit of dense plate armor. The plate mail was a masterwork, fitted to perfection to its wearer's dimension. It moved with Galseric like a second skin, black and gleaming with golden sigils.

For an odd second, Omen focused on the wide riveted plates protecting Galseric's feet. *Those pointy toe covers should hinder his movement. Trip him up. What a bizarre choice for fighting on foot.*

As Omen neared him, the eerie energy swarmed outward from Galseric like the tentacles of the great leviathan they had fought at sea. The insubstantial mass swirled shadow-like, striking out at any opponent who neared. Warrior after warrior collapsed — untouched by any weapon — driven down by the force emanating from the eldritch king. Only Templar managed to hold his own against Galseric, but as Omen approached he could see his friend struggling just to stay on his feet.

"Drive him into the water!" Omen shouted to Khylar and Nikki, who were closing in. *Maybe those stupid toe things will get stuck in the wet sand.*

Templar leaped back before Galseric's axe could cleave him in two, and Khylar brought his sword hard against

133

Galseric's extended upper arm. Under normal circumstances, the arm under the plate would have broken, but
Galseric, unhurt, just pulled up the axe, catching Khylar
with the spiked pommel. Khylar stumbled back, a deep
dent in his armor's breastplate.

Omen shot out a wave of psionic energy at Galseric,
hoping to drive him back. At the same time, he unleashed a
swift combination of blows with his two-handed sword. He
hit Galseric in the neck, slashed across his chest and
brought the sword up again, cutting Galseric's thigh in an
effort to force him down onto one knee. Omen's every blow
landed true, but Galseric took little notice. He kept advancing, seemingly untouched by the crushing strikes. Omen's
psionic blast hit against a solid shield, unable to break
through.

Physical force isn't working! Omen realized at the first
touch of that shield. *He has too much power.* Omen
searched for a weakness — a direct way to attack Galseric's
mind — but no matter how hard he pushed, he couldn't
snake past the protective shield. There was nothing to latch
onto — no thought, no consciousness, no mental pattern to
break. *It's like there is no mind on the other end! Just raw
power — raw hatred. Like a force of nature.*

Nikki bashed his mace against the back of Galseric's
knees just as Galseric took another wide swing with his
axe. It turned the strike just slightly, and Omen caught the
axe against the blade of his sword and twisted it aside —
the glancing blow only hitting his shoulder. The crushing
strength behind the axe vibrated through his bones and
drove him down as if he'd been hit by a falling boulder, despite his deflection.

Nearly incapacitated, Omen went down to one knee. His

right shoulder had taken most of the force, and his arm felt as if it were on fire all the way down to his hand. The music in his mind shifted as he forced a pain-blocking pattern to the forefront of his thoughts even as he scrambled back to his feet. His head spun, and he braced against the burn in his throat. *I'm not barfing!*

The pounding black force twisted around him, ramming against his mind, the whispering growing louder as it drilled through his own mental shield. It tried to pluck the song out of his head — the pulsing music that Omen used to hold his psionic pattern securely in his mind. But he knew the tactic well — his father had used it against him, pulling away the music chord by chord, disrupting the sound. 7 had taught Omen how to move through it, how to claim notes and tunes from the sounds around him, how to clasp his patterns in his mind no matter what pounded away at him. He employed every trick he knew, desperately clutching on to his shield as he fought back.

Something dark and hateful battered at the gates of his mind. And with each wave of power, Galseric struck Omen with his axe, driving him farther back. *There's nothing to fight against — no consciousness! No thoughts — just sheer violence.* Without the familiar constructs of a mind to access, Omen could do nothing but try to hold back the force pushing against him. *My attacks are doing nothing!*

Omen staggered away. This time the attack shifted — instead of pulling away the music in his head, it amplified it, twisted it into a loud cacophonous blare. The awful clamor consumed him, and a sudden flare of colors overwhelmed his senses.

He swung his sword back and forth blindly, connecting once. The force against his sword shook through his hands.

He thought he sensed a pack of wolves on either side of him. *No, not a pack of wolves. My companions.* Reality and odd visions overlapped in Omen's perception, but he knew that his friends had fallen on Galseric while Omen concentrated on only one thing. *I'm going to make his brain explode!*

Heat. He conjured heat with a familiar domestic pattern and sent it straight at Galseric's skull — tiny darts meant to penetrate bone. *Heat. Burn.* The flaring music of the psionic pattern made the air around him sizzle as it struck the unrelenting force in front of him. *Burn! Burn!*

Templar slashed his bone blades up and down Galseric's body, still seeking a weakness, or trying to create tiny flaws in the armor. Beside him, Liethan had appeared, wielding sword and shield in tandem to strike out at the armored king. More than once, the Corsair blocked one of the blows aimed at Templar or Omen — Omen could see deep dents in Liethan's shield and long furrows where the axe blade had nearly cut through.

Khylar, in concert with Nikki, brought hard, powerful blows down on Galseric's arms and wrists, trying to cleave through the armor with the blade's sharp edge.

Nikki, for his part, strategically bashed his mace against Galseric's joints — but blow after blow seemed to have little effect.

A shuddering shock wave moved through the air, and a moment later large black spiders the size of raccoons began pushing their way up through the fine-grain sand at their feet. They swarmed out from Galseric's position in concentric circles, attacking anyone in their way. *Reinforcements? Maybe he's worried.* Exhilaration briefly flashed through Omen even as he had to dodge Galseric's next strike to swing at a spider attempting to climb his leg.

"We've got them!" Liethan shouted out. "Stay on him!"

Nikki and Liethan both turned their attention to the spiders so that Omen, Templar, and Khylar could stay on Galseric.

"I hate spiders!" Nikki called out. "Die! Die! Die!" he punctuated every blow as he smashed the spiders swarming toward Omen.

Galseric's axe arced toward Omen's head, and he barely managed to turn aside, deflecting the blow even as he lashed out again with another psionic push. *Can't reach his mind. Have to stop him physically.*

But Galseric pressed forward unfazed, swinging his great axe relentlessly. None of the blows they landed staggered him — none of Templar's burning magical strikes injured him. He was unstoppable.

Exhaustion gnawed at Omen, and he could tell his companions were slowing down as well.

"Get out of the way!" Templar shouted at Omen.

Omen stumbled back, but still the flat of Galseric's axe caught him in the side of the head.

Omen felt himself dropping. For a strange moment he was tumbling off Kadana's tower again, the fall slowed as he drifted feather-like to the ground.

"Ooooomy!" he heard Tormy's cry as he had back at the Deldano hold.

Tormy. If I fall now, what will happen to Tormy?

Omen slammed into the damp sand. His head bounced twice. Sharp pain spiked through him and blacked out his vision.

He forced his eyes to open. The clear cloudless sky tinted his vision with azure blasts. A shadow passed over him.

A fuzzy orange cloud?

Omen sat up abruptly, the pain sloshing from the back of his head down into the rest of his body and turning instantly to nausea.

A long, sharp cry and high-pitched yips assaulted Omen's ears, but he'd never been happier.

Before him, Tormy reared up against Galseric. The giant cat's paws flew through the air rapidly.

"Yeeeeeee!" tiny Tyrin wailed with shocking volume and swung precariously from the curled fur behind Tormy's ear.

Galseric took a step back, toward the ocean. Then he took another. *He doesn't know what Tormy is — it's confused him.*

Khylar rained a combination of hard blows against Galseric's head and chest.

Galseric seemed to recover from his momentary confusion, and with an almost annoyed gesture, Galseric swept Khylar aside with his gloved hand and glanced over his shoulder at the ocean.

Cool, thin hands propped Omen up.

Kyr had crept next to Omen's side during Tormy's surprise entrance. "Time to go," Kyr said as he helped Omen to his feet.

His head once again clear, Omen saw that the surging flanks had come to the aid of the weakened middle of Khylar's line. *They followed Tormy into battle,* Omen realized with something akin to pride.

Reinforced, Khylar's troops engulfed the enemy like ants swarming a frosted layer cake. Many of Galseric's warriors struggled to stand their ground, but many more turned and ran toward the ocean where the water teemed with writhing

138

serpents splashing around the shallows.

Galseric's fleet of ships bobbed up and down not far from shore, but with a sudden bang, the biggest of the ships burst into flames. *Bang.* Another exploded. *Bang.* Another. *Bang.* Another. Engulfed in the blaze, Galseric's fleet drifted together, floating pieces creating a surreal inferno.

Omen could almost feel the heat on his skin.

Galseric turned again toward them — shadows teeming around him. *He's angry!* The king raised his axe, advancing on Tormy.

Omen grabbed his fallen sword, stumbling forward to aid his cat.

"Not the air, Omen!" Kyr shouted to him. "It's too light!"

And despite everything — the sheer nonsensical words his brother called out — the desperation of the situation — the fact that Omen realized that even one blow of that axe would split open his cat — Omen's mind sang in triumph. He knew what Kyr meant! He knew exactly what he was telling him as if he had spelled it out in detail.

His giant cat hopped to one side, barely avoiding Galseric's axe as Omen reached out with his mind, attacking not the warrior, but the very ground at the man's feet. Omen reached deep into the sand, and with one mighty pull he ripped open the earth. Water and sand rushed upward in an explosion of power, and Galseric — unstoppable, unmovable, untouchable — flew with it, thrown from his feet as the very ground beneath him disappeared.

And behind him in the water, something rose from the waves. With flames dancing on the ocean behind her, the dripping figure seemed more goddess than woman. But woman she was. And friend.

Shalonie!

Chapter 9: Cypher

SHALONIE

When Shalonie had shared her idea, she hadn't imagined herself riding on a giant turtle's back through a bay teeming with poisonous sea monsters just a few hours later. Perched precariously on her mount's yellow-green shell, wet hair plastered around her face and dripping down her neck, she shivered from both fear and cold as she scanned the writhing sea beasts all around her.

The waters were swarming with creatures that looked to be a cross between eels and jellyfish — serpentine bodies with large teeth-stuffed mouths and long trailing tendrils covered in poisonous fibers that could blister and burn her skin. She knew she was protected from the poison well enough — she'd been told that the tendrils' wiggling fibers were not long enough to pierce through even the thinnest cloth. Already outfitted in knee-length stockings, leather breeches, and a long-sleeved shirt, she'd also slipped on leather gloves to protect her hands. But her face was still exposed, and she didn't relish the possibility of those tendrils accidentally scorching her skin.

The sea turtles were strong swimmers, but she didn't want to risk weighing them down. *Don't need to be dragged under the waves in case things go horribly wrong.* So she had given up her hardened leather jerkin and warm cloak but had kept her sword and the metal Cypher Rune she carried.

Glancing across the waves, she saw Dev not far from her, also perched on a giant turtle's back. He too had removed all of his armor and most of his weapons, keeping only a slender sword. And of course, he carried the metal rune she'd given him.

And somewhere back on the beach, she imagined, the other companions carried their runes as they marched into battle.

Dev gave her a wide, encouraging smile across the waves. *He can't possibly have done something like this before in his life, but he's riding the turtle as easily as his horse.*

The Teyledrine had assured her that these particular sea turtles were the giant eels' only natural predators, and the eels had an instinctive fear of the creatures. Shalonie didn't exactly trust the faerie warriors' overconfident assurances to keep them safe, but as promised all the eels veered away from the turtles. *But it would take only one bold one to get us.* She was protected from the poisonous tendrils, but the nasty teeth could still bite off a sizable chunk of flesh.

And my arm aches. A violent shiver shot through her body. Omen and Templar had managed to close the wound inflicted by the wyvern, but the skin around the mending scar had turned black and blue. Without any opportunity to rest and heal, Shalonie was starting to appreciate the frailty of her own mortal flesh.

How did I get here? she wondered, not for the first time. Of course, when she thought about the others — all of them heading into a battle they couldn't possibly win — all on the faith that she could do what she claimed she could, she felt sick to her stomach. *It will work! It has to!* she repeated to herself over and over, attempting to ward off the sheer terror threatening to paralyze her.

It had begun innocently enough. Both she and Omen had had the same thought — that they'd seen a situation like this before . . . in Khreté.

"I have an idea," she had told those gathered, and Khylar had led them back into his tent to hear the details of her plan. While Khylar and the Teyledrine didn't know Shalonie, her companions had given her their full attention, which seemed to be enough.

"If you can't remove the creature from Galseric's body, and you can't take the ring off his hand, why not just trap his body?" she'd explained. "The creature controlling him is obviously tied to the ring — it must be trapped inside it, and since we've never heard of it before, it must have been dormant all these years, probably since the time of the first Covenant. It needed someone to put the ring on — it needed a body to control. If you can't stop the creature itself, just stop the body it controls."

"How?" Khylar had demanded. "It isn't stupid — we can't lure it into a cage."

"No, but we can build a cage around it," Shalonie had snapped out her answer.

"Impossible!" Lady Morcades had proclaimed, her pale face cast in shadows by the candles lighting the tent.

When Shalonie had first seen the woman she'd mistaken her for Indee — Morcades bore such a strong resemblance. Tall and fair with long ebony hair that hung in a thick braid down her back, and eyes as blue as the ocean, the faerie woman was beautiful in a way Shalonie knew she herself would never be. Exotic, seductive, and yet possessing a regal bearing that left no doubt in anyone's mind that she was a noblewoman, even if the gown of dark blue silk twined

142

with silverleaf had not been mark enough. But more than that, Shalonie had sensed power — something dark and chaotic that made Shalonie quake uneasily. And she hadn't missed the way the rest of the Teyledrine and creatures of the Autumn Lands had avoided Morcades' gaze.

They fear her . . . Kyr too, and the cats, Shalonie remembered. *They moved away from the group to avoid her. Dev didn't like her either.* The Machelli's eyes had hardened when he'd seen the faerie sorceress.

"What you are suggesting is impossible," Lady Morcades had informed Shalonie. "The only cage that would be strong enough to hold him would be a summoner's entrapment circle. Those take hours to cast — if not days or even weeks. He would see it upon the ground — and even if we were able to hide it in some fashion, he would feel its power long before he ever stepped onto it."

"I'm not suggesting a summoner's circle," Shalonie had countered. "I mean the principle is the same — but this would be made of Cypher Runes. If you engage him directly in battle, and then surround him with people each carrying one of the runes — we could trigger the trap instantly. He'd never even know it was there until it was activated."

"Cypher Runes!" Morcades had ranted. "There are few who even know that name, and none who possess the knowledge of how to use them — that knowledge was lost eons ago during the Unsung Wars."

Shalonie had startled at the pronouncement. *Unsung wars!* It was the first she'd ever heard of the term — indeed Morcades was one of the first people she'd ever come across who possessed even a passing knowledge that Cypher Runes even existed. *And she seems to know some sort of history about them that I do not.*

"Shalonie possesses the knowledge!" Omen had jumped in immediately. "We've seen her use them — if she says she can build a trap for Galseric, I believe her."

Shalonie had cleared her throat nervously, wishing momentarily he hadn't revealed her shaky skill so brashly. *I can't be afraid of her. I have work to do.* "I just need to figure out the calculations." She decided to forget about Morcades and whatever threat she could pose in the future. "I can create the runes ahead of time, then we carry them into battle, surround Galseric and trigger them."

"Aside from the fact that you are suggesting we engage Galseric directly in one-on-one combat — something no warrior in a hundred years has survived," Khylar had told her, "he is not the only threat on the field. The thing that possesses him controls all of the creatures in his army — and it continuously infects more and more each day, taking over their minds. Even if it cannot control Galseric's body, it still has the entirety of its forces to turn against us."

"No," Shalonie had replied, nearly sure of herself. "The trap should contain it utterly, should cut the creature off from the influence it holds over the army." She'd pulled out her notebook and had begun jotting down some preliminary calculations.

"It can't be as simple as surrounding him with runes," Morcades had disparaged.

"No, not simple," Shalonie had agreed. "I'm going to need a lot of things to make this work — first the time of day . . ." She had scribbled down more calculations, trying to figure out the best option. "Midnight would work, but noon would be best. That way I can use the sunlight as part of the equation. So this has to happen at high noon — when the sun is directly overhead." She had looked up in alarm,

144

staring at Khylar. "The sun still rises and sets the same way in these lands, right?"

He'd nodded. "It does. What else do you need?"

"Well, there is certainly enough power on a battlefield itself — I can use that. But I'll need the four elements combined as well."

"The typical combination of the elements is a cauldron of water over a wood fire," Morcades had informed her.

"How is that all four?" Omen had cut in. "Isn't that just fire and water?"

"The wood itself is earth and the air is the smoke," Shalonie had clarified. "Well, actually it's the oxygen making the fire burn, but most people just assume it's smoke. Still, this is problematic — getting a fire on a battlefield is easy enough, but we can't exactly cart out large cauldrons of water — and we're going to need a lot of it."

"There's an entire ocean of water," Omen had stated as if not understanding the issue.

"The elements must be together. Can't exactly light the ocean on fire," Shalonie had explained.

They were all silent a moment as they'd tried to collectively figure out a solution to the dilemma — at least Morcades' suggestions let Shalonie know that she was willing to entertain the idea that this might be possible. *That's something at least.*

"Would burning ships work?" Dev had suggested with a smirk. The Machelli had been staring out the tent opening toward the ocean where they could see the dark shapes of numerous ships on the horizon, silhouetted in the moonlight.

"Yes!" Shalonie had nearly jumped up and down with nervous energy. "But how are we going to light them on fire — they're too far away for spells or arrows — do you have war engines?"

"Not here," Khylar had replied. "But we do have men who could reach the ships." He'd glanced at his aunt. "The frog men could certainly get on board."

Frog men. Half man, half frog? Shalonie had wondered if they were like the rabbit men or Puppy. *Nothing in this land is as you expect.*

"I can make some form of liquid fire if you have the ingredients," Dev had offered. "Dwarven redstone, salamander oil, dragon spark — there are so many ways to create liquid fire. I could keep those ships burning as long as you like."

"They'd also need to all start burning exactly at noon," Shalonie had informed him.

He'd frowned at that. "There are ways of making timers with wax and other chemicals, but I'm not certain they'd be accurate enough."

She'd pondered the problem. "Liquid fire just needs a spark, right?" When Dev had nodded, she'd picked up one of the wine goblets from Khylar's table and used her lead stylus to sketch a quick rune into the side of the goblet. A moment later a web of tiny sparks of lightning had shimmered over the surface of the vessel — causing her to drop it at her feet.

The looks of astonishment on the Teyledrines' faces had been satisfying.

"I should be able to time that to happen exactly at noon," she'd stated, pleased. "If your frog men can get the explosives on board — we'll have our elements. Now I just need something to carve the runes into — once I work out the equation."

"Such as?" Khylar had asked.

"Metal would work best," she'd decided. She'd held out her hands, her palms perhaps twelve inches apart. "And at least this large — but it will have to be something easy to carry into battle. And preferably something fairly conductive."

Omen had reached across the table and lifted up a dinner plate. In the firelight it had looked like reddish gold. "Would this work?" he'd asked. "I believe it's copper."

Shalonie had grinned. "It's perfect — and it already has a smooth surface — easy to carve into. Once I have everything ready — we'll need to surround Galseric at high noon. Then all you need to do at that point is drop the runes on the ground in a circle at his feet."

"Do I need to trigger these the same way I triggered the others?" Omen had asked.

But Shalonie had shaken her head as she'd thought of the intricacy of the calculation she was attempting. "No, this isn't a matter of just pushing power into it — it will already have all it needs to make it work. I'll have to trigger this one — with an incantation or maybe musical notes."

"Absolutely not!" Omen had protested, and to Shalonie's surprise the rest of her companions had echoed his words. "Shalonie, we're talking about marching directly into the front line of battle against terrible odds. You don't belong on the battlefield — it's far too dangerous."

Shalonie had opened her mouth to protest, though she could see a unified front among her companions. "But what about Nikki and—"

A sudden thought had occurred to her, bringing her protest to an end. Though she certainly had more fighting experience than Nikki did, neither Nikki nor the others in

147

her company were mortal. She was.

"I would concur," Khylar had agreed with a frown. "This is no place for a mortal. Even possessing immortality, we have lost countless Teyledrine to this enemy. Immortal lives forever scattered, leaving empty husks. Who even knows —"

He broke off as well, a haunted look at the back of his eyes. "On this battlefield not even immortality will protect you — this enemy has the ability to rip your soul asunder and completely sever your connection to your body, immortal or not."

Shalonie had shivered, realizing finally the danger she was putting her companions in, as well as the danger to herself. But she was no coward and would not back down. "I have to be there," she'd insisted. "Too many factors involved — and the battlefield is too unpredictable. If something goes wrong or there is some new element thrown into the mix, I'll need to be able to alter the equation on the fly — and since I can't change the runes themselves, I'll have to change the incantation that activates them. That means recalculating the equation — no offense, but I can't teach any of you how to do that in a single night."

She'd plainly seen the frustration in Omen's eyes as well as the worry in her other companions. They had all learned enough, she'd guessed, to know that what she was proposing wasn't going to be easy.

"I realize that this plan is a risk — but does anyone else have a better one? The Autumn Gate has to be closed if we wish to save the mortal lands. And if we don't stop Galseric, the Autumn Dwellers will be slaughtered — and I doubt very much he will stop with the Autumn Lands. If the Teyledrine have been fighting him for a hundred years without success — surely you can all see the reason for trying something different — something new."

They'd been silent as they mulled over her words. It was Omen who'd broken the silence. "Dev, Shalonie . . . can you both swim?" He'd grinned, motioning to the map on Khylar's table. "I have an idea, but I doubt any of you are going to like it."

Which was what ultimately led to Shalonie's predicament now — riding on the back of a giant sea turtle through the eel-infested waters. She and Dev had gone to Morcades' tent after Omen had explained his battle plan; Morcades, a sorceress, had a well-stocked apothecary with her — supplies to make any sort of potion required on a battlefield. She'd had all the ingredients necessary for the liquid fire Dev had promised — and under her watchful eye, Dev had concocted the necessary bombs for the attack.

While he'd worked, Shalonie had gone through sheet after sheet of paper in her notebook, working out the required equations for the Cypher Runes. And then she'd taken the magically imbued stylus Morcades had given her and carefully carved the runes into the surface of the copper plates she'd collected. Even as she'd carved, she'd recalculated the equation over and over in her head, terrified of making a mistake. *No second chances. Either I get this right, or we're all doomed — and the mortal world with us.* Despite the chill, she'd started sweating the moment she'd put stylus to copper.

This was just supposed to be a rescue mission of one man, she'd thought darkly to herself. *How did it become a dire threat to the entire world? Did Indee know — is that why she hexed Kyr in the first place?*

More than once she'd found her mind drifting to Kyr,

wondering if once again he'd given her some strange prophetic phrase that might at least tell her if they had some hope of success in this endeavor. But the boy had seemed happily occupied by the cats and the strange creatures surrounding them, heedless of any danger. On the matter of their near future, he'd stayed silent.

Hours later, once the bombs were completed and she'd finished the last of the copper plates — she'd returned to her group. The bombs themselves were given to a troop of very tall, thin men who possessed bulbous eyes and freakishly large mouths — not quite the *frog men* she'd been expecting, but she could certainly see the resemblance. Their long fingers and the toes of their bare feet were thickly webbed and designed for swimming. They'd taken Dev's instructions in silence as he'd doled out the bombs.

"You have to get them on board the ships before high noon," Shalonie had explained, not entirely certain how much they'd understood since none of the frog men had spoken a single word. "The rune etched into their containers will activate them — the liquid fire will ignite. You have to be off the ships before then."

Still silent, the frog men had taken the bombs and disappeared into the darkness. If all went right, they would climb down the far southern horn of the bay near the swamps and slip into the open sea.

Shalonie then bid the others farewell — touched as all of them came forward to hug her. They had already received their instructions on what to do with the copper plates — she'd have to trust in their abilities to make it into position at the correct time. *So much could go wrong.*

And then she had followed Devastation Machelli into the night — two Teyledrine warriors accompanying them as they headed off on a journey that would take them far around the outskirts of Galseric's army and down through the southern horn of the bayside crescent into the swamplands. They would then take a route through the ocean, trusting their companions to hold Galseric at the shoreline away from the mountain and the open Autumn Gate. She and Dev would come up behind him through the water — his attention would be focused forward away from the sea.

She hadn't expected to find the turtles waiting for them at the ocean side. The Teyledrine warriors had explained the dangers in the water, and that swimming would be inadvisable. The turtles — though entirely ordinary-looking as far as Shalonie could tell — were clearly intelligent and able to communicate with the Teyledrine. Like the rest of the plethora of strange creatures of the Autumn Lands, they were more than willing to aid in the endeavor before them. *I'd love to classify the creatures of the Autumn Lands one day.* She'd refocused on her mission immediately, a small part of her grateful that she'd been capable of having a thought that reached past the immediate.

When Shalonie had stripped out of her jerkin and leather cloak and then slipped into the water, one of the large turtles had immediately swum over to her, letting her grab hold of the upper ridge of his shell and climb aboard its back. Though their land-dwelling kin were known for their slowness, the sea turtles moved swiftly through the saltwater. Shalonie had to grip tightly to keep her place. For a light second, she'd shared a grin with Dev, both of them realizing at the same time that, were it not for the circumstances, the ride would be a lot of fun.

The turtles had stayed submerged enough that they were largely hidden from the sight of the shoreline, Shalonie and

Dev keeping only their heads above water. Someone would have to be specifically searching for them to spot them moving through the dark ocean. And as the battle had already begun, all the attention of the army was focused on the advancement of Khylar's troops.

Heart pounding in her throat, Shalonie watched the battle as they neared the shoreline. The sun was nearly overhead. It would just be a matter of moments before the liquid fire ignited — if everything had gone according to plan, the frogs would have placed the devices already and made their escape. But until the moment actually came, she had no way of knowing if they'd been successful.

If they failed, there won't be the proper combination of elements — my runes won't work. She'd gone over and over the incantation in her head — trying to devise the best combination to activate the Cypher Runes as well as figuring out contingencies if something went wrong. For this, the power would come from the surroundings — from the combination of the four elements, from the energy rising off the battlefield — the fear, the terror, the rage, even the death and blood. The sheer force of the power would be extraordinary, and she intended to turn all that back on the creature inside Galseric. But the power needed to be channeled; otherwise, it would erupt into sheer chaos.

Her runes would control the energy, but first she'd have to activate them. She'd have to channel all that power directly into them. *And that's the trick — the activation sequence itself has to be part of the equation.* Musical notes would have worked, she imagined. In calmer situations, music would be extraordinarily powerful. The sound waves of each individual note could be planned out in detail, like numbers in a mathematical equation.

152

However, even having spent her entire life studying music, Shalonie couldn't count on herself to be able to hit the notes perfectly in the rush of battle. If she hit a *C* when she meant to hit a *D-minor,* the equation would fall apart. *Omen might be able to manage something like that — or 7 or Beren, but not me.*

For her, it would have to be words of power along with the magical constructs of ordinary spell casting — the sort of magical patterns sorcerers used. Most spells were cast in one of three languages: Sul'eldrine, Nightspeak, or Dawn's Tongue. And while she would have felt more comfortable using Sul'eldrine, she couldn't be entirely certain the gods would favor them in this endeavor. There was a good chance the gods were angry at the sheer violation of the Covenant.

And Khylar even hinted that he'd done this specifically to vex the gods — to force them to act. But the gods do not care to be manipulated. Under the circumstances Shalonie felt it was far safer to use Dawn's Tongue — and certainly the power of the noonday sun would be far easier to channel using that language. *There's nothing dark about this spell — I'm doing this to save lives, not end them.*

"Get ready," Dev called to her from across the crashing waves — they'd already moved into the ocean surf and were being driven forward toward the shoreline by the force of the icy water more so than the power of the turtles. Another violent shiver ran through her, and her heartbeat pulsed like the percussive pounding of a kettledrum. The battle raged upon the beach ahead — countless men and creatures crashing upon one another in the savage fray. Galseric's army charged ahead, driven by mad rage.

As Shalonie and Dev neared the shore, she could feel a

strange pulsing power moving through the air like the incessant booming of terrible thunder.

"Do you feel that?" she called to Dev, wondering what it could be.

His face spasmed with worry. "It's Galseric's power manifesting," he called to her. "The creature possessing him is getting angry."

Shalonie's eyes sought out the shape of Galseric on the battlefield. He wasn't hard to spot. It wasn't so much that he was a tall man — most of the Teyledrine were — or the black, sigil-covered plate armor he wore — a mark of his nobility. Rather it was the shadow that radiated out from him. It rose from his body like a black cloud, swirling around him and pulsing with a reddish light that flared with each crash of thunder.

Staring hard, she could see that same misty cloud hanging over the forms of his army upon the field — enormous moving tendrils of smoke or mist crawling over the beach, casting shadows and reddish light over all. *We shouldn't be able to feel it here — he's not trying to control anything in the ocean. How strong is this creature?*

She could see her companions — Omen and Templar fighting side by side. Nikki and Liethan were near them, guarding the flank while Khylar moved alongside them. They all slowly advanced on Galseric as they tried to push him back toward the shore.

They're pushing his minions back — but he's not moving.

Droves of incomprehensibly strange creatures moved to confront her companions — every shape and size imaginable. The bizarre denizens of the Autumn Lands raged under the control of the creature that had possessed their king.

154

As Shalonie watched, unable to act, Omen and Templar took down creature after creature. Nikki and Liethan protected them, warding off blow after blow with their shields and getting battered in the process. Khylar, surrounded by his own loyal warriors, moved alongside them.

From the vantage of her position out at sea, Shalonie saw Khylar's front line beginning to collapse. They'd relied on the charging force of the strange armor-skinned behemoths to drive forward — but few of the enormous beasts were still on their feet and moving.

In the space of a moment, Galseric himself moved forward — wielding a great axe in his hands as the shadows and tendrils of power all around him grew and rose skyward, whipping about him like a cloak in a terrible windstorm.

Shalonie's companions surged forward to meet him, but even from her perch on the sea turtle, Shalonie could feel the awesome force of energy pushing back at all of them. Lightning cracked across the sky — fire and tendrils of black energy ripping through the multitude of creatures on the battlefield.

Some of that is Templar's magic — some the Teyledrine's — but I think most of that is Galseric himself!

She watched in terror as Galseric engaged her friends in combat. His axe rained down upon them with merciless blows, driving them back as Galseric moved forward. It wasn't until Shalonie saw a physical shifting of the black mist around Galseric that she realized that Omen was using his psionics against him — pushing him back with the full force of the Daenoth's terrible mind powers. For a moment it looked to her as if Omen's body was wreathed in flames. *He's trying to burn Galseric!*

155

And though Galseric wavered under the weight of the psionically enhanced blows of Omen's sword, she realized to her shock that beyond a tiny stumble, Galseric was largely unfazed by the attack. *How is that possible?*

She knew enough about the Daenoth's psionics to realize that they had few equals in the world. Galseric, at the very least, should have been slowed. *Even if the creature is capable of withstanding the assault, Galseric's body should succumb to the onrush of energy.* A terrible gnawing thought ate at her, growing monstrous in the back of her mind. *What is this thing?*

They were close to the shore now — the sun nearly overhead. She looked up.

Noon.

From across the crashing surf, Dev waved to her, glancing over his shoulder at the ships even as he drew his sword from its sheath. She saw him toss aside the sheath in the foaming water and pull the copper plate she'd given him from his belt where he'd secured it. She drew her dragon-scale sword, pulling out her own copper plate, the words of her incantation sharp in her mind as she thought of all the calculations she'd worked into this spell.

But if I'm wrong about this creature — wrong about what it is . . .

Her heart lurched in her chest; her stomach churned with true terror. The calculations and this entire spell hinged on her belief that this thing was one of the creatures from the Age of Blood, one of the many creatures imprisoned here in the Autumn Lands during the first Covenant — when the Elder God Damien, The Redeemer, had first died and his blood had stained the earth. This was one of the creatures Cerioth had unleashed upon the world when he'd broken

156

the first Covenant thousands of years ago, bringing about the current Covenant. But even as she watched the battle and saw the power swirling out from the form of Galseric, she began to doubt herself — began to doubt that she truly understood what was happening.

And then, Omen went down. Galseric's great axe swung toward her friend as the full force of the pulsing black shadows swarmed forward and encased Omen and the others within its confines.

Heart in throat, she watched as a large orange blur leaped across the sand, arching through the air. *Tormy!*

Astoundingly, the cat reached Omen just before Galseric could aim his killing blow. Templar pulled Omen back from the fray as the cat hit the shadowed king squarely with all the might of his giant paw.

Shalonie marveled as instead of the black mist swirling forward to swallow the cat, it swirled back and away as if the creature inside Galseric had flinched. Tormy's fur blazed like fire in the sunlight as the cat slashed sharp claws, scratching and hissing.

Though she doubted Tormy truly caused much damage, Galseric backed away — a single step only into the water. The others took it as encouragement and swarmed closer. Just as Galseric glanced over his shoulder toward the water's edge where Shalonie and Dev were now setting foot on solid ground and rising up out of the crashing water, the boats behind them exploded.

Dev's bombs sent liquid fire spraying across the hulls. They went up like angry funeral pyres, and already Shalonie could feel the driving force of the elements she'd combined gathering within the confines of the copper plate she held in her hand. She saw her companions reaching for their own plates — no doubt they too could feel the pulsing energy move through them. Even without her activation incantation, they were already responding to the combination of elements she'd worked into her calculation.

It has to work! She swore as she pushed forward. There were a handful of creatures in her way. Dev moved alongside her, cutting his way forward with his sword, keeping the creatures away from her. The others stepped into place to surround Galseric. Reinforcements arrived just then. Khylar's troops cut off the enemy army from the shadowed king. They would have only moments to do what was necessary — only a few moments before they'd be swarmed again. She saw an explosion of sand and water burst upward from the ground directly beneath Galseric's feet.

Omen! Shalonie thought with a flash of pride as she saw Galseric fly backward — finally knocked off his feet by the only blow that had landed. Her friends moved in quickly, copper plates held in their hands.

Galseric wasn't fazed for long — rolling to his feet despite the full suit of plate armor. He turned and shot a quick glance to the sea at the burning ships.

And then Galseric spotted her approaching from the blazing surf. He met her eyes, and for one brief moment they were locked there suspended in time as she held out her copper plate. The others had already circled around him, had already dropped their plates into place on the ground. She had only to drop hers and complete the incantation — that was it, it was time.

And then Galseric smiled.

In that single instant, that gnawing terror inside her soul raged forward as she understood in a flash of insight that she had been wrong — all of it was wrong. She knew this

158

thing, or rather didn't know it — didn't recognize it even in the depths of her soul — there was no word for it, nothing except the blind hatred that raged about it. But even everything she'd ever known of hatred — her every understanding of emotion at all was incapable of describing this thing.

It was alien — utterly alien in a way she could not perceive — which could only mean one thing. This wasn't a creature of the Covenant — this wasn't something bound by the current Covenant of the Gods, or even a creature bound by the first Covenant — wasn't a creature held back from the world by the sacrifice of the Elder God who had died. This was something older — something she could never even hope to understand — and something she realized in that single instant she had no hope of stopping.

"Galseric, I know you can hear me," a voice rang out — a musical, sweet voice that sounded a thousand ways wrong because it was speaking in Kahdess, the Language of the Dead. To her horror Shalonie realized that Kyr had come with Tormy — that the little boy and his small kitten had come to join the group. She nearly collapsed from the visceral flare of horror that coursed through her. In one terrible moment, she understood what she had done.

There was no threat to her — nothing beyond her own mortal death. She had the easy path — she would die, and it would be swift and final and ultimately unmarked because, in the grand scheme of things, she meant nothing at all.

But the others — Omen, Templar, Khylar, Liethan, Nikki, and Kyr — they were all immortals. She and the cats could escape the fate before them — maybe Dev too if he had only his Shilvagi blood to bind him to this world. They could find escape. But the poor, dear boys she'd been traveling with — they would find no escape. The creature within Galseric would take hold of each one of them and burn the world with their hands, their minds, their powers.

"I know you can hear me, Galseric!" Kyr said again, his voice rising above the screams of battle and the crashing of the ocean surf. "You have to fight — just for one moment. One single moment is all that matters — just resist for one single moment and your nightmare will end!"

And then Shalonie remembered hearing the same thing once before — Kyr had grabbed her hand at the doorway of the chamber of Khylar's father Charaathalar and had stared so earnestly at her as he'd uttered more nonsense in her direction. "It's just the one single moment that matters. Ignore all the rest of it."

She hadn't understood what he'd meant — how could she after all? His words had made no sense out of context. But now, thinking back, remembering what Omen's parents had done to stop Charaathalar and the Night Lord — she understood. Frantically she thought of her incantation, thought of the calculations she'd made — the ones already carved into each of the copper disks at Galseric's feet. In a second, it would be too late; her mind worked furiously.

Staring into the face of Galseric — seeing that creature look back at her — hearing Kyr's words, she saw her opening. She saw the brief single instant those eyes shifted and changed and understood then that Galseric — the Teyledrine King — was still there, still alive, still listening to the world around him and that he too had heard Kyr's words.

She dropped her copper disk into the sand and shouted — screaming out the words of the modified incantation she'd constructed in her mind — so different from what she'd intended, her only hope — their only hope. And King

160

Galseric, staring back at her, understood as well. He fought against the creature who held him with all he had — just for one moment, one single, ghastly moment.

Her Cypher Runes burned. Blazing light burst upward in a column toward the sky, energy exploding all around them, throwing all of them back as the ring of copper plates in the sand around Galseric's feet erupted in a shower of blinding sun-white light and sand that shot upward like an inferno. The electrical charge in the air stunned all of them.

Shalonie, thrown back into the wet sand and crashing surf, whipped her head away from the light, squeezing her eyes shut as the sand rained down on her, and lightning danced across the surface of her skin. Her nose registered the smell of salt and burning hair.

Her ears were ringing, the sounds around her muted and distant. She thought she heard shouting — thought she heard voices crying out to her. Hands lifted her up — her body numb. She turned painfully, the sight before her unnatural, heinous — wonderful.

Galseric stood fully encased in glass — the copper plates that had lain at his feet were now embedded into the block of glass along with his unmoving body. The force of power, the heat of the electricity that had sparked through all of them had turned the explosion of sand into glass, freezing him completely. The shadow was gone — the black pulsing cloud nowhere to be seen. Galseric's army fled. Khylar's forces gave chase, needlessly. All around her, men and creatures cheered resoundingly — her own dear companions smiling and shouting, clapping her on the back. It was Omen and Dev who had lifted her and were holding her up.

Her body shook uncontrollably. Her eyes burned, tears

welling within them as the strength left her limbs. She sank back down into the wet surf, unable to stand as her legs gave out. Her hair was plastered around her face, her body wet from the ocean and coated in sand as she stared with utter horror at the glass-encased king. Everyone around her cheered. They didn't understand.

"Shalonie!" Omen knelt beside her.

The others came forward to surround her; Khylar stood nearby uncertainly.

"Are you all right, Shalonie?" Omen asked. There was blood on his face, dripping from a wound on his scalp — she wondered if he even knew he'd been cut.

She shook her head in denial. "I was wrong," she said simply. "I was wrong."

"About what?" Omen asked, voice clipped and hard.

They have to understand. I have to make them understand. "Omen, I'm sorry. I thought I knew what the creature was. I assumed it had to be from the Age of Blood — from the time of the First Covenant. One of the creatures the gods locked away so that mortals could live."

"But wasn't that . . ." Omen searched. No doubt, he hadn't studied this footnote to history overly long — even though as a son of Cerioth it was a part of his heritage. It was Cerioth after all who had broken that first Covenant. "I don't know . . . a really long time ago?"

Her heart fluttered with shame. "But I was wrong — the creature wasn't from then — it was already ancient by the time any of that happened. It had nothing to do with the mortal world. There was no way I could stop it. Not with my simple little equations and spells."

She identified the looks the companions exchanged immediately. *They are refusing to hear me.* All of them looked

162

from her to the glass-encased king, a bit of smug satisfaction on all of their faces.

"But Shalonie, you did stop it," Omen told her slowly, speaking carefully as if she were a very small child.

Shalonie's shoulders slumped. "No, I didn't. I couldn't stop the creature, I couldn't even stop Galseric. I did what your father did in Khreté, Omen. I stopped time."

She could see from their expressions that none of them truly understood. "If Kyr hadn't spoken up, I'm not sure I would have even thought of it." She stared out across the sand where Tormy was seated just out of reach of the water, Kyr crouched in front of him, Tyrin perched upon his shoulder.

"But what does it matter how you did it?" Omen asked lightly. "It worked! You stopped him. That was the plan — to trap his body."

"No." She wondered why they didn't understand what she was saying — what a terrible risk she'd just forced them all to take by agreeing to her foolhardy plan. *Maybe they don't want to understand.* "All I did was stop a single moment in time — just one moment, nothing more. And even then you can't really stop time — not completely. You can just slow it down — that's all I did, I just slowed down one small single moment of time around Galseric."

"Slowed it down?" Khylar demanded, coming forward. "For how long?"

She paused, not entirely certain, though she supposed she could calculate it out to the day if her brain didn't hurt so badly. "A few years perhaps," she replied.

"A few years!" Khylar roared, taking several steps toward her. Liethan and Nikki both stepped in front of him, stopping his motion. "We have been fighting him for a hundred years! What good are a few years? A few years! That's nothing in the Autumn Lands!"

"I didn't use the Autumn Lands as a point of reference!" she snapped at him, her nerves frayed beyond her control, her anger rising as the terror and guilt inside her warred with each other. "I used the mortal world as the reference point."

"What does that mean?" Khylar demanded gruffly, though she thought he should know without asking.

Surprisingly, Omen had figured it out immediately. He rose to block Khylar from Shalonie. "You've been here a hundred years, but only a few weeks have passed in the mortal world. I imagine a few years in the mortal world means many centuries here."

"Certainly that should buy you time enough to figure out what to do with him," Shalonie said. "Seal him up in a tomb, bury him beneath a mountain, throw him into a volcano."

Khylar paused, seeming appeased by the information. "Can he be moved?" he asked, his wheels already turning.

"Yes," Shalonie confirmed. While there was some component of real glass in the bubble around him, formed by the superheated sand that had exploded — she knew the glass encasing him was far more than that. Until her single moment of frozen time ended, his prison would not break.

"And now you have to keep your promise, Khylar." Omen turned on the Kharakhian king without losing a beat. "Close the Autumn Gate and return home."

They all saw it — the indecipherable look Khylar threw them, the way he glanced back at Galseric, the gaze that swept over the still-battling armies as his troops harried the fleeing hoard.

"Of course," he stated smoothly. "A promise is a promise, after all."

Kneeling in the sand beside her, Shalonie felt Dev shift and mutter a quiet curse under his breath.

Chapter 10: Triumph

DEV

Devastation Machelli took a bite of warm, buttery puff pastry and let the subtle sweetness of the apricot kernel paste spread over his tongue. He half-closed his eyes and for a moment shut out the pandemonium of King Khylar's triumphant victory parade.

In the short decade since its completion, the capital city of Caraky had never seen such an elaborate affair. The wide streets were lined with both citizens and visitors from the outlying towns. Shops closed temporarily, merchants stood in front of their businesses, wringing their hands in a complex roundelay of fret and anticipation. Happy swallowtail flags fluttered in the breeze, black and silver and blood red — the colors of the Set-Manasan dynasty patterned in repeating threes.

Wonder how this "victory" is being sold to the citizens of Kharakhan. Amazed how fast they spread the word. It's only been a week since the beach. As far as Dev could discern, the people had never known that their king had disappeared. Many had just barely figured out that the Autumn Dwellers were an existential threat.

"Say, Riverboy . . ." Curious, Dev addressed the Machelli Guild apprentice standing next to him. "What does the city make of this triumph?"

When they'd arrived in Caraky a week ago, right after Khylar had kept his promise of closing the Autumn Gate and returning home, Dev had reported to the Machelli

Guild House at Avarice's prompting. To Dev's deep vexation, Master Finagle — the Caraky guild master — had foisted two young apprentices on him for the duration of the victory parade. Dev hadn't bothered explaining that he was, in fact, one of the heroes being honored. He knew without being told that Avarice didn't want him participating in the elaborate and highly political affair.

Heroes. Dev sniffed, unintentionally blowing pastry flakes on his sleeve. *Never cared for being put on display like a painted poppet, and Avarice doesn't want the Machelli coat of arms displayed for Khylar's purposes.*

Dev snapped up the last bite of the treat like a hungry dog and brushed the crumbly remnants off his tunic.

"Don't be shy, youngling," Dev goaded the younger of the two apprentices. Neither of the boys was actually related to the Machelli family; they were born and raised in Kharakhan. He was curious to see what they were made of. "What's your opinion?"

"It came on very suddenly," Riverboy said, clearly hoping his answer would impress. He nodded his tightly curled black mane for emphasis.

The slightly older boy stepped closer. "There's more to this triumph than meets the eye," Rat, as scrawny and grey as his name suggested, said with measured caution. "And you, Devastation Machelli, know more than you let on."

Dev raised an eyebrow. *Need to watch out for that one.*

"Master Finagle said you arrived in Caraky last night," Rat explained. "But I believe you arrived with Khylar's troops last week and have been camped on the Field of Victory outside of the city as the arrangements for the triumph were being made."

"What makes you think that?" Dev was intrigued.

167

"The apricot knots," Rat said simply. "That pastry was created by the Caraky pastry guild to honor the return of our king and the defeat of the Autumn Dwellers. The first orders were delivered to the Field of Victory and King Khylar three days ago. The knots have only been available here in the city since this morning. After the first cock's crow to be exact. Yet, at the pastry cart, you asked for the knots by name, without inquiring what they were called first. And, while you clearly enjoyed the knot, you weren't surprised by the unusual flavor nor did you ask how the baker had accomplished the subtle interplay of sweet and bitter notes."

For a kid named Rat, he's remarkably eloquent. "You know a lot about the pastries," Dev said dryly, a little put off by the boy's accurate assessment. *How predictable of me — I'm getting complacent.*

Rat showed his long teeth in a self-satisfied smile, which made him look even more rodent-like. "I've been working as a baker's assistant in the guild kitchen since Lord Fel'-torin arrived in Caraky. Master Finagle thought . . ." He paused and studied Dev's face. "I'm sorry. I have annoyed you."

Now I'm annoyed, Dev thought. *He reads people too well — must have grown up on the streets.* Dev forced a good-humored smiled. "Not at all. But I am still waiting for an answer. What do the people of Caraky make of the triumph?"

Rat scanned the eager crowd.

Dev and the young Machelli spies had taken position on the side of the First Plaza, not far from the city gate. The parade route had been demarcated as running the diagonal road from the Victory Gate to the castle, which rose in the

168

exact center of the city as if it had been placed using an oversized protractor and a compass.

The geometric layout of the streets isn't accidental either, Dev thought and felt the slight queasiness he always associated with dark magic.

"The citizens of Caraky are a curious lot," Rat said, leaning heavily on the double meaning. "Don't you agree, Riverboy? You grew up here."

That took Dev by surprise. "I was under the impression that Queen Indee'athra Set-Manasan had the city built from nothing," he probed. "How could you have grown up in a city that didn't exist? You are more than a decade old, though not *much* older judging by the few lonely hairs on your chin."

Rat snickered, though he had no facial hair whatsoever.

"My people and I are river folk. Generations back," Riverboy said with a ring of pride. "That's why I carry the name Riverboy. And I was half a decade old when the first cornerstone of the castle was placed."

"Your people helped build the city." Dev surmised, intrigued.

"My people labored to build the docks," Riverboy said. "We know the two rivers well. Know well the conflux . . . and the danger it holds. We know protections of the rivers spirits that are as old as the drops of water that make up the stream."

That's the old religion. Spirits in every tree, bush and creek. Fits right in with Machelli superstition.

"What are you doing in the Machelli Guild, then? Why not profit from the river?" Dev strained to see over the heads of five burly men, a blacksmith and his apprentices by the look of their thick arms and leather aprons.

169

"My family does many things around the river," River-boy said evasively. "My father paid my apprenticeship in full."

Rat threw Riverboy a jealous look. "You lucky pig," Rat grumbled, apparently without meaning to because he clamped his mouth shut quickly and with a sharp snap of his molars.

Which means Rat is indentured under contract — River-boy is free to walk away. Dev could sympathize with the boy's resentment — though he himself would never agree to work under contract. Not even for the Machellis.

"Now, let's focus." Dev spoke like a pedantic school-master, fully aware that he'd been the one to sow the seeds of unrest between them. "We have a job to do. Go collect knowledge, mugworts."

The boys split up and wiggled away through the crowd like tadpoles swimming through murky water.

Dev blew out a heavy breath.

Without much effort, he scaled the side of the building and scrambled over the roofs toward the mouth of the plaza. The light stone, he noted absently, had come from the dwarfkin mines on the eastern shores of the country.

No expense spared.

The unique architecture of Caraky was another concern. *It's like nothing I've ever seen before,* he thought. *Yet, it's uncomfortably familiar. Like something from a recurring dream.* Grinding down on his teeth, he studied the buildings across the boulevard.

Tall columns. Symmetrical. Triangular pediments. Domed roofs. Not to mention the grand spherical temple in the Second Plaza, like a planet in the sky. Why do I keep thinking Indee is trying to tell us something with the design

170

of this city?

And of course, all of it stood beneath the presence of the great Mountain. He glanced over his shoulder, westward at the looming beast watching over all of them. There wasn't a single place in the city that the Mountain could not be seen, and though Dev knew it was quite far away, it looked close enough to reach out and touch. Once the sun passed the noonday mark and headed downward in the sky, the Mountain would cast its shadow over all of them. He knew it was possible to tell the date by the movement of the peak's shadow down the great central boulevard.

The unexpectedly harmonious flourish of battle horns snatched Dev's attention back to the parade in progress.

He took out his spyglass, a favorite among his tools, and without straining his eyes, scanned the triumph's tip as it crossed through the Victory Gate.

First came the musicians, trumpets, and percussion, to set the pace — an upbeat swell invented to lift emotions. Then came the beauties: glittering white unicorns, golden does with wings like polished ivory, long-bodied felines led on silver leashes by tall Teyledrine girls in jewel-toned robes, and tiny winged creatures that shimmered brightly and dropped red and pink flower petals ahead of the gleaming chariots and rows of striking warriors.

Then came the things that fueled nightmares: dark, splotchy millipedes the size of sheep, men with the heads of ants, along with crawling insects with the heads of men. There were hoofed monkeys and winged rats.

Wonder if Rat feels some kinship to those flying vermin.

Shaggy wolves with swirling shells encasing their bodies took up the rear of the creature parade.

Dev wished he'd remained on the ground to hear the natter as the humans of Caraky first beheld King Khylar's train of supernatural and otherworldly attendants. Even up on the roof, Dev could hear surprised gasps and could see the frantic pointing, the feast for the eyes a sensory overload for even the most hardened and stoic Kharakhian. *In Khreté they were terrified by the arrival of Tormy — called him a manticore. What must the people of Caraky be thinking?*

He saw more than one fierce Kharakhian warrior back away from the roadside. Men and women everywhere were making the warding sign against evil. One wily merchant had thought ahead and was selling holy symbols to the crowd — the lightning bolt of The Redeemer, the dark heart of Cerioth, the blue moon of The Lady, and others Dev wasn't certain he could identify. *The Kharakhians still worship all the gods — the six elder gods and every younger god in the sky and down below.* He had to admire such practicality — worship them all, for fear of offending one.

Wonder if they understand that this spectacle isn't just a momentary aberration but is their future, he thought, his cynicism unchecked.

When the battle in the Autumn Lands had ended, the enemy army had been routed. That in itself hadn't been much of a feat — with the removal of Galseric, most of his army could no longer even remember anything beyond a vague feverish nightmare. To a being, they could not remember why they had been fighting in the first place. Many of the creatures of Galseric's army had simply surrendered on the spot — or in the case of the more animalistic of creatures, returned to their homes without understanding what had happened. Within two days Khylar had fulfilled his bargain — he'd returned to Kharakhan and closed the Autumn Gate.

Dev's companions had been satisfied by the end results — but that was because they didn't see the trick for what it was. They didn't truly understand what had happened — was happening still — and what long-term repercussions it would have. *The others think Khylar will now set his mind to rounding up all these misplaced Autumn Dwellers and return them to where they belong — and how kind of the Autumn army to accompany the Kharakhian king to aid in the effort.* Dev, however, knew that the young king's loyalty lay with the Dwellers of the Autumn Lands now and not with the people of Kharakhan.

Meet your new masters, lowly human scum. Dev hoped he was wrong.

As the triumph continued on its route, Dev spotted a wagon weighted down with a large oval glass tub. A number of the frog men who had aided with the destruction of Galseric's fleet splashed around, waved their webbed appendages, and flicked their long tongues in the air like undulating ribbons. *I hope you like frogs, Riverboy — because they will quickly become the new rulers of your beloved river.*

Next came Dev's companions, spearheaded by Omen wrapped in a cloak of the dark blue colors of Lydon. He rode a white horse, artistically harnessed in black and silver. Tormy trotted next to him, orange head raised high, fully appreciating the applause and cheers from the crowd. Kyr, also in Lydonian blue, rode Tormy with ease and cradled Tyrin in the crook of his arm. Templar and Shalonie followed on their own white horses — Templar wearing his father's colors and crest — a black cloak emblazoned with the silver lightning bolt of The Redeemer. Shalonie wore a gown the exact shade of Sundragon gold, expertly made for

173

her by some faerie seamstress. The glittering dragonscale sword hung from a jeweled belt around the girl's waist.

Along either side of Shalonie rode Nikki, in the green livery of the Deldanos, and Liethan clad in the blue and gold of the Corsairs. Scores of Teyledrine warriors flanked them, heavily armed and armored, all wearing the scarlet red cloaks of the Set-Manasan house.

A delicate chariot made of finely spun white filigree came next. A pair of spindly magic constructs of smoke pulled the chariot smoothly as if it were gliding on ice. The smoke creatures shifted from equine to feline to lupine to amphibian as they rolled ahead of the white chariot like a bank of dense fog. Morcades held silver reins with one perfectly pale hand, but from the white wrist up, the sorceress was covered in scarlet paint — her arms, neck, face, feathered headdress and flowing robes the deep color of blood. *Almost the Set-Manasan color but not quite — just slightly off.* The image burned the back of Dev's eyes like a searing flame.

What magic is she spinning with her appearance?

Before he could dwell on the acid rising in his throat, Dev beheld King Khylar standing tall and straight on his own chariot drawn by two black horses. Dressed in simple black pants and a loose white shirt, Khylar looked young and worn and the most human of all his followers. He wore a red cloak to match his soldiers', though his was emblazoned with the black unicorn of the Set-Manasan house. With his spyglass, Dev could make out the dark shadows of exhaustion under Khylar's eyes. *You're worried, little king, aren't you? You know something is off — you just can't quite put your finger on what — not with everything going exactly as you planned it.*

174

Puppy, Khylar's constant companion, stood behind him proudly and held a wreath of green leaves over Khylar's head. White berries were mingled among the leaves. The young creature's fur had been brushed to a shine, and he wore the silver and black vestments of a court squire. Puppy smoothly changed the arm that held the wreath, without dipping or dropping the ornament.

The wreath of an emperor, Dev thought. *Got that tradition from his mother — just one little problem. He's supposed to be king of a single human kingdom, not a conqueror of multiple lands. Wonder if he knows Morcades is playing him like a lute.*

As the triumph passed through the plaza and headed to the castle, Dev surmised that more information was to be gained on the ground, and he climbed down to join the crowd and listen to their reaction to the spectacle.

He met Rat and Riverboy at a cider wagon on the Second Plaza.

The parade had turned into a citywide feast, with revelers snapping up food and drink from the smartly placed vendor wagons along the route: pies, pastries, drink, sweets, and any variety of grilled meats and exotic fruits, much of it autumn fruit from the recently affected orchards.

"What have you learned?" Dev asked and handed each boy a cup of cool cider.

Riverboy's eyes were still wide as saucers. "Those are Autumn Dwellers in the parade . . . monsters!" he stated with a trembling voice. "Are they captives or . . ."

Dev slapped the back of the boy's head, making him flinch. "Focus!" Dev ordered sternly. "Fear will get you nowhere except killed. Focus on what you know absolutely — not what you fear. If you can't do that, you have no place in the Machelli Guild."

Rat didn't laugh at the dressing down of his compatriot, but steeled his round shiny rodent-like eyes and took all emotion out of his face. "The people are torn," Rat said with calculated ironic derision. "Some are afraid; some are delighted. None have any idea what this means."

"I want both of you to watch the markets very carefully over the next few weeks," Dev instructed. "Watch if there is more selling or buying. If the good folk of Caraky are in the mood to accept their king's new lifestyle and the Dwellers that brings, they will stock up on goods and hunker down for the long haul."

He put a hand on Riverboy's shoulder in a gesture meant to appease the boy. "If you see a lot of selling — goods, furniture, art, and especially property — then the people of Caraky are getting ready to run."

"What if we see both?" Rat asked, trying to work out the answer for himself but failing.

"You *will* see both," Dev said. "I want you to suss out which you see more. More buying or more selling."

"Will you stay in the city?" Riverboy asked, working hard to disguise the nervous tremble in his voice.

Rat is smart, but this boy is intuitive. He's right to be terrified.

"I have a little assignment of my own, which I shall be following out of town before too long," Dev said, trying to keep it vague but interesting. "I will tell Master Finagle that you both did very well today."

He looked at Rat. "There is no reason to tell him anything else. Correct?"

Rat bobbed his head, and Riverboy visibly relaxed, relieved that Dev's reprimand would not be relayed.

176

"The world is a complicated and dangerous place," Dev told the two boys in parting. "Sometimes the most protected place you can be is right in the center of the storm."

Dev handed his wooden cup back to the serving girl at the cider wagon and lost himself in the ever-swelling and increasingly raucous crowd.

It took him longer than he'd expected to get back to the guild house — the streets were too crowded with rowdy revelers for easy passage. In the end, he'd taken to the rooftops again, finding movement across the heights much easier — out of reach and sight of the citizenry.

Two guardsmen stood before the door of the guild, both wearing the Machelli wolf-head crest. From the looks of them, tall, muscular, stern-faced, they were directly from Scaalia — perhaps called in specifically because Master Finagle had figured out that things were no longer going to be quite the same in Caraky. While the Machelli Guild was powerful in its own right — more so because of Avarice's connection to Indee — any guild house master worth his salt would realize that precautions would be needed in days to come.

The guards inclined their heads to Dev, one of them opening the door for him to pass inside. Dev slipped into the foyer, noting the young servant boy who had manned the entrance hall already racing down a passageway to summon Finagle. Dev followed, having little patience to call on. He intercepted Finagle coming down the hallway from his private quarters.

"You have some means of communicating with Avarice, yes?" he demanded of the man before Finagle could speak.

Taken aback, Finagle paused before answering. "We have a scrying mirror, but it requires the magic of the house sorcerer, and can only be used under dire—"

"Send for the sorcerer," Dev cut him off. "We need to talk to Avarice, and we're running out of time."

Perhaps it was the urgency in his voice, or simply his reputation alone, but Finagle only hesitated a moment before he sent the servant boy off again in search of the sorcerer.

He motioned Dev to follow him downstairs into the main cellar. The stone walls of the cellar were free of the usual hex marks found in the upper floors of the guild house, and the lanterns along the walls were already lit with thick candles. Likely, this area had been set aside for the practice of magic and had its own hidden protections.

Finagle removed a large key ring from a pouch at his belt and fumbled through the collection of keys until he found an ornate silver key which he fitted to a door off the main cellar entrance. Pushing open the door, he entered — Dev only a step behind him.

A thick blue carpet covered the floor, and in the center sat a solitary chair with plush cushions. The chair faced the far wall where an extremely large mirror had been fastened — the mirror matched the one Dev had seen in Avarice's office. Running from floor to ceiling, the mirror was surrounded by a silver-trimmed frame carved with the shapes of running wolves.

A moment later an older man entered. He was grizzled and worn, his beard thick and nearly as white as his hair, heavy lines around his silver eyes. He carried no weapon, and wore no armor — but his clothing was of fine make, and he bore rings upon all his fingers. Machelli sorcerers were rare — the people of the clans more suited to physical battle than scholarly pursuit. But Dev knew enough to realize that this was not someone to be trifled with. And judging by the man's age, he was likely a contemporary of Avarice's father.

"This is Grave Machelli," Finagle introduced. "Devastation here needs to speak with Avarice."

Dev heard the way Finagle emphasized his name. While he was fairly certain that none of the Machellis really knew if he truly was who he claimed to be, they were all under direct orders to aid him if possible. They all walked a fine line between security concerns if he were an impostor, and Avarice's wrath if they failed to do as she asked.

Grave, however, seemed unsurprised by the request. "Of course," he acquiesced quickly. "Stand just there." He pointed to a spot directly in front of the chair as he moved toward the mirror and off to one side, out of direct line of sight. Dev had to smile at that. Grave could activate the mirror without being seen, and all Avarice would notice would be Dev standing in front of it. Any potential blame would fall on his shoulders alone.

Finagle seemed to realize it too and moved quickly off to the other side of the room, out of the line of sight.

Dev took up the appointed position and turned his attention to Grave. The man reached out one gnarled hand and touched the surface of the mirror with his fingertips. Immediately, Dev could feel the swirl of magical energies rising in the air — the surface of the mirror turned white with light and began to pulse in a steady rhythmic pattern. A low hum sounded through the room.

It took several moments of waiting, but without fail the white light within the mirror changed colors and began to coalesce and swirl. A moment later the surface cleared and instead of staring back at his own reflection, Dev found himself staring at the reflection of Avarice Machelli, dressed in a rust-colored gown, her long black hair braided and hanging over one shoulder. She inclined her head to him, her gaze flicking briefly to the right and then to the left as if asking him if there were others in the room.

He tilted his head in confirmation, tapping his fingers twice against his sword hilt. "A full triumph, my lady," he told her with a smile. "You missed quite a spectacle — Omen and all his companions in full colors."

The twitch of the muscles in her jaw was visible, and Dev suspected she'd just resisted the impulse to spit with annoyance. "Please tell me he wasn't wearing the Machelli coat?"

"No," Dev assured her. "I'd warned him ahead of time. He was in Lydonian colors. Kyr as well."

Her eyes flashed at that, and she smiled. "Kyr? Really?" She seemed delighted. "That means Khylar is unaware that Kyr is the heir to the Venedrine throne. Which means his source of information is faulty. Anything more?"

"Khylar wore an emperor's wreath," Dev replied. "Green leaves — white berries. An Autumn Lands plant I'd guess."

Something hard shifted in Avarice's eyes. "Poisonous Feybloom," she proclaimed. "It's actually from the Winter Lands, and is often used in very dark magic." She looked away briefly, her face fixed in deep thought. When she'd looked back, he could tell she'd come to some decision. "It's likely he means to knight Omen and the others. He needs alliances to claim as his own — which is going to put Templar and Shalonie in very awkward positions. You need to get them out of there, tonight, and you're going to need help to do that. Kadana will be best."

"You want me to use the portal we came through at the

Mountain of Shadow?" he asked. While the great Mountain was clearly visible, he wasn't entirely certain he'd be able to find that portal again. *Not to mention there's still the small problem of getting through the cluster of wyverns.*

"No." She waved away his suggestion. "That portal is only stable one way — Kadana would be hip-deep in monsters otherwise. It would likely fling you to the far side of the country. Not to mention, it's on the other side of the Mountain — it would take you too long to get there."

She glanced off toward the left side of the mirror's edge. "Finagle!" She barked out the guild master's name in a commanding tone.

The man, still well out of sight of the mirror, jumped in alarm. He quickly came forward and inclined his head to the reflection in the mirror. "My lady," he greeted.

Dev heard the hesitation in the way he spoke as if not certain how to behave after having hidden from view. Grave too looked concerned.

"Devastation, my son, and his companions are to be given full access to the portal," she ordered the man, her tone leaving no room for questioning. "Dev, there's a stable portal in the lower cellar of this guild house. It's stable both ways so you can use it both coming and going. It will take you to a farmhouse about five miles south of Kadana's keep. Get a horse there, ride to the keep, and bring Kadana back to the portal. Tell her what's going on. She'll help you get the others out of the castle. And do it before Templar causes an international incident. I can deal with Indee's anger — I don't want to deal with King Antares."

There was a stable portal here all along! He bit back any smidgen of indignation. *But I guess Kadana's portal took us straight to the Mountain. Could have done without*

181

the wyverns though.

"I'll leave immediately," Dev assured her. A part of him rather wished he could see the alarming events unfold. But keeping Avarice happy was ultimately of more value to him than any entertainment he could glean from seeing the Terizkandian fight. A moment later the mirror flashed white again and then went dark. When it cleared, Dev found himself once again staring at his own reflection.

Finagle and Grave exchanged a long look before the guild master turned to Dev. "I'll show you to the portal, Devastation," he said — this time there was no hesitation in his voice and no emphasis on his name. Avarice had left no room for doubting his identity.

As he followed the guild master down yet another set of stairs, he calculated the timing in his mind. Five miles to Kadana's keep, time to explain what was happening, five miles back to the portal, and then they would have to get across the city and into the castle. It would be well into the victory feast before he could retrieve everyone. *But any plans for knighting the others wouldn't happen until tomorrow at the earliest. Expedience aside, Khylar is a noble — they need their pageantry. And that takes time to plan.*

Chapter 11: Feast

OMEN

By the time the triumph through the city of Caraky had come to an end, the sun had reached its most prominent place in the sky. Omen fought to keep his eyes from drifting closed with boredom as the outlandish procession took what seemed to him like an excruciatingly long time to arrive in the courtyard of the Set-Manasan castle. The fully assembled gathering of courtiers waited breathlessly, their anticipation showing on their sweat-glistening faces.

Not quite sure what to make of your king, are you?

Omen recognized a few Kharakhian nobles, lords and ladies who had been attached to Indee's retinue when she'd visited Melia in the past. But the greater number was unknown to him, though he noted that most of the attendants were young — Khylar's age.

Well, Khylar's age before he spent a hundred years battling Galseric.

A stern-looking, singularly older Kharakhian, Khylar's seneschal by his chain of office, marched straight from the castle steps through the throng of people and creatures and bowed deeply in front of Khylar's chariot. If he twitched at the sight of so many oddities, Omen could hardly blame the man.

Khylar exchanged a few words with Puppy, who barked a laugh and hopped off the chariot, victory wreath loosely held in hand.

Together with the seneschal, Khylar and Puppy proceeded up the long stairs to the wide, recessed entrance of the grand hall.

Lined up between the columns, a row of armored warriors in Nelminorian colors flanked a tall, sandy-blond man in dark scale and woven leathers. Lord Fel'torin, Caythla's husband, had been the acting ruler of Kharakhan in Khylar's absence. Since it was only a four-day journey by boat from the shores of Nelminor to Kharakhan — he would have arrived in Caraky shortly after Omen had left Melia.

Fel'torin's a good guy. Wonder what he makes of this?

Even from where he stood, Omen could see the white gleam of Fel'torin's distinctive grin. Omen flashed back to the overheard heated discussion between Indee and Caythla.

"You will tell your husband to go to Kharakhan . . . You will tell him to rule in my stead, in Khylar's stead until such time—"

"If Omen isn't going, I'll send Fel'torin after Khylar and one of the Set-Manasans can rule Kharakhan . . . Fine, I'll send Fel'torin to Kharakhan. But don't think you've heard the end of this."

The angry words spooled about in Omen's brain, catching on the events in the Autumn Lands and the sights and sounds of the day like wool strands on dry coral.

Is this what Indee had in mind all along? Or did it all get away from her too?

Fel'torin seemed no worse for the experience and clasped Khylar in a welcoming bear hug as soon as Khylar's boot touched the top of the uniformly carved steps.

There was no denying the impact of the moment: Khylar, the battle-proven and victorious king, returning home with riches and miraculous visitors from another land, greeted by his much-trusted and beloved brother-in-law, a man who was a magnificent king in his own right and one of the heroes of the Nelminorian Wars, and thereby one of the saviors of Kharakhan.

Every person and creature in the courtyard burst into spontaneous applause, number of appendages permitting, and cheered as the two rulers embraced.

There's one for the history scrolls.

Omen shielded his eyes against the sun and studied the building that served as backdrop for Khylar's spectacular return. Running from the tops of the columns and framing the entrance, a horizontal frieze featured muscular unicorns battling fierce gryphons and long, scaly wyrms.

Symbolic of the Set-Manasan dynasty taming Kharakhan, Omen vaguely recalled his history lessons. He let his eyes roam over the castle, appreciating the architectural details.

The massive rectangular main structure had the same uncluttered and elegant lines as all the buildings in the city, but unlike the strict symmetry every other structure in Caraky seemed to adhere to, the castle defied the rules. Only one tower rose at the north side of the castle, but it shot into the sky nearly twice as high as the rectangle of the main castle stood long.

Tallest structure in the city, Omen thought. *And since the castle is on a hill, I bet you can see all of Caraky from the top of that tower. And it would be the most vulnerable target if ever Caraky is attacked by dragons or any other flying enemy.*

A small shudder shook through him. *The battle is over — we're not going to be attacked again.* He tried to shrug it off, but the unease churned in his stomach.

"There will be a spider in the tall tower," Kyr commented casually.

"Shush," Omen said quickly as if speaking to one of the cats.

Hope that's just blather and not . . . He couldn't help but throw a wary look toward Lady Morcades who stood near Khylar. She too was staring up at the tall tower.

"Where's the dinner, Omy?" Tormy purred next to Omen's ear. The big cat, Kyr still seated in his saddle, had wiggled closer to Omen's horse without Omen even noticing his approach. The cat scratched briefly at the belly strap of his saddle with one hind leg as Kyr clung to the silver pommel.

Also still mounted, Omen reached out from the back of the white horse and stroked the soft fur behind Tormy's ears with his fingertips. To the horse's credit, it stood steady and stoic despite the proximity to the great cat. "Won't be long now," Omen said, wanting to reassure the cat. "They'll take us inside, and to the great hall, I think. We'll have dinner—"

"And then we'll go home," Kyr finished his sentence. The boy looked pale and thin. He'd covered both of his hands with leather gauntlets, hiding the hex.

Omen's heart contracted slightly. "Soon, Kyr," he said. "I promise. Really soon."

They were met by servants then, stable boys coming to take their horses, prompting the inevitable conversation, "No, Tormy is not to be taken to the stables, and yes, he is going to the feast." A few swift turns of the large cat, accompanied by several tail whacks to the head cleared out the gaggle of servants attempting to *aid* Omen and Kyr with their *beast.* Before they departed, however, the fussy servants informed all of them that they were required to change their clothing yet again before the feast.

Argh, more nonsense.

Templar managed to rescue Liethan and Nikki from overly helpful courtiers but was unable to save Shalonie from a fate of expensive silks and pin curls. The companions all spared a moment of sympathy for the poor girl as she was shuffled off by a group of ladies-in-waiting who'd apparently been ordered to drape her in another new gown and fix her hair. The look of suffering endurance on her face spoke volumes.

Can't get involved. Everyone for themselves. Omen hoped the forced primping wouldn't take too long because he had little hope of holding Tormy and Tyrin back if the cats grew hungry enough to search out their own food. *Could be a problem.*

Luckily, just before the cats reached the end of their stomachs' patience, they were all led to the great hall where a feast fit for a glutton awaited them. They were all politely but firmly directed to a raised platform — the heroes of the celebration with King Khylar seated in the center. Omen surveyed the crowded hall.

How did Khylar's people throw all of this together in a week? Some of the nobles had to travel from the other side of the country to be here. It occurred to him that his group was not alone in risking travel by portal. *If portal use is widespread, the Kharakhians are inviting trouble at every turn. I guess Kadana warned us.*

Dish after local dish was placed before them and sampled — or gobbled greedily by Tormy.

Kharakhian delicacies continued to be served long after Omen had eaten his fill, though he forced himself to eat beyond his capacity for the sheer fun of trying to figure out ingredients by taste.

Hours later Omen, nibbling the corners off a sweet plum tart, watched Tormy laboriously roll onto his back and expose his full, fluffy belly to the warmth of the fire. Though the summer heat had returned to the country, the dark innards of the castle were cool enough to make the cat seek out the flames.

The fireplace in Khylar's great hall ran along the length of the room and curved around both corners. The resulting space allowed for three spits in a row, and the castle's cooks busied themselves roasting game fowl, venison, and several entire pigs. Having the bulk of the food prepared in front of the honored assemblage kept things lively, especially since three brick ovens also graced the far side of the hall. Bakers and bakers' assistants scurried about with long, wooden shovel-like tools, which they used to slide dough lumps into the ovens and rescue loaves of bread and a delightful variety of pastries from the heat.

One oven was dedicated to a flat round doughy specialty from Omen's mother's homeland. Omen watched in fascination as one cook tossed a dough oval in the air, slapped it down in the flour, flattened it out, and covered it with sliced meats and cut peppers and tomatoes. Omen's mother had recently attempted to recreate the favorite food of her youth, but Omen had found the burnt-to-a-crisp, dry cracker-like bread covered haphazardly in meaty char rather unappetizing.

She's usually a pretty great cook, but that thing was a disaster. Probably didn't help that the cats kept bugging her to put mice on it as a topping.

Omen followed the preparation with rapt attention as the

188

cook brushed the dough round with sparkling green olive oil and vibrant tomato sauce before carefully laying out concentric circles of thinly cut dried meats, crumbles of sausage, and sliced vegetables. The cook, dressed in stark white, then sprinkled a broad layer of grated cheese all over his creation and shoved it into one of the ovens. Before too long, the most incredible aroma wafted toward Omen.

They must be feeding more people than just us if they're still cooking so much. Wish I wasn't already so full.

Kyr pointed. "Is that like what Avarice made that one time? The Scaalian bread?"

Omen nodded. "I bet it tastes a whole lot better not burnt."

"I like Avarice's cooking," Kyr said protectively. "Hers is probably just an old family recipe."

Omen decided not to argue. Kyr would eat pretty much anything Avarice gave him, no matter how badly made.

"Old family recipe is being the most likelynessness." Tyrin pushed himself into the conversation. "But one little bite of deliciousnessness today is not being disloyal to Avarice's cooking." He gave a slow blink of his amber eyes and licked his pale pink tongue over his whiskers.

"I supposed it would be all right to take a bite," Kyr agreed hesitantly.

"How are you two still able to eat anything at all?" Omen was genuinely baffled and a little concerned. He wagged his finger at Tyrin. "I don't want you throwing up later."

Tyrin eyes rounded in outrage. "I is not a barfing cat!"

The timing of his outburst corresponded to a natural lull in the clamor of the room with near scientific precision.

Everybody heard that, Omen thought with chagrin. No

more than a second later, the entire hall burst into peals of merry laughter.

"To cats that don't barf," a familiar, and very loud voice shouted from the back tables. Rows and rows of honored guests raised their drinks and shouted, "To cats that don't barf!" The waves of laughter continued.

Omen looked up to see his grandmother Kadana standing on a long table, holding up a tankard in salute. She took a deep gulp. *How did she get here? I thought she'd still be back home.* He was happy to see her.

"And to our blessed King Khylar!" She waved her arm to encourage everyone to join her in the toast.

Omen saw the pleased smile on Khylar's face as he saluted Kadana with his wineglass.

Then Omen caught a quick flash of silent communication pass between Shalonie and Kadana in a glance. And he noticed that Morcades, seated to Khylar's right, had caught the look as well.

What's going on there? He decided not to explore the uncomfortable hunch and turned his attention back to the party in progress.

The feast continued for many hours past midnight, and both Kyr and Tyrin, having finally eaten their fill, had curled up next to Tormy by the fire.

After speaking to more people than he was able to remember, Omen had joined the musicians and spent song after song exploring the limits of Beren's faerie lute. It thrilled him to work the strings and anticipate the melody lines of the unfamiliar pieces. Wrapping his tongue around the Kharakhian lyrics proved another matter, but he persevered to the obvious enjoyment of the Kharakhians. But after a bit, he switched to Melian and sang a few verses from

190

"The Maiden and the White Rose."

At least no one here knows it well enough to give me grief about getting all fifty verses right. He looked over to Templar, but the Terizkandian prince had better things on his mind. He sat in what seemed like deep conversation with a pretty lady-in-waiting dressed in red, white, and silver.

"Careful of those Kharakhian girls," his mother had always told Omen, but he decided to leave Templar to his better judgment. *Whatever that might be.*

There were requests for other songs, some familiar, others not. Omen delighted in learning the new ones from the Kharakhian musicians. He later offered up a song he'd been working on — about a faerie maiden trapped within a rose briar. It was well received by the increasingly inebriated crowd.

"Nice ballad, my boy. But I think it's time to leave." Kadana sidled up next to him during a break in the music and handed him a tankard of ginger brew. "I'm hearing rumors," she clarified her urgency. "I hear Khylar wants to knight the lot of you, and he plans on asking you to stay at court."

Omen felt himself go pale, then flush. "That's a problem." He drank down a quick swallow of the spicy liquid. It burned his throat at first, but then his vocal cords felt soothed and refreshed.

"One of Beren's fail-safe recipes," Kadana said jovially. "How I ever got bards for children and grandchildren, I will never know." She guffawed, one hand on his shoulder, and leaned forward as if the belly laugh was curling her in on herself. "Your mother would have a fit; on the other hand, you can't say 'no' without starting something with that damn faerie witch," Kadana whispered.

Omen wasn't sure if she meant Indee or Morcades.

Kadana leaned in closer as if to place a grandmotherly kiss on his cheek. "Play another song on that magic lute of yours — think about sleep and exhaustion. Khylar looks about ready to drop anyway, and once he retires for the night, we can leave as well." She spoke quickly and quietly in his ear.

"How do we leave the castle without being noticed?" Omen asked under his breath as he searched through his repertoire for something appropriate. He knew a Lydonian lullaby that might do the trick — the song was slow and melodious, and the lyrics were vague enough that few people would realize it was meant to soothe children.

Despite trying to focus on *sleep and exhaustion* like his grandmother had urged, Omen felt a surge of excitement flare through him. *She wants me to use the magic in the lute to affect the crowd — like I did with the Bower Dames.* Guessing that most of the people in the room were either too drunk or too exhausted to notice a subtle manipulation of magic, he suspected it would be safe enough to try.

And it's not really making people do something against their will. It's suggesting they do something they already want to do. Just a little earlier. He knew he was rationalizing.

"We leave the same way I got in without being invited." Kadana grinned. "Secret portal."

Omen began his song, plucking away at his lute while Kadana moved off to one side, all but disappearing into the shadows near the fire. As he sang, he cast a careful look around the room — Templar and Shalonie were nowhere in sight. Neither were Nikki and Liethan, he noticed after several long moments. There were others making their way from the hall as well — the night had grown late and even the seemingly inexhaustible cooks and servants were now sagging with fatigue from their long day's labor.

Omen could feel the gentle power in the lute as he tried to do as Kadana had asked. He focused on sleep — the song made it easy enough, and he started to feel the tingle of magic moving through his body as his song began coaxing the power from the lute. It felt different this time — gentle, quiet, easy. He wondered if this was the trick to using the magic. *Let the song itself do all the work.*

At first, he wasn't certain if he was affecting anyone, but then he saw more than one person yawn suddenly. A few minutes into his song, Khylar too gave a tired sigh and rose, waving to the remaining guests and then retiring for the night. His departure signaled an end to the festivities, and the remaining balance of guests hurried away as well.

As Omen wound down his song, he glanced briefly over to the fire where Tormy still slept like the dead. Kadana was crouched down next to the cat, carefully extracting Kyr from Tormy's heavy paws. The boy came awake at a gentle shake, smiling up at Kadana and nodding his head when she whispered to him. He lifted the sleeping Tyrin from where he was curled in Tormy's ruff, patted Tormy's flank briefly and then shot Omen a quick smile. Kyr followed Kadana from the great hall, disappearing through one of the exits into the bowels of the castle.

Omen finished his song, giving one last glance around the hall. Yawning servants were slowly clearing the tables and the two remaining musicians with him were asleep in their chairs. *Not bad — I put everyone to sleep — wait, that's not supposed to be a good thing for a performer.* He

193

grinned in spite of himself.

Time to find my grandmother.

Slinging his lute over one shoulder, he crossed to the fireplace and gently bent down to shake Tormy awake.

"But I don't want to get up," Tormy complained bitterly. "I is liking the fireplace."

"I have a nice fireplace," Lady Morcades said, seemingly materializing out of thin air, "in my chamber."

Omen took a startled step back, almost tripping into the fire. *She wasn't there a second ago.*

Morcades stood so close that he could smell the tiny red roses woven through her hair and the lavender oil on her pale skin. She'd clearly bathed and changed since the triumph, none of the scarlet paint remaining on her body. Instead, she was draped in a white gossamer gown and looked unnervingly like a young faerie girl instead of the dangerous sorceress he'd avoided in Khylar's camp.

"Omen," Kadana poked her head around the corner of the hall at that moment.

Omen breathed a sigh of relief.

"Could you help me find my spectacles?" his grandmother asked. "I think I dropped them in the coat room." Kadana took several steps closer, putting her body in front of him and Tormy. "Grandchildren," she said to Morcades, "they can be so helpful . . . Don't you agree?"

Omen thought he saw Morcades' eyes flare a mantis green.

Ouch — an age joke. Bet she didn't like that.

Omen almost chuckled as Morcades swept out of the room without another word.

"I didn't know you wore spectacles," he said lightly.

"That's a dangerous woman," Kadana said, nearing a

scold. "Don't let her corner you alone."

"I wasn't al . . . alone." Omen stumbled over his words. "Tormy's here."

Kadana threw a pointed look at the snoring cat. "Comatose isn't here."

"He was talking to me a second ago," Omen said quickly and shook Tormy's front paws. "Get up, fur face. We're leaving."

While Tormy stretched and yawned, Kadana laid out their escape route. "We have to get to the lower kitchens. Shalonie and Templar left through the maze gardens about an hour ago. No one stopped them. Guess assumptions were made." She smirked. "Liethan took Nikki to The Lady's temple. If questioned, he'll say he's looking for his cousin. Tara is an uncomfortable topic for Khylar, so I am sure Liethan won't be stopped. I took Kyr and Tyrin to Dev."

"Dev?" Omen said. "He hasn't been here all day."

"Your mother strictly forbade Dev's participation in the parade," Kadana supplied quietly as they walked past cleared tables and empty chairs. "She didn't want to provide Khylar with an official Machelli endorsement."

"But I was part of the triumph."

"She knows that couldn't be helped," Kadana whispered, indicating the two guards barring the west exit. "Besides, here you're considered a Lydonian prince and not a Machelli. Politics . . . Don't worry; your mother agreed that you should continue to be part of Khylar's retinue until after the triumph. But now, it's time to leave."

They approached the two soldiers who stood on either side of a large, arched exit.

"Lady Kadana," one of the guards addressed her respectfully. "We were instructed to tell you that you and Prince Armand—"

Omen groaned at hearing his given name.

The guard shifted uncomfortably.

Probably nervous about offending us. Omen gave him a benevolent smile.

"That you will be staying in the tower." The man pointed in the opposite direction. "When you are ready to retire, the hall to the tower is that way. I can escort you if you wish."

"Very good," Kadana said. "But our cat is in dire need of some warm cream before he goes to sleep. This is the way to the lower kitchen?"

The other guard nodded. "Would you like us to summon the kitchen maids?"

"I is getting cream?" Tormy perked up.

"I don't think we can wait," Omen told the man quickly, playing up a tremor of concern in his voice. "Tormy gets very irritated when he doesn't get his cream. And when he gets irritated—"

"He's been known to tear limbs off of strangers," Kadana finished. "Armor doesn't really stop his teeth." She gave the two men a meaningful glance.

Both guards quickly stepped aside and let them pass without further conversation.

"Cream is good — but maybe I is having fishies too," Tormy pondered out loud as they hurried down the stairs to the lower kitchen. "I is maybe eating a little cream cheese if you is thinking I should eat cream. And I is maybe washing it down with a little cup of milk . . ."

"We're not stopping to eat," Kadana said sharply. "We're leaving through the kitchen garden . . . the others are already waiting for us at the portal."

196

Tormy let out a little, disappointed *meow.*

"You said it's a secret portal . . ." Omen searched, but Kadana said nothing else.

They arrived in the large lower kitchen to only the glow of a cooking fire, surprising a young kitchen maid who'd been dozing in a wooden chair. She jumped to her feet as they entered.

"Don't bother yourself," Kadana snapped. "The cat saw a mouse in the garden."

Omen wondered why his grandmother kept lying to the servants. *Maybe she's trying to create confusion. Or maybe she just likes to lie.*

The girl curtsied awkwardly and then busied herself with stoking the fire.

"Is we not eating anything at all?" Tormy whined as Kadana pushed open the wooden kitchen doors into the garden. Omen knew the cat could smell the butter in the crock even if it was covered with a red-checkered cloth. He scooted him past the long butcher block table and into the garden.

The moon gleamed in the late night sky as the stars flickered in what looked like an inferno in the firmament.

Too many stars, Omen thought. *Guess the seasons are still working themselves out. Wonder how my father is going to explain that away.* He chuckled softly to himself. His father never cared for unnatural phenomena having a one-word answer — magic.

Dev and Kyr were waiting on the far side of the garden, hidden in the moon-cast shadows of the garden wall. Tyrin, perched on Kyr's shoulder, twitched his tail excitedly as they approached. "We is being quietlynessness," the little cat whispered, whiskers flaring. "Dev is saying we is tricking the guards."

Dev flicked a wary look toward the cat before retrieving Omen's great sword from the shadows along the wall. "The others have the rest of your belongings," Dev explained as he handed the weapon to Omen. "Liethan and Nikki were able to get most of it out earlier, but I thought it best you keep your sword with you. Just in case."

Alarmed, Omen glanced at his grandmother. "You don't actually think we have to fight Khylar's guards, do you? They're our allies. They wouldn't try to forcibly keep us here."

Kadana's eyes narrowed. "Indee is one of your mother's closest allies, and yet she hexed Kyr. But it's not the guards we need to worry about."

"We should go," Dev warned. "The sooner we get to the guild house, the safer we'll be. Tormy, Tyrin — you have to be very quiet. We're sneaking away . . . You understand?"

Both cats looked affronted. "We is cats." Tormy lashed his tail back and forth. "We is understanding quietedly-ness."

Omen slipped his sword strap over his shoulders, shifting his lute to the side so that the great weapon rested firmly across his back. Placing a hand on Kyr's back, he motioned the boy to follow after Dev and Kadana toward a small toolshed near one of the garden gates. Tormy crept along behind him, paws silent against the loamy garden dirt.

A hidden doorway behind the shed led to a narrow room filled with wooden crates within the inner garden wall. After crowding inside and closing the door, Dev lit a single candle. In the flickering firelight, Dev shifted aside a wooden crate, revealing a trapdoor beneath it. When opened, it revealed a wooden stairwell leading down into a long dark tunnel.

"Should just be big enough for Tormy to squeeze through," Dev estimated, eyeing the large cat. "I think you've grown since we left Melia."

"I is very growingnessness," Tormy agreed proudly. "On account of the fact that my saddle is not fitting very well anymores."

Great . . . need a new saddle. Maybe I'll get something designed with a set of armor for him.

Omen watched as Dev disappeared down the stairwell, taking the candle with him. Kadana urged Kyr and Tyrin to go next.

"I thought Indee had this castle built," Omen whispered to his grandmother. "Surely Khylar knows about this passageway."

"I'm sure he does," Kadana agreed. "But he's not the issue at the moment. Now come along." She disappeared down into the darkness, leaving Omen flustered by her words.

If we're not sneaking away from Khylar, who are we sneaking away from? More and more he was beginning to wonder if Dev and his grandmother knew something that he didn't. "Come on Tormy, follow after me as quiet as a mouse."

"As a cat," Tormy hissed. "Mouseses isn't being quiet, on account of the fact that they is squeaky."

The dark passage below was narrow — almost too narrow for Tormy whose furry shoulders brushed the walls. Luckily it was straight, the ground smooth so that they did not stumble in the darkness.

Must lead under the outer walls, Omen guessed by the

direction they were traveling.

A short while later, they reached another stairwell which led upward. Exiting through a narrow doorway — Tormy had to force his way through — the six of them found themselves out on the streets of Caraky in a dark alleyway behind a series of shops. Dev immediately snuffed out his candle, and then headed toward the edge of the alley to peer around the corner.

It was late, the moon high in the sky, dawn was only a few hours away. The few people who were moving through the streets predominately weaved home from the taverns, pickled in spirits. Nonetheless, Dev led the group from one alleyway to the next, keeping clear of the main streets. To Omen's relief, the cats and Kyr stayed quiet and, as far as Omen could tell, passed unseen.

We're heading toward the guild quarters, Omen noticed. He'd seen guild flags flying from one of the southern neighborhoods as the triumph rode down the main boulevard. But as they neared the central street containing the guild houses, Dev stopped them, holding up a raised fist and then motioning them all to slink back into the shadows. Grabbing Kyr's hand and pushing Tormy back, Omen retreated immediately, wondering what had caused the alarm.

They all crouched low, and Dev raised his hand to point. Omen's eyes narrowed, and a chill ran down his spine. On the far side of the street, perched upon the roof of a nearby house, was a shadowy lump, strangely misshapen with numerous spindly legs and glowing red eyes. But as that glowing red gaze moved up and down the street as if searching for something, Omen saw the eyes flash from muted red to fire-yellow.

Yellow eyes! That's some sort of Night Dweller. He felt

the tension in his companions — even the cats were aware of the nature of the creature on the rooftop. Tormy's entire body, tail, and whiskers were utterly still, the cat fixed on the creature as if ready to pounce at any moment.

After a few minutes of silent waiting, the creature moved on, spindly legs extended as it skittered across to the next roof and proceeded farther down the street away from them.

Monster beast spider! Omen shuddered as he sharply recalled Kyr's warning earlier that day about the spider in the tower.

Dev motioned to them; they crept closer, leaning in to hear his words. "We're going to have to run for it," he whispered. "I see more trouble along the rooftops farther down. We're only about a block away from the guild house, so we should be able to make it before the critters catch up."

Then those things are looking for us! Omen ground his teeth together, wishing now that Kyr was somewhere safe. Quickly he unslung his sword, holding the sheathed weapon in his hand so that he could draw it quickly if necessary.

They waited for Dev's signal. He crouched by the alley exit for several heartbeats, and with a sudden motion of his hand, urged them all forward. They sprinted after him as he crossed the street, heading unerringly toward the guild houses. Dev's footfall was completely silent, as — surprisingly — was Kyr's, perhaps because of his elvin heritage or his slight form. Tormy's velvety paws were silent as well, the cat for once moving with the hunting grace unique to prowling felines. But Omen heard both his and Kadana's steps against the cobblestone, and a moment later he heard the skittering click of spindly legs against the tile of the surrounding rooftops. From the corners of his eyes he could see moving shadows.

There's dozens of them! he realized, his skin growing cold and clammy at being hunted.

Ahead of him, Dev turned a sharp corner, Kyr following directly behind him. As Omen too rounded the corner, he saw the bright light of torches up ahead — the guild houses along the main road all clearly lit. Only one guild house, however, had guards standing out front. Omen recognized the Machelli wolf's head insignia emblazoned upon their livery. The guards had their swords drawn, and they scanned the rooftops as they held open the heavy wooden doors to the guild house.

"Hurry!" they shouted as one.

The spidery shadows were closing in — several dropped down from the rooftops nearby. Two more approached the guards from the other end of the street, yellow eyes burning malevolently.

Dev didn't hesitate. He bolted through the doorway of the Machelli Guild House — Kyr with Tyrin followed, then Kadana.

"Get in, Tormy!" Omen yelled to his cat, slowing briefly to let the large feline rush past him. He followed swiftly, the guards leaping in after them.

The main foyer of the guild house was ablaze with lantern lights. The guards slammed the doors shut behind them, and Omen saw every single arcane sigil painted on the walls of the guild flare to life, burning like beacons all around them. The guards barred the doors.

Heavy weights struck the doors, one after another, and beyond the thick stone walls, high-pitched shrieks cut through the night. The sigils flared brighter with each heavy thump, and they all waited in breathless silence as the wooden doors shook from the pummeling force.

And then silence fell — the pounding stopped, the shrieking faded, and the sigils burning around them dimmed and softened, until finally growing dark. Omen let out his breath in a quiet huff, his racing heart beginning to calm.

The Machelli hex marks actually work! He imagined his mother would be delighted to hear the news. *Of course, she probably already knows that.*

"What in The Redeemer's name was that!" a man's voice quavered. Omen turned to see an older, dark-haired man standing nearby, his silver eyes wide.

"Get used to it," Dev said, the words ominous.

What is that supposed to mean? The muscles in Omen's arms and back convulsed with anxiety. Kadana, he noticed, looked unhappy, but not terribly surprised. "Khylar didn't send those things," Omen stated definitely. Though he didn't know Khylar particularly well, he was certain Khylar considered them friends.

"No," Kadana agreed. "Those were summoned by someone who practices necromancy and infernal magic. We should get going. I want to be back inside the walls of my keep before dawn."

Necromancy and infernal magic . . . Does she mean Morcades?

"The others are waiting downstairs with your belongings," the silver-eyed man said, voice still shaking. "What do we tell the king's men if they come looking for you?"

"Tell them that Omen was summoned home immediately by his mother and Queen Indee'athra to remove the hex on Kyr's hand," Dev instructed. "Regardless of what else might be going on here, Khylar won't want to cross his mother. And if they ask how we got home, simply tell them that 7 came for them. Let Khylar think 7 has created some sort of portal to Melia or Lydon, but you don't know the location."

The Machelli man nodded. "We'll spread rumors throughout the city. By lunch tomorrow it will be common knowledge." The plan of action had steadied him, and he almost smiled.

"Let's go home," Kadana urged. "It's going to take Shalonie at least two weeks to get that Cypher Rune Portal built, and the sooner we start the sooner you can get back to Melia."

Omen and Kyr followed her into the depths of the guild house, Tormy falling silently into step behind him.

Home sounds good right about now. Thought leaped over thought as Omen tried to sort through the night's events. *It's high time we got that hex mark off Kyr's hand. Maybe Mother knows what's going on with Khylar. I hope Shalonie doesn't want me to help with the math for the Cypher Runes.* He shuddered, picturing pages and pages of equations. *Maybe someone else can help her out.* He stifled a yawn and let the "secret" portal's magic close over him.

Chapter 12: Calculations

SHALONIE

Shalonie sat in the patch of colored sunlight coming through the stained glass window of the large tower chamber Kadana had set aside for the portal. She held one notebook in her hands, scribbling down her latest calculations, while Dev's private communications notebook rested open in her lap. Beside her on the table were a number of metallic devices she'd been using throughout the day — a clerical starlave, a nautical solverten, an astrologer's vetrenci, among others — all devices designed to show her current position in the world relative to the sun and the stars as well as calculate the four cardinal directions as accurately as possible.

She was well-versed in all of the instruments' uses, but it still bothered her that the numbers Omen's father 7 had sent were more precise than the numbers she'd figured out herself. He'd calculated her position out beyond a thousandth of a fraction. *How does he do that?*

7 had claimed that he could be more precise if she thought it necessary, but he'd also assured her that the portal's magic didn't actually require more exact numbers. *Just rub it in!* He was right, of course. In fact, the portal's magic didn't require anything beyond the numbers she'd already figured out, but she enjoyed the security of working with his more precise calculations. *But how did he manage so quickly?* It bothered her.

Annoyed, she set aside her equations. Then she picked

up Dev's notebook from her lap and placed it on the table. "Very well — you are correct," she wrote in her sharp, precise script.

A few moments later, words began to appear on the page underneath her remark, scrawled in the bold hand of 7 Daenoth. "Don't fuss. I told you I would show you how I came up with the numbers once you returned to Melia."

She twisted the stylus in her fingers. There were few people who were capable of holding their own with her on an intellectual level. 7 was one of them, and she knew better than take offense at his remark. "I assume you finished your telescope," she wrote in reply.

"I did," he wrote back. "Once Omen and Tormy were out of the house and weren't shaking the foundations with their constant reckless abandon, I was able to get the stabilization spells in place around the tower. And Avarice finished the mirror — which is a thing of beauty I might add. You'll be impressed."

Shalonie was certain she would be — 7's extraordinary engineering ability along with Avarice's creative use of magic had resulted in a number of impressive creations. "Well then, if we're satisfied with the numbers, this is the Cypher Rune for Kadana's keep."

She carefully wrote out the Rune — adding an occasional notation to her drawing so that 7 would know what to pay the most attention to. It was a complicated Rune — a symbol made of a dozen other symbols all interconnected and part of a careful mathematical calculation that would allow her to connect Kadana's portal to the one in Melia. She already knew the symbol for Melia by heart.

Still, this would be the first time the two of them would be working entirely alone on their ends of the connection.

She and 7 had worked side by side when they'd set up the first portal between Melia and Lydon, and then the second between Melia and Terizkand. However, this was the first time she was drawing the portal entirely by herself; all 7 needed to do was add the extra Cypher Rune to the existing portal in Melia to connect it.

"I'll have it in place by the time you're ready," 7 assured her. "How long do you think it'll take you to finish the portal on your end?"

She glanced at the wide floor before her — all the carpets had been removed and the floor had been swept and then scrubbed clean. The floor itself was made of large stones that had been smoothed out with a layer of clay plaster forming an unbroken surface.

She'd already drawn the numerous rings of the portal in dark chalk, and would now spend the rest of her time working on the actual Cypher Runes that would form the portal itself.

Once she was done with that, Kadana's master stonemasons would come in and tile over it with tiny mosaic stones to form the Cypher Runes in black and white stone. Protection spells would be cast over top of that — along with whatever defensive spells Kadana would require to make certain no one entered the castle without her knowledge.

"It will take me at least a week to draw out everything," she wrote back in her book. "I'll keep you updated."

"Don't exhaust yourself," 7 replied and then signed off.

Shalonie set aside the book, knowing Dev would likely be along to collect it later. When he'd given her the book, he'd also given her a rather impish grin along with permission to read the rest of it.

Curious, she'd leafed through some of the pages, seeing

that — as promised — Dev had detailed the events of their journey to Avarice who occasionally answered back. But she found herself laughing only a few pages in, realizing why Dev had made the offer to her — she doubted even Avarice had bothered to read the full extent of his reports.

He didn't just report on the events of their journey — he wrote everything down. There was page after page of mundane, boring conversations between Kadana and her crew with nothing more than "move that rope," "tighten that sail," "the wind is coming from the north," "the stew's too salty." And among those conversations were the inane ramblings between Tormy and Tyrin: "You is twitching your tail too much," "I is not twitching my tail," "You is . . . I is seeing it," "No you isn't, that is not being a twitch," "Yes it is," "No it isn't, it is being a flick — twitches is looking like this." And on and on.

"Stop!" Avarice had written at one point.

"I believe my instructions were 'excruciating detail', my lady," Dev had replied back. "I would hate to fail in my duty."

And no matter how much Avarice commanded him to stop, he continued on in the same manner until Avarice finally gave up. Likely the most annoying part, Shalonie suspected, was the fact that interspersed with the inanity were some very astute observations about the more important events, information Avarice would find extremely valuable, as long as she took the time to sift through the rubbish. Dev's cheekiness was obviously well-balanced with his cleverness. Shalonie guessed that Avarice was well aware and allowed him the leeway more in keeping with a favored family member than an annoying employee.

"Can I help you with any of this?" a voice asked from

the doorway of the tower, and Shalonie looked up in surprise. She'd been alone in the tower most of the day, and the two days prior, as she worked on the calculations. And after explaining the type of work she needed to do, she hadn't expected anyone to join her. Omen, Templar, and Liethan had all gone practically cross-eyed when she'd attempted to explain the calculations necessary to build this portal.

Nikki Deldano stood in the doorway, a familiar-looking notebook clutched in his hands. It was the book she'd given him on the road from Khreté. She'd been surprised he hadn't already returned it, guessing that like the others he'd lost interest after the first few pages. It had been written as a reference book for her — not for others — and certainly not something anyone beyond a mathematician might find remotely interesting.

"I've been reading it," Nikki said quickly, holding the book up to show her.

"Really?" She could hear the doubt in her own voice and guessed Nikki did too. "How far have you gotten?"

"Halfway," he said swiftly, his expression eager. A fraction of a moment later the eagerness slid away as if he were unable to sustain it. "Well, the first time anyway. I had to start over when I realized that . . . well . . . you see . . . some parts of it were hard for me to understand so I started over again. Actually I started over a few times — but I'm making headway." The eagerness was back again.

In spite of everything, Shalonie had to smile at that. *How honest of him! Not a trait normal in a Kharakhian.* "How many times have you started over?" she asked.

His lips thinned as if he were not entirely certain how to reply. *He wants to lie,* she thought in amusement. She could see it in his eyes. Though his features and coloring were very like his father's, Beren Deldano could look her straight in the eye and lie so convincingly even she believed it despite knowing he was talking nonsense. Nikki lacked Beren's guile — his eyes gave everything away.

"A few . . ." he started and then shook his head like a dog shaking off water, unable to finish his statement. "Twenty-five times," he admitted. "I keep getting stuck on this one part."

"Which part?" she asked, genuinely curious.

"You said, 'beyond the representational elements of the Runes themselves they can be used in conjunction with constantly changing variables that require a derivative of the representation based on the other elements present in the equation,'" he told her, still clutching the book tightly in his hands.

Shalonie stared at him, dumbfounded. *Not only can he read it, he quoted that word for word. Even made sense of it. Did he memorize it?*

"That's in the first paragraph," she told him. "Which part confused you?"

His cheeks flushed red at her question. "Well . . ." he began. "It's the derivative part. Is that a math thing, like doing your sums?"

Shalonie fought hard to suppress a spontaneous smile and took a deep breath. "Yes," she answered. "It's a math thing."

Nikki nodded as if he'd guessed that much. "And do you learn that before or after multiplications?"

"After," she replied gently.

"Oh," he let out a deep, forlorn sigh. "I guess that's why I don't know it yet. I'm still working on my multiplications. I can do the single numbers — but not the bigger numbers.

You have to put down zeros and carry things, and no one ever really explained that part to me. I kept the books in the tavern — and that's just sums and differences."

She could sympathize. "I keep the books in our Hold as well. Multiplication is really just a faster way of doing sums."

Nikki looked startled by that. "You keep the books in your . . . Hold?" He hesitated over the word. While he'd certainly asked a number of questions about Melia and the positions both she and his as-of-yet unmet father and siblings held in Melia, the concept of the dragon-guided Melian oligarchy was clearly foreign to him. "I thought you would have an accountant to do that sort of thing so you could do your more important work."

"We do," she told him. "But my mother has some rather odd hiring practices — our accountant is a baker's apprentice, not a bookkeeper, so I always have to correct his numbers after he's done. Usually it's easier to just do it myself the first time. Besides, keeping the books is an important job. It's our duty to our people and the Sundragons to keep accurate records."

Nikki was staring at her as if she'd just sprouted wings and flown away. His green eyes gleamed with light. "You're amazing!" he exclaimed.

Shalonie laughed dismissively, guessing where this conversation was going. Being quick with numbers hardly made a person amazing — and certainly after her rather spectacular miscalculation in the Autumn Lands, she could hardly laud herself as infallible. It had been sheer luck that any of them were still alive — and while she'd tried to explain to her companions repeatedly how badly she'd failed them, they had just refused to understand.

Her own certainty in her abilities had nearly led to the destruction of the Covenant of the Gods and possibly far worse had Galseric actually entered the mortal world. "Yes, yes, I'm very clever," she replied tonelessly.

"No," Nikki stated immediately.

Shalonie looked up, waiting for him to elaborate.

Nikki flushed bright red then but straightened his back determinedly. "I mean, yes of course you're clever and all . . . but that's not what I meant. It's just that you seem to care so much — about your friends, your country, your people, even about Kharakhan. You care what happens to people — you care what happens to the world, and you spend all your time wondering how you can make it better. We have scholars in Khreté, but they don't do anything. They just sit around writing books and scrolls that no one is allowed to read. They just talk to each other — couldn't even be bothered to talk to anyone who isn't like them. But you . . . you go out into the world and do things — help people — save people. That's . . . amazing."

Shalonie flushed deeply, certain this was the first time anyone had ever praised her for something other than her intellectual abilities. "I was hardly alone," she reminded him.

He grinned. "Yeah, but all of this would have failed without you — and we all know that." He took a step farther into the room. "And I do want to help. I know I can't figure out any of your equations, but if there's anything else I could do, I will."

There had been a weight on her soul these last few weeks as she'd pondered the events of the Autumn Lands. The understanding she'd come to when she'd realized what precisely had taken control of Galseric — the knowledge that a creature like that even existed — that there was something in this world so far beyond her understanding, a power that could literally destroy everything. It terrified her. What's more, it confused her and led her to believe that her understanding of the world was flawed, and that the very foundations of the Covenant she'd thought held the world in balance were far shakier than she'd ever imagined.

She recalled the unease of her Hold Dragon Geryon when they'd discussed the magical protections that surrounded Melia. She'd thought then that he'd been far more worried than was warranted. Now, she feared that the Sundragons' disquiet was rooted in even greater threats.

Nikki Deldano's earnest face and his genuine offer to aid her lifted some of the accumulated weight and the stark loneliness from her. She smiled at him.

"How's your penmanship?" she asked.

"Good!" he said enthusiastically. "I can write with a quill without dripping ink."

"And can you copy what you see on a page?" She stood and crossed over to him, showing him the very complicated diagram she'd worked out earlier with 7. She knew most of the characters on the page would be unfamiliar to him. But then again, he didn't need to know what they meant to copy them down.

"I'll do my best!" he promised.

Shalonie motioned toward the circles she'd drawn on the floor. "Then let's get to work. This is going to take time. And if you want, I'll explain multiplication to you while we work."

"Brilliant!" Nikki exclaimed in delight as if she'd just promised him the moon.

The Deldanos are going to love him, Shalonie thought as

she handed over a piece of dark chalk and set about explaining what needed to be done to get them all home to
Melia.

Chapter 13: Hex

OMEN

Omen waited impatiently as Shalonie explained the workings of the portal to Kadana. It was a beautiful piece of masonry. The stonemasons had done a spectacular job laying down the black and white stones. The master mason had placed the actual Cypher Runes themselves with excruciating care while his apprentices had finished the white stones around them — all under the watchful and exacting eye of Shalonie. It was a work of art in the end, concentric circles within circles, the runes precisely set along the rings themselves.

She'd set up a ring of glass oculerns on the floor that were actually embedded into the tilework of the portal. Each had a small glass and copper lid that opened so that a sunstone could be secured on the inside. All were filled at the moment, casting the room in a bright golden glow that blended perfectly with the colored light coming in through the stained glass window of the tower.

"I used the sunstones to power the entire thing — since you have so many of them," Shalonie explained. "If you want to shut it off, just remove the stones from the oculerns. Even removing one of them should be enough to stop anyone from using it."

Omen's grandmother looked impressed, satisfied by the measures Shalonie had taken. The portals in Melia and Lydon were both powered by his father's magic, not sunstones. And the one in Terizkand was powered by a strange magical artifact King Antares had provided — a large ruby that was carved in the shape of a skull. *Creepy looking, but it does the job.*

"Are you all ready then?" Kadana asked, turning toward the others. She and her daughters would be using the portal themselves to travel to Melia, where they would then take another ship to the Corsair Isles to meet up with her husband and sons. She wanted to be there when Nikki was introduced to Beren for the first time.

And they'll probably talk Shalonie into going with them to the Corsair Isles to set up the next portal, Omen realized. *Been too long since I've been there. Bet Kyr would love it.*

He laughed at himself. *Not even home yet and I'm already planning my next trip.*

"How do we know it works?" Templar asked then. "Have you tested it yet?"

"It works," Shalonie assured them. "7 came through earlier this morning and then went back. It's fine."

"Then let's get going," Templar said cheerfully. "Remember, step off the portal the moment you get on the other side. Bumping into someone coming through hurts . . . a lot."

Omen chuckled at the remark, knowing where it was coming from. He and Templar had tested that theory out when the portal to Terizkand was built. Two people couldn't actually appear in the exact same location — a force literally knocked the other person out of the way — hard.

"Ready Kyr?" Omen glanced down at his brother who was standing next to him, Tyrin clutched to his chest, Tormy beside them both. The two cats were eager to get back to Melia, though Omen suspected their enthusiasm

216

had something to do with a particular Melian summer dessert they'd been talking about for days. *And it's finally fully summer — instead of pseudo-autumn. Too bad it won't last much longer — not really ready for another autumn.*

Kyr was still wearing the leather gauntlet covering his hexed hand. The mark itself had stopped growing the moment they'd entered Caraky with the missing king, but it did still bother the boy — more so than it had initially. Omen suspected it itched — and while Kyr was capable of ignoring pain, the itch made him twitchy. Omen had caught him more than once scratching at the black marks until his skin bled.

"I can hear the ocean," the boy said with a smile, which Omen imagined meant, "Yes, of course, dear brother, I'm ready. Let's depart."

Omen gave a decisive nod to the others and then stepped onto the portal. He felt the familiar pull he'd come to associate with the activation of a transfer portal. His skin felt taut as if stretched by tiny pincers, and for a moment his sight went completely white as if a blazing light had flared around him. When his sight cleared, he found himself standing on the familiar transfer portal in Daenoth Manor. His father and mother waited nearby.

Quickly, Omen stepped off the portal. Tormy followed, then Kyr and Tyrin, and then the others one by one. Their arrival sparked a chain reaction of chaos, which was only punctuated by an overly happy Tormy and Tyrin who tore around the room greeting everyone in sight all at once — including the very people they'd been traveling with.

In the midst of the excitement, Avarice and 7 managed to welcome them. To Omen's surprise both of his parents hugged him, both pleased to see him, and judging by the "well done" that came from his father, approving of his performance over the course of the journey and its, to his mind, questionable conclusion.

Glad to be home, but something . . . something . . . He could not identify the uneasy feeling that gnawed at him, didn't know what had prompted it.

"No Lilyth?" Omen asked after the initial chaos had abated. His sister was nowhere in sight.

Irritation flickered through Avarice's eyes. "She's pouting. She still has several months on her grounding and was angry when I told her you weren't allowed to bring her any presents."

"That is being all rightnessness!" Tormy insisted happily. "Templar is bringing Lily a prize, so she is being happy."

Omen threw his friend a look of surprise. "You brought my sister a present?"

Avarice's brow furrowed in disapproval.

Templar waved one ring-adorned hand through the air dismissively. "I always bring her presents," he explained. "She told me she'd poison me if I didn't. And considering she actually did poison me once, I took her threat seriously."

"Honestly," Avarice's voice was laced with heavy annoyance, "it was just a little bit of poison and hardly did you any harm." Her frown smoothed away a moment later. "Fine, just make sure she doesn't know that I know that you gave it to her."

While 7 led the majority of their group from the room, amicably chatting with Kadana and Shalonie and shooing both hyperactive cats toward the larger gathering rooms of the manor, Avarice drew Omen and Kyr aside.

First, she pulled Kyr into a tight hug, which he returned

enthusiastically. "And how's your poor hand?" she asked the boy.

Kyr quickly held up his gauntlet-covered hand. "Filled with ash and dust and angry thoughts."

Omen spotted the almost imperceptible tremble in Avarice's fingers as she stopped herself from making a warding sign against evil at Kyr's words. "That doesn't sound good," Avarice said solemnly, smoothing Kyr's tousled blond hair down. Her silver eyes flashed with unspoken warning toward Omen. "Indee is waiting in the gold parlor. She'll remove the hex."

Righteous indignation rose up in Omen's chest, and he smiled grimly. "Good!" he blurted out. "I have a few things to say to her."

He'd thought long and hard about all the things he would say to Indee — not only about what she'd done to Kyr, but also about the fact that she'd known all along that Khylar had not been kidnapped, essentially forcing him to make a decision between protecting the Covenant and protecting his brother. That he'd managed to do both instead of just one or the other was largely the outcome of extraordinary luck and Shalonie's cleverness.

"I'm sure," Avarice said mildly, her voice deceptively calm.

"I'm angry!" he informed her, surprised that she didn't already know that. "I'm furious. Wouldn't you be if she'd done this to you? She lied to me, tricked me, manipulated me. Don't you think I have a right to be angry!"

"Of course," Avarice replied still using the mild tone that Omen was fairly certain meant that she didn't believe him. "Of course, I'd be furious. You have every right to be mad."

"And I'm going to give her a piece of my mind," he told

his mother — warned her, really. He felt it was necessary to put his foot down on this issue even though he'd always been very cautious not to go directly against his mother's wishes. He knew from experience that rebellion against Avarice never ended well. *This is important — too important to back down, even if she tells me I have to for some political reason.*

"I would as well," Avarice agreed. "I'd let her know exactly how I felt under similar circumstances. I completely understand."

Surprised that his mother wasn't challenging him, Omen stared at her for a moment. While he was far taller than she was, there had always been something about his mother's stance and demeanor that nullified the advantage of his size. Even Tormy backed down from whatever mischief he was involved in with nothing more than a look from his mother. And yet on this point, she appeared completely accepting. He wondered if the details of their past adventure — related to her through her spy Devastation — had, in fact, won him a certain degree of respect.

"Good," he proclaimed with satisfaction. "I'm going to tell her that she had no right to put so many innocent lives in danger — that she should have told me right from the start that Khylar had not been kidnapped. That she had no right to hex Kyr, that . . ." He continued on for some time, detailing all his grievances.

Avarice listened patiently, only raising one dark eyebrow now and again in response. "Come then," she replied after he'd wound down. "Best not keep her waiting. It will be far more effective if you don't have to chase after her all over Melia."

Her hand still on Kyr's shoulder, Avarice led them both

from the room and away from the general noise of the others who were now in one of the larger halls on the west side of the manor. Instead, she moved Omen toward the north wing and the gold parlor — a sanctuary set aside for Avarice's private meetings. It was richly appointed, filled with exquisite furniture all done in golds and creams. Fine silk curtains covered a glass doorway that looked out at a circular patio replete with a flower garden brimming with full-petalled roses and fragrant lavender. The floors of the meticulously charming room had been covered in expensive carpets from Frelzaire, and the walls were lined with delicately patterned paper decorated with drawings of cream-colored roses. It was a room designed for ladies in fine dresses, one very few men ever entered.

This was where Avarice had tea with Arra Corsair or Omen's grandmother Queen Wraiteea. It was where the Hold Ladies of Melia were led when they visited, and it was one of the few rooms in the manor that Tormy was absolutely forbidden to enter for fear the overly large cat would destroy the priceless vases and spindly-legged tables and chairs with one sweep of his tail. It was a room that Omen had only entered on very rare occasions.

He noticed now that his mother had taken care to dress herself for the occasion — she wore a silver and blue gown of her own design — high-waisted, with a long flowing skirt and tapered sleeves that covered her hands with pale lace. Her long black hair had been set in a careful design, tiny braids forming a thin cap over waves of curls, all interwoven with very thin strands of silverleaf chain and a flare of perfect sapphires that caught in the sunlight as she moved. Standing beside her in his traveling gear, his large sword strapped to his back, his leathers and armor scuffed and scratched from the battles he'd fought, he felt suddenly grubby and barbarous.

Omen shot a quick glance at Kyr who was happily trotting beside Avarice as if he hadn't a care in the world. He dutifully wore his sword at his hip — Omen kept reminding him every morning to retrieve it. And he had on the fine coat Avarice had made for him. It was none the worse for wear, his mother's spells keeping it in surprisingly good form despite the travel and the battles. Kyr's boots were probably scuffed up and muddy, but a quick glance down at the boy's feet revealed that Kyr was no longer wearing them. His feet were utterly bare as they had been for much of their stay in Kadana's castle. Apparently, Kadana's girls had shown him the joy of splashing around in frog ponds, and now it was all Omen could do to get him to keep his feet out of every body of water they saw.

Two Melian servant girls waited just outside the gold parlor, and they curtsied quickly to Avarice as she approached.

"Your swords, boys," Avarice told both Omen and Kyr. Omen quickly released the buckle on his sword belt's strap and removed the large weapon from where it hung against his back. He handed the weapon over to one of the girls who bravely took it with a polite nod. Her arms sagged at the weight, but she kept a straight back and maintained a cordial smile. Omen also removed the weapon belt from around his hips, giving up his daggers. He handed it over slowly, along with his gauntlets.

Kyr did the same, passing his sword and gauntlets to the other girl gingerly as if the items were made of spun sugar. The black hex mark twined around his left hand and fingers stood out in stark contrast to his pale skin. The servant girl took in a sharp breath, then quickly cast her eyes to the ground. But Avarice did not reprimand her. Omen felt his indignation and anger at Indee returning all the more forcefully. Kyr, delicate and barefooted, stood in the hall like a branded lamb being led to slaughter.

Avarice pushed open the door and gestured for Omen and Kyr to enter. The heavy honey-and-apricot fragrance of his mother's prize roses flooded over him.

Bathed in diffused sunlight, Indee was waiting for them, but she was not alone. Two attendants flanked the queen — Omen recognized them immediately — Aiena and Elisiena, two of the youngest Untouchables from the Temple of the Sundragons. Though it wasn't unusual for Indee to keep ladies-in-waiting with her, it was highly unusual for the much-revered Untouchables to act the role of servant. But the moment Omen laid his eyes on Indee seated in an overstuffed chair near the open garden door, he understood why the Untouchables were present.

Indee held two small figures, one in each arm, wrapped in downy white blankets. The little forms were infants from the size of them, mere weeks old. *Babies? Baby Sundragons! Twins!* Omen's mind sorted out the information even before he had a chance to realize the meaning of his discovery.

"Aww," Kyr cooed immediately. "How sweet."

Indee, dressed in a gown of gold and white, her long black hair fixed upon her head in a delicate cascade of curls and crowned with a thin golden circlet, was the very picture of contentment and motherhood. She smiled widely at Kyr's spontaneous gentle adulation.

Omen had almost forgotten she'd been pregnant — certainly hadn't expected this, to find her with twin babies in her arms.

And of course she'd have Untouchable ladies-in-waiting. No one else would be allowed to even touch the babes, save the immediate family.

His eyes shifted directly to the children — they looked human enough, plump and pink-skinned, not even the telltale sign of scales around their temples to mark them as Sundragons. But of course that wouldn't matter, in human form or dragon form, they were still Sundragons — wondrous, adored, sacred.

"Sorry to keep you waiting, Indee," Avarice said offhand as they entered the room. She moved toward the chair opposite Indee and sat down in a delicate fall of silk and lace. Kyr sank to the floor beside Avarice, leaning his head against her chair as he continued to gaze curiously at the two babies. But his eyes inevitably drifted toward the table between the two women and the tea set and tray of coconut macaroon cookies upon it.

Indee's cat Fog was seated on the table, preening on a small blue pillow, tiny grey tail folded elegantly around his body. A small dish of cream sat in front of him and a plate with a half-nibbled macaroon next to it. The little cat reached out one dainty grey paw and pushed the cookie off the tray and toward Kyr. The boy snatched it up, blithely devouring it in one bite.

Got to teach him to stop eating cats' leftovers!

"Omen," Indee greeted with a regal tilt of her head, her voice pitched low. "Welcome back."

For a moment Omen didn't know what to say, all his words and angry retorts fleeing as he stared at her. Instead of unleashing the fury and frustration of the past weeks on the wicked queen, he squeaked an undignified, "Twins?"

Indee could not have looked prouder. "Yes, a boy and a girl. Caught me off guard as well. My darlings are the first set of twin Sundragons born in centuries. Meet Phaethra and Phaedron." She carefully turned both infants just slightly so that Omen could see which was which — though to him there was little difference between the two.

"We is being very quiet," Fog informed Omen sternly. "On account of the fact that the baby dragons is sleeping. We is not raising our voices or being hoppity, and we is sitting on a pillow and being quiet. I is very good at it."

"Yes," Indee said indulgently to the little cat. "You are being very good — a most perfect kitten."

Fog's ears perked up, and he began purring contently. "Is you liking the baby dragons?" the little cat asked Omen. The kitten gave him a very sharp stare — one that reminded him surprisingly of his mother.

Aside from his sister, Omen had little experience being around babies — he'd been five when Lilyth was born and vaguely remembered being more annoyed than pleased with the arrival of the small screaming person. While these two were not screaming, Omen was surprisingly relieved that he wouldn't be asked to hold one of them. "They're lovely," he agreed, and both Indee and Fog seemed well satisfied with that.

"I believe Omen had something he wished to tell you, Indee," Avarice said then. She poured herself a cup of tea and refilled Indee's cup as well. She patted Kyr on the head and set another teacup in front of him, filled it, and then handed the boy another macaroon.

Indee looked expectantly at Omen, her dark eyes gleaming. "Yes?" she asked, the soul of patience and grace.

"I . . . I . . ." Omen began, but there were no words waiting for him, nothing at all that came to his mind. A helpless glance at his mother showed a faint smile on her lips. His stomach twisted. His mother had known this would happen. She knew him too well. *Which was why she was so supportive of my outburst earlier. She knew I wouldn't be able to confront Indee . . . not with the babies right here.*

"Would you please remove the hex from Kyr?" he asked then, giving up and just accepting that he'd been skillfully outmaneuvered by the two women.

"Oh, yes of course!" Indee said with concern as if she'd utterly forgotten the whole point of the trip. "Oh, you poor dear boy, look at you." Her dark eyes were fixed on Kyr with a look of motherly concern. She motioned toward the two Untouchables who immediately came forward to take the children from her arms.

Then Indee held out her hands to Kyr. The boy reached across the table with his hexed hand, placing it gently on Indee's palms. The black marks on the boy's pale skin stood out all the more in the sunlight streaming in through the window. Indee clasped Kyr's hand between her own and closed her eyes — a faint red light rose from their joined hands. Omen detected movement on Kyr's skin. The marks twisted, slithering around like snakes. And then, not a moment later, they were simply gone — vanished like mist evaporating off the boy's skin, leaving his hand spotless and unmarked.

When she was done, Indee carefully inspected Kyr's hand — as if checking to see that she'd gotten every trace of the hex and searching out lingering effects.

"How does that feel?" she asked Kyr tenderly.

Kyr gazed solemnly up at her, his large sunset violet eyes unreadable. "Do not go down the sunless path. It leads to only sorrow and shadows."

Indee sat back, startled. Her eyes narrowed as she looked at Kyr with genuine alarm. Despite everything, Omen felt a twinge of satisfaction at the uncertain look. Where he had failed to give Indee the tongue-lashing he had dreamed of, his brother had succeeded in forcing a genuine reaction from her.

"What?" she asked breathlessly.

"Indee?" Avarice leaned forward in concern, setting her teacup down. Omen thought he saw a faint gleam of pleasure in his mother's eyes. She too recognized Indee's momentary shrinking response as a victory of sorts.

Indee, eyes still on Kyr, shook her head imperceptibly. "Those were the exact words my father said to me when I was a child — the last words he ever said to me. Where did you hear them?"

"Magic leaves whispers and echoes and there is never any silence," Kyr told her. "I can't shut off my ears — I tried ripping them off once, but they grew back. Can I have another cookie?" He'd directed that last question at Avarice. She lifted the plate of macaroons and offered another to him.

"I see," Indee said sitting up tall, hands falling to her lap. "Aren't you full of surprises?"

"Omen, why don't you take Kyr and Fog to wherever Tormy and Tyrin are," Avarice suggested then, motioning to the small cat still seated on his pillow.

Fog looked up, a happy cat smile of his grey face.

"Yes, take Kyr and Fog," the little cat agreed. "I is needing to talk to Tormy and Tyrin and hearing all the news I is going to tell them."

"Right." Omen bowed to the inevitable. This meeting

was over — all without one word of his epic rant being spoken. Kyr rose and scooped Fog up in his hands, placing the little cat on his shoulder where Tyrin typically rode. Omen led him from the room after another brief bow of his head to his mother and Indee.

Beyond the doorway, they could hear the peals of laughter coming from Tormy and the others. Kyr grinned and took off down the hall in an excited run.

Omen paused. He stared after them.

"You all right?" a voice asked.

Omen turned. The two servant girls had disappeared with his weapons. Instead, he noticed Devastation leaning against the wall as if waiting for him.

In the short time since they'd returned, Dev had already cleaned himself up and changed his clothing. He looked a bit more like the young courtier Omen had seen that first day in his mother's office rather than the rugged traveling companion he'd grown accustomed to.

Omen was struck again by Dev's resemblance to his mother. Indeed Dev seemed to have gone out of his way to play up that similarity. He was now wearing a high collared tunic of silver and blue — the exact shade as his mother's gown; the shirt beneath had tapered sleeves with lace at his wrists. His soft moleskin breeches were offset with fine felt boots etched with a silver wolf's head pattern, and while he simply wore his black hair brushed back from his face with no adornment, Omen noticed thin silverleaf chains with sapphires in his ears. Further, he bore no weapon that Omen could see — though he'd learned from their trip that meant nothing. Regardless of what he wore or how he looked, Dev was a Machelli through and through.

"I had all these things I wanted to say to her," Omen told

228

the man. Despite everything, even knowing he was still technically his mother's spy, Omen had come to trust Dev's judgment. "And there she is with those two little babies, and I said nothing. Which was of course the whole point of this little setup, I suppose."

Annoyance rushed through Omen. "It isn't right," he told Dev then. "What she did — lying to us, tricking us, hexing Kyr. She didn't need to do any of that. I would have done the right thing no matter what — so would Kyr and Tormy and Tyrin and the others. That's the part I don't get. Did she think I would just let the Covenant be destroyed — abandon the world, abandon people in need?"

"Perhaps," Dev replied. "Not everyone is so willing to do the right thing as you put it. In fact, most people can't be bothered — or actively do the wrong thing."

"Well, it's still not right . . . and I wanted to tell her that." Frustration welled up inside him.

"Omen, she owes you a favor," Dev pointed out. "She knows it, you know it, the dragons know it, the Corsairs and the Deldanos know it, and more importantly your mother knows it. And that's a very powerful position to be in."

"I suppose," Omen groused. *It's not like I'm the sort of person who will press that point — but my mother is.* He felt somewhat cheered at that thought. No doubt his mother would use this to her advantage.

"Where did you get the fancy clothes?" he asked Dev instead. "You didn't have those with you all this time, did you?"

"Of course not," Dev replied. "They were up in my room. Your mother left them for me."

Which of course meant that for whatever reason Avarice

229

wanted Dev to dress like her. "Wait a minute . . . your room? You live here? Since when?"

Dev waved his hand dismissively. "Oh, I've been around — coming and going for some time now."

"How did I not know that?" Omen was certain he'd never seen Dev prior to meeting him in his mother's office. *He also could be lying — he likes lying. Seems to take great pride in it.*

"You're not very observant," Dev pointed out.

A thought occurred to Omen, and he glanced briefly from Dev to the closed door of the gold parlor. "Are you meeting with them? Why? I thought you've been writing to my mother all along — what more could you possibly have to tell her?"

Dev chuckled at that, a mischievous grin stealing over his face. "Omen, having someone to collect information is all well and fine, but it's a lot more effective when you can dangle it in front of important people and let them know exactly what you know."

More plots within plots — how am I even related to my mother or him? "I hate politics," Omen said defiantly.

Dev gave him a sympathetic look. "Nasty business. Best avoided at all cost." He moved forward to knock lightly at the door. From beyond, Omen heard his mother calling out, "Come in, Dev!"

Dev threw Omen a cheeky wink as he opened the door and disappeared inside.

Still annoyed Omen stared down the hallway after his brother and Fog. He supposed he should go make certain neither he nor Tormy were getting into trouble. *My mother and Indee can have their little private meeting with Dev, and I'll—*

"Join us, Dev," he heard his mother's voice state clearly from the other room, and he turned in surprise. Dev had failed to shut the door — leaving it opened a crack.

That's odd . . . he's usually more paranoid than that . . . doesn't forget the little details . . . Omen stepped closer.

Chapter 14: Secret Weapon

DEV

When Dev entered the gold parlor, he immediately drew the attention of both Avarice and Indee. Avarice, looking over his attire, gave him a faint nod of approval. The clothes had been waiting in his room, and he'd immediately understood. Avarice wanted to make certain that Indee knew exactly who he was — a Machelli, loyal to Avarice — and Avarice alone.

Indee's eyes narrowed to slits as she studied him. He caught the way her gaze moved from him to Avarice and then back again. Their resemblance to one another was uncanny — and not something he could, in fact, explain himself. He had no clue who his parents were; no idea why he looked so much like Avarice Machelli. Truthfully until he'd met the Machellis, he hadn't even suspected he had any family at all. But the Machellis all insisted that he had Shilvagi blood, something they could apparently smell, disconcerting as that sounded to him. Shilvagi blood meant that he had to be directly related to the clan. Whether he truly was or not, the association had suited his purposes. Still did after all these years.

"Join us, Dev." Avarice motioned toward one of the overstuffed, cream-colored chairs against the far wall. He retrieved it and scooted it next to Avarice, before inclining his head to both women. Avarice poured him a cup of tea as he sat down. She handed over the cup and saucer graciously.

"Dev?" Indee asked. "Hardly a suitable Machelli name?"

"Short for Devastation, my lady," he informed her.

A sharp flare of annoyance flashed through Indee's dark eyes. "Of course it is."

He glanced over at the two bassinets and the babies inside. The young Untouchable women were standing beside them, and he couldn't help but think they were hardly suitable bodyguards for such precious infants. *Indee could stop any threat before it started. And this is Melia — there isn't a person in this city who wouldn't die to defend the baby Sundragons.*

"Congratulations on your children," he said to the woman. Such niceties were expected after all.

Indee smiled. "I have been blessed," she agreed. "Now, I understand you have news for us."

"Yes," he replied, pausing to take a sip of tea. *Jasmine.* He glanced briefly at Avarice who gave him a subtle nod. *She wants me to tell the truth. All right then.*

"I've given Indee the highlights of your journey," Avarice explained, "but there are some points that need clarifying."

"Apologies, my lady," he offered quickly, his own humor getting the best of him. "I thought I was quite thorough — but perhaps I skimped on the details. I will endeavor to be more forthcoming in the future."

Avarice's lips quirked at that, and he could see that while she was mildly annoyed, she was also not unamused — indeed she seemed somewhat torn between the two emotions. "Yes, you are an excellent writer," she commented dryly. "But to the point — we were actually both curious about something you said about your encounter with the Aelaedrine."

233

That surprised him. Of all the things he'd expected to be asked about, their encounter with the Aelaedrine was not one of them. He'd thought for certain both Avarice and Indee would be far more interested in Khylar's actions and the political climate of Kharakhan. It had occurred to him that they also might bring up the subject of Indee's first husband, Charaathalar, and what had become of him. No doubt the presence of an active Nightling in the king's chambers must have alarmed them.

"The Aelaedrine?" he questioned. Granted the Ae-laedrine queen certainly had said a number of rather intriguing things about all his companions — most notably the comments about Templar's grandfather, but Dev knew he had relayed the conversation in great detail. He knew no more than that.

"You said the Aelaedrine bowed to Tormy and Tyrin," Avarice pressed. "Did you mean that literally?"

The cats! That's what surprised them! He set his teacup down on the table with an audible *clink.* "I did, my lady. Prince Cuillian himself even dropped to his knees in front of them. And the term they used — Tau el Faigntha — Shalonie said it translated to, 'the ones who are blessed or sacred.'"

Dev saw the strange look Avarice and Indee exchanged and found himself wondering what he had missed. He'd thought the fuss only an oddity of the faerie folk rather than something meaningful.

"The Aelaedrine are the eldest of all the faerie races," Indee said. "They possess secret knowledge I can't even guess at. If they think the cats are something more than they appear, then I'm inclined to agree with them."

"Lovely," Avarice's voice dropped in tone, and she set

234

aside her own teacup. "Giant, important balls of fluff running around and breaking things in my house."

Indee smiled at that. "Perhaps you should find some means of shrinking Tormy. Fog is not so hard to manage."

"We also have a small one," Avarice pointed out. "And believe it or not, he's more work than the big one. Far too clever for his own good."

Which was why, despite himself, Dev had grown to like the little cat so much. *That mouth on him is priceless.*

"Now," Indee changed the subject abruptly. "What of my son?"

Dev glanced again at Avarice, receiving another subtle nod. *She wants it unvarnished.* And certainly he felt no need to spare Indee's feelings. "Compromised," he said simply.

He saw Indee's eyes harden as she studied him, trying to assess if he was telling the truth. He was aware that Indee could employ magic to determine if he was, but he doubted very much she'd use such spells in front of Avarice.

"Explain," Indee commanded.

"Your son's loyalty is no longer to Kharakhan or its people," Dev replied. "It is to the Teyledrine. In fact, I'd go so far as to say Kharakhan has been invaded — and any war that might have been fought to prevent this invasion is long over."

"Khylar would never betray his people," Indee declared, though she didn't sound entirely certain.

"Khylar has not," Dev agreed. "To him, the Teyledrine are his people — and besides I do not believe he is acting entirely of his own free will — despite the fact that he thinks he is."

Khylar rebelled against his mother only to fall under the

influence of an even more powerful woman. Idiot.

"You are referring to this Lady Morcades?" Avarice clarified.

"Yes." His hands tightened on the arms of his chair. He'd held nothing back in his description about Morcades in his missives to Avarice. He knew Lady Morcades' type far too well — had known it the moment he'd laid his eyes on her. *Evil — pure and simple.*

"And you believe she holds more influence over Khylar than I do?" Indee pressed. "More influence than his own mother?"

"Your pardon, my lady," he replied with a false humility that he knew both women could see through. "Lady Morcades is not someone to be underestimated. Kyr named her a spider the instant he saw her. I think it is an apt description."

"And we're giving an insane boy's words such credence?" Indee asked, surprised and looking at Avarice for confirmation.

Avarice's jaw tightened. She glanced out the open doors to the garden, inhaling the scent of roses in the air. Two deep breaths. Songbirds chirped among the blooms.

In the stillness, Dev thought he could hear the buzz of bees.

"You have not spent much time around the boy," Avarice said, finally. "Beyond what you saw today. It would not be wise to ignore his words . . . Any of his words."

Indee swallowed slightly. "Save for the fact that you Machellis are superstitious as can be," she mocked, attempting to cover up her disquiet.

It's not superstition when the world is literally out to get you. Dev knew from personal experience exactly what darkness lurked in the shadows. "Not just the Machellis," Dev corrected, self-assured. "I think you'll find that along with Shalonie, the Corsairs, and the Deldanos, even the Terizkandian royal family are likely to give Kyr's words credence. Kyr may speak out of turn, and his words may be jumbled up between the past and the future — but most of what he says turns out to be alarmingly true."

"And do you have evidence beyond the boy's assertion that she is a *spider* — to believe her influence over my son?" Indee challenged.

Dev supposed he could explain how he was very rarely wrong about such things — but he didn't care to delve into his own dark history. "Lady Morcades is unnerving. The cats would neither talk to her nor even look at her, and both Shalonie and Templar were immediately mistrustful. Indeed, there were many among Khylar's retinue who, while utterly loyal to Khylar, would not even turn their gazes to Morcades. She terrifies them. She is the sort of *person* that one grows more leery of the more time one spends in her presence. You must know people like that." Dev snatched up a shard of sugar crystal with thin silver tongs and sweetened his tea. He watched the sugar start to dissolve as the room stayed silent. He could hear the buzzing of the bees again.

"And yet in spite of all of this," Dev went on after a time, "your son actively sought Morcades' counsel. And as strong as your influence on him might have once been, the witch has had one hundred years to weave her spells around him. She resides in the Caraky castle now, at his side. As his advisor . . . Or more."

"I see." Indee lowered her dark lashes for a moment, veiling her eyes. "And what of Tara Corsair? Was there any

237

sign of her?"

Surprised that the Corsair girl was of interest to Indee, Dev shot Avarice a penetrating look.

She too seemed caught off guard by the question.

"No, my lady," Dev replied. "Liethan found no sign of either Tara or her sister. Nothing pointed to foul play either — all evidence suggests they both left of their own free will. But where they have gone, or why they left, remains unknown."

"You think Tara could influence Khylar where you could not?" Avarice guessed, and Indee tilted her head dismissively.

"Perhaps," Indee contemplated out loud. "Though, if Morcades has somehow been influencing things since the beginning, that may explain the conflict in the first place. Tara is a very gifted priestess — her ability to see into a person's soul is extraordinary. It gives her great insight. She would have unmasked Morcades immediately. I had hoped that whatever happened between Khylar and Tara was little more than a minor squabble that could be easily remedied — but I suspect now it was . . . more." She pursed her lips for a second. "And it pains me."

The two women fell silent at that, both deep in thought. Dev waited patiently until Avarice smiled at him as if pleased with his performance.

"Thank you, Dev," she said, her tone one of dismissal.

He rose to his feet, inclining his head to both women. "My pleasure," he replied, sending Avarice a flashing grin to let her know he meant it. *Delivering shocking news is always fun — the more shocking the better.*

With that he turned and headed for the door, leaving the two ladies to concoct whatever plans they might for the wayward King of Kharakhan.

Dev closed the door firmly behind him to shut out any further sound of discussion inside, and then he paused, expectantly.

Omen was leaning up against the wall in the exact place he had left him. The young Daenoth had a rather peculiar expression on his face.

"Omen," he mocked, keeping his voice pitched low. "Were you spying? Listening in on a private conversation?"

Omen scoffed. "You left the door open. You wanted me to listen in."

Delighted, Dev motioned Omen away from the door. They began walking toward the distant sound of laughter coming from Tormy and the others. "Why, you make me sound utterly devious and underhanded." Dev chuckled. "It's like you know me better than my own mother."

"You said you didn't know who your mother is." Omen said, unimpressed.

"I don't," Dev agreed. "But if I did, I'm certain you'd know me better than she ever could."

"They're not going back, are they?" Omen changed the subject.

Dev took in a shallow breath and tilted his head back, stretching his tight neck muscles. "If you mean the Teyledrine and the Autumn Dwellers, no, they're not going back. Not ever. You didn't make that part of your deal with Khylar."

"My deal?" Omen stopped dead in his tracks. "What's that supposed to mean?"

"Your deal for helping Khylar," Dev replied. "You agreed to stop Galseric in exchange for Khylar returning to Kharakhan and closing the Autumn Gate. You never said he

239

had to send the Autumn Dwellers back."

Omen looked momentarily stunned by the news. "So this is my fault?"

"Hmm . . . Of course it's not your fault," Dev huffed. "Don't go taking blame for someone else's failings. This fault lies with Khylar, and with Indee, and with the Autumn Dwellers themselves. Certainly with Morcades. And if you really want to argue the point — with the gods for failing to make certain that people stayed where they belonged when they wrote the Covenant in the first place. And I assume it was the gods or magic itself that chose Khylar as the Gatekeeper. That was probably a mistake, but who am I to second-guess how the world works."

"But what's going to happen to all the people of Kharakhan?" Omen hit a panicked note. "To my grandmother, all my family, and all those soldiers in her castle, all the farmers, all the people in the cities?"

Dev waved his hand through the air. "Prince Cuillian had it fairly accurate when he said that they would likely die. It is what mortals do. It's not as if this is the first upheaval Kharakhan has suffered and survived. They've fought war after war over the centuries, and I imagine they will go on fighting."

"But the odds are against them," Omen said, his face ashen. "They have no hope against the Autumn Dwellers — especially if their own king isn't backing them. And what happens when that spell around Charaathalar and the Night Lord wears down? How do they fight that? What if Galseric frees himself and—"

"Omen!" Dev cut off the rapidly escalating tirade. "It isn't really a matter of what if . . . it's a matter of when. But you know all that — so does Avarice and Indee and Kadana and your father. What happens is, you deal with it. I told you that immortality is no blessing. The threats against immortals are far greater than the threats against mortals. All mortals have to do is die — and as terrible as that sounds, it isn't the worst thing that can happen to you. But you're also one of the few immortals who actually has a chance of changing things — making them better."

There was a worried gleam in Omen's eyes. "How do I stand against all that? How do I beat those odds?"

Dev just laughed. "You learn, you grow. I mean you just spied on your mother and Indee. I didn't expect you to get to that point for years yet. I'm very impressed."

"You're easily impressed," Omen remarked dryly.

"Not really," Dev spoke truthfully.

They both heard a loud crash up ahead, followed by Tormy's voice crying out, "Oops!"

"Ah yes, the blessed Tau el Faigntha, your secret weapon." Dev found the idea that there was more to the cats than just fluff and giggles enchanting. "Perhaps we should go see what trouble they've caused this time."

"I do have a Tormy, a Tyrin, and Kyr," Omen said, more to himself than to Dev. "And Khylar, Morcades, Galseric, and the Night Lords don't. We'll all be fine."

Dev had to smile. Despite everything — his own pessimism, his cynical view of the world, his understanding that no matter how bad Omen thought things were, they were far worse — Dev felt a new, faint glimmer of hope at Omen's optimism. And, until now, hope hadn't been something he'd thought himself capable of feeling anymore.

Chapter 15: Harps

OMEN

Abalmy summer breeze played over The Harps' outer courtyard and whooshed into the belly of the tavern itself. The soft air brushed over Omen's face like a caress.

Good to be back, he thought as he surveyed the over-crowded room. *That's a lot of people. Good thing Jarlen added more tables outside.*

Omen stepped around two bards he knew from the Deldano school, greeting them as he passed. He slid into an empty chair at his usual table by the hearth. Kyr, his parents, and sister were already seated.

Omen snatched a small fried roll from his sister's plate and popped it into his mouth. The crispy appetizer fell apart on his tongue, the sharp and salty flavors of cheese and ham mingling with the creamy sweetness of mashed potato. "I might have added chives," he said.

Omen noticed 7's lips twitch. He knew his father was perpetually amused, if not a little baffled, by Omen's preoccupation with ingredients and culinary techniques. *Everybody likes to eat. Why not have fun with it?*

"Chives would work," Lilyth agreed. "But used sparingly." She smiled a surprisingly sweet smile and pushed her plate between them. "Have another. I'm saving my appetite for dessert."

He took another roll. "Thanks, Lily." *She's being genuinely nice. Maybe she missed me? Might have a few days*

242

of peace before she's back to her usual obnoxious self.

Lilyth's eyes were fixed on Kyr working an untouched part of the tabletop with the new Kharakhian dagger Templar had given to him. "I love these carvings," she said and ran the flat of her hand over the detailed image of Shalonie. "Did Kyr do all of these?"

"Every cut." Omen didn't bother hiding the pride in his voice. His eyes came to rest on Kyr's dexterous fingers as the boy shaved a curl of wood from the table's surface. He noted both of Kyr's bare hands — no gauntlets. Pale skin, whole and healthy — there was no sign of the hex. A warm glow of satisfaction filled Omen. *We did it. We saved him — no matter what happens with the Teyledrine.*

"She's got pretty ears," Kyr said as he thrust his nose nearly against the image he was working on. "I have to get them just right."

Lilyth leaned forward, her dark curls brushing the tabletop as she studied the carving with growing interest. "That's a cat. . ." she breathed.

Kyr had carved the head of a fluffy cat with neatly folded-over ears.

"A new cat—" Lilyth corrected herself, barely managing to suppress a squeal. She bounced up in her chair and quickly sat back down on her hands. Her eyes lit up with delight; she looked away and bit her lip in a desperate attempt to control her excitement.

Omen knew that the girl was convinced that any new cat arriving in Melia would have to be hers. Lilyth clung firmly to the belief that it was her turn. *And she's also certain that Mother won't be able to say no. Good luck. The cats are harder to discipline than Lily.*

"Kyr is really very talented," their mother said, clearly

243

taking note of the subject of Lilyth's exuberance but not commenting. Avarice sipped light golden liquid from her wineglass and patted Kyr's arm gently.

"We'll get you more art supplies, little lamb."

Kyr smiled but didn't look up.

Omen leaned over and kissed Avarice's cheek. "Thanks," he murmured.

On the floor of The Harps, proprietor Jarlen couldn't have been more solicitous. Omen watched, impressed, as the man effortlessly catered to his many guests, running from table to table to ensure that everyone was pleased. *Bet working a room like that is harder than it looks.* Omen noticed several young servers he hadn't seen before. *More staff. Things must be going well.*

Jarlen's oldest daughter, Neria, arrived at the table with Tormy's large blue pillow. "Is Master Tormy not joining us tonight?" she asked, looking disappointed.

"He'll be here," Omen reassured her. "He's still playing outside."

The girl snuck a peek out the large open doors.

Just beyond The Harps' patio, Tormy chased around the grassy clearing of the park, providing endless entertainment and mirth for the patrons seated outside.

Kadana's daughters, Tokara and Caia, little Tyrin, Tess and Chant Deldano, and a pack of at least four dogs bounced around with utter delight. The dogs, belonging to Tess, wiggled and bowed, showing not the slightest fear of the giant cat. In turn, Tormy played with abandon, though Omen could tell how very carefully the enormous feline set down each paw — sensitive to the size of his playmates. *He's never once stepped on Tyrin. The cat has got extrasensory perception.*

Tess had brought along several dog toys, and the four Deldano children took turns throwing. Once a toy left a hand, a wild chase would start, cats and dogs thundering after their airborne quarry.

Omen was surprised to notice how equitable the actual retrieval was. *Is Tormy letting the little creatures win?* Omen wondered as both Tyrin and a medium-sized golden dog carried a ball and a duck toy back to Tess and Chant respectively. *How does Tormy know to do that?*

Once again he was struck by how little he actually knew about his cat. *Tau el Faigntha. Whatever that means.*

Quiet music wound through the air, catching Omen's attention. He turned toward the stage where Beren Deldano was seated, dark hair falling across his half-closed eyes as he bent his head to study the strings of the lute he was playing. *I hope he doesn't want his magic lute back.*

When Omen had first arrived in the park, leaving the cats to play while he headed toward the tavern to join the rest of his family, both Kadana and Nikki had fallen into step with him. All three of them had heard the unmistakable sound of Beren's music as they neared the open doors of the tavern.

"That's your father playing," Kadana had told Nikki with a proud smile. "Guess you'll meet his music before you meet the man."

Nikki, who'd been terrifically nervous about meeting his father, had listened as if entranced. "That's the most . . . beautiful sound I've ever heard."

"Yes," Kadana had agreed. "Beren is a great musician and a highly gifted singer." She'd paused for a second, torn momentarily before she'd decided to speak again. "Beren can be extremely charming and when you meet him, you'll love him instantly. As well you should." She'd taken a deep breath. "But, I need you to promise me something."

Nikki had slowed his gait. "What is it?"

"Try not to be too disappointed when Beren moves on to the next thing that catches his attention."

"What?" Nikki had sounded slightly offended.

"Beren's heart is true," Kadana had said. "But he is like a butterfly, blithely flying from one exciting event to the next. Which means, he sometimes forgets about people, even though he loves them. He forgets."

Omen had felt deeply embarrassed and had picked up his own pace, unwilling to listen to any more of Kadana's warning to Nikki. *Argh. Too personal. Too personal.*

"I'm serious, Nikki," Kadana had said, though the words seemed to cost her something. "Please know that you are my beloved grandson and your place is with your family. Either here in Melia or with me and my children in Kharakhan. The choice is yours. Beren is lucky to have you as a son, but don't let Beren decide one single thing about your life or your happiness." She'd grasped his hands.

They'd both stopped, and Omen had been torn between the rudeness of listening in on their conversation and the rudeness of walking away. *I promised Nikki I'd be there when he meets his family.*

"Understand?" Kadana had asked emphatically.

Omen had paused to wait, compromising by turning his attention toward Tormy and Tyrin who were bouncing around with the pack of children and dogs. He'd been grateful that his mother had taken Kyr ahead with her. *Kyr was so antsy to get back to carving that table. Wonder why.* Omen had sighed inwardly. *Kadana might have hesitated to speak of such private matters in front of my mother . . .*

Odd, really. Kadana is usually extremely tight-lipped about touchy-feely stuff. She must really be worried.

The realization had sparked sudden worry inside Omen as well. *If things don't work out with Beren, Nikki can always stay with us,* he'd decided definitively. *What's another brother in the house?*

Omen needn't have worried.

When they had finally arrived at The Harps, a gaggle of Deldanos, all tall and green-eyed, had surrounded Nikki as if he were visiting royalty. Beren's wife, Nekarra, had taken the young man's hand, walked him to the center of the room, and beckoned him to sit at the head of the table clearly reserved for the family. Kadana had joined them, sitting at his left, while the younger Deldano children had run off to rejoin Tormy, Tyrin, and the dogs outside. Omen had noticed his cousin Bryenth in deep conversation with Beren's eldest daughter Dari, and he'd waved in greeting. Beren, still in mid-song, had just winked at all of them and continued to play.

Now as Omen sat beside his family, Kyr happily carving, Lily dreaming of cats to come, and his parents watching the spectacle of the entire Deldano clan welcoming yet another child into their fold, he found his thoughts drifting to summers past: the beach, picnics in the park, a field of lavender in full bloom. He hummed softly to himself as he drifted off in a sort of daydream for a moment. Bright, happy memories swam through his mind. Noting his own distraction, he shook his head as if trying to clear water from his ears.

7 gestured to the raised platform. "Beren snuck onto the stage shortly before you walked in. He wanted to make certain everyone was in a good mood before Nikki arrived."

He felt the gentle touch of his father's mind, and heard the clearly sent message, *He's manipulating emotions.*

Just like the blasted faeries! Can't get away from it. The dream-like memory of their dinner in the Summer Lands awoke.

"Shouldn't somebody stop him?" Omen said earnestly, though a note of guilt buzzed in his head. *I did the same thing at Khylar's feast . . .*

"Beren's not hurting anything," Avarice said, surprising him. "And he plays in public so rarely. His bardic magic is really no worse than having an extra glass of wine. Just loosens everyone up a bit. Besides, I don't think he can actually help affecting people with his music."

Omen felt the light hum of his mother's spell weaving. *A shield . . . is that what I need?* He quickly wove a psionic shield around himself, using a basic pattern that he'd been taught when he was very small.

"You're getting faster," 7 commented. "Traveling has obviously done you some good." His father sounded pleased. *But this is bardic magic, not psionics. The shield won't work. You need to learn a pattern to control your emotions.*

Avarice chuckled. "I can show you a little guarding spell later. In the meantime just enjoy yourself — as I said, it's harmless."

Beren's performance was delightful. Omen could tell the entirety of the tavern's guests agreed. A general sense of peace and well-being emanated from every man, woman, and child.

Beren's music is making everyone happy. Whether they want to be or not, Omen thought. A quick glance down at Kyr showed the boy still blissfully focused on his carving, unconcerned about the music. *I suppose if something was truly wrong, Kyr would speak up. He'd probably—*

Omen cut off the thought with a twisted smile of bemusement as he realized he'd grown to rely on his little brother and the cats to keep his path true. *And here I thought it was my job to protect them.*

Beren strummed a familiar chord on his lute, starting a new song. A lively murmur moved through the tavern as the patrons realized that this song was going to be a true performance. *The Maiden and the White Rose,* Omen realized with glee. *This is going to be phenomenal.*

Beren started the familiar song with all its lightness and intricacies, but within a few verses the song evolved. The melody mostly retained, he affected an inspired key change.

He moved it up by a semitone. Boosts the energy, but in lesser hands it would sound dissonant, trite. And he's changed the harmonies. That's going to put that song to bed for a long time. Nobody is going to want to touch it.

Thunderous applause from all corners of the tavern rewarded Beren when he ended the piece. The consummate performer, Beren immediately started on a Melian round that Omen recognized as the song Beren typically played to end his sets. Most everyone started singing along.

Kyr hummed along to the melody but kept busy carving the tabletop instead of paying attention to anyone or anything around him. He'd finished the cat and was now working on a new figure.

"Who's he carving?" 7 asked, also admiring the boy's work.

Servers rushed around their table, removing empty plates from the right and in proper fashion bringing in the next course from the left side. *Jarlen trained them well.*

"Thank you," Omen said and smiled down at his plate.

Melian summer crisps. Apricots and honey. Yum. But they're messy. He turned his attention back to Kyr's carving, tilting his head to get a better look. Though the shape in the wood still had no details, there was enough of an outline that he could discern the form of a woman, a throne, and a crown of stars.

"Looks like Kyr's carving the queen of the Aelaedrine," Omen informed his father.

"You met a faerie queen?" Lilyth said with a pout, Omen's words drawing her thoughts away from her potential cat. "No fair!" She turned the pout on her mother, her good mood evaporated. "No fair that Omen gets to do everything, and I get to do nothing. It's because I'm a girl, isn't it? How is that right? Just because I'm a girl you treat me like I'm worth less than a horse in your stables."

"That comparison doesn't even resemble reality," Avarice said, looking at her daughter calmly. "We have extravagantly expensive taste in horses, dear." She took a bite of apricot crisp, not one flake of the crumbly pastry dropping from her lips.

"And you wouldn't believe what Omen spent on Tormy's saddle," a new voice quipped.

They turned to see Templar approaching. The prince tilted his head toward Avarice and 7 in polite greeting but slid into a chair at the table without waiting for an invitation. He snatched up an apricot crisp from the plate and popped it into his mouth. Dressed in an elegant doublet of dark blue velvet and silk, jeweled rings on all his fingers and a thin circle of silver at his brow, he looked every inch the proper prince despite his manners.

250

"Usually one waits to be invited!" Lilyth exclaimed at his blatant theft of the crisp she'd been reaching for.

"I'm a Terizkandian," Templar apologized insincerely, placing one hand over his heart. "Apparently we're extremely rude — I do my best to maintain our reputation, but it is exhausting when it goes so unappreciated."

Lilyth opened her mouth to scold him again but snapped it shut a moment later, as if uncertain how to reply. She glanced toward her parents, but both Avarice and 7 seemed more amused than annoyed.

Breea, Jarlen's dark-haired daughter, slid a goblet in front of Templar. The girl curtsied, a bright blush staining her cheeks.

Was she waiting for him?

"From your private cask, Lord Templar," Breea said.

"Thank you, Breea." Templar gave an appreciative nod. "Please bring a taste for my friends as well." He raised his wine to 7. "You'll like this. It's from Ardeen at the southern end of Terizkand. Very rich. Very rare."

"Ardeen red," Avarice said, impressed. "What a lovely treat." She hailed Breea before the girl could leave the table. "None for my daughter or the boy." She pointed to Kyr.

Lilyth made an annoyed sound. "I don't want any anyway. Alcohol just tastes bitter and awful."

"And you would know that how?" 7 asked, suddenly very interested.

Lilyth crossed her arms and fell silent.

"So how did it go with your father?" Omen asked Templar.

His friend had returned home to report to his father immediately after they'd arrived that morning. Omen was surprised to see Templar back in Melia so soon and wondered if something had gone wrong. He could never quite figure out the odd family dynamics of the Terizkandian royals — they seemed fiercely defensive of one another and equally contentious. Despite his friend's jovial arrival, Templar seemed harried — worry lines round his eyes.

"Oh, brilliantly!" Templar proclaimed with a dramatic wave of his hand. "I lied and embellished in all the appropriate places of course, and he was most impressed. Patted me on the shoulder and said, 'Son, I'm proud of you.'"

Omen perked up at that. "He did?"

"Well, he called me an obnoxious miscreant," Templar amended. "But that's what he meant. I mean, all my sister has ever done is liberate thousands of our people from a centuries-long enslavement by brutal man-eating giants. I helped save the entire world. I'm certain I'm the favorite now."

Attempting to read between the lines, Omen tried to puzzle out King Antares' response. "Did he not believe you?" he asked, perplexed. "I mean, we did technically save the world—"

"Omen!" Avarice's sharp tone cut him off. "Don't let people hear you say that."

Startled, Omen sputtered. "But we did . . . I told you . . . the Covenant was . . ."

The downturn of his mother's lips stopped him; she trained her silver gaze on Templar. "You didn't actually tell your father that, did you? Did you actually use the words 'saved the world?'"

"No, of course not!" Templar scoffed. "I told him we'd prevented an epic cataclysmic event that would have toppled the kingdoms of the world and destroyed all mortal life as we know it. Saying we saved the world would just be bragging. I may be a rude, obnoxious miscreant, but I certainly don't brag."

Despite Templar's bravado, Omen saw the flush of color staining his friend's face at his mother's disapproving stare.

"And what did your father say then?" Avarice asked in a tone that made Omen think she already knew the answer. *Why is she going after us like that? I thought she was pleased.*

Templar shifted uncomfortably in his seat, his eyes downcast. He twisted one of the rings on his left hand. "He told me that if I was now in the world saving business, he had a number of jobs for me to do, things to fix, people to save, towns to liberate. And then he handed me a list — a long list." He scowled at Omen. "They're like chores, Omen. Lots of chores! It's horrifying."

Lilyth tittered at Templar's expense.

"That's pretty much what I thought," Avarice said. "Your father is going to keep you very, very busy from now on. You go around telling people you've saved the world, and they'll never let you rest."

"But—" Omen tried to say something.

"Don't worry," his father added. "Where Templar goes, you go. He helped you and Kyr after all. You can help him with his list — assuming you don't get a list of your own."

Shouts of greeting erupted from the Deldano clan, interrupting them. Omen looked up in time to see Liethan Corsair enter the tavern.

His friend paused, grinning happily, and waved back at the Deldanos before he hurried over to Omen's table. Liethan politely inclined his head to Avarice and 7 and charmingly complimented Lilyth's beaded gown as he casually slipped into a chair at their table. After a few rushed

pleasantries, he leaned in toward Omen and Templar, looking very serious.

"I may need your help with something," Liethan began.
"The weirdest thing happened." He snatched up Templar's
wine goblet and downed the contents. "Turns out, two of
my uncles are in port — they're going to be taking Kadana
to the Corsair Isles shortly. In any event, I told them about
our trip and they contacted my mother and Aunt Arra with a
scrying mirror and told them all the news — mostly about
Tara. She hasn't been found yet and—" He shook his head
as if trying to get himself back on track. "In any event," he
repeated, "the long and the short of it is, they gave me this
list of things to do — a really long list — places to go,
things to do, leads to investigate, people to help — and
something about treasure. I'm pretty certain there was
something about treasure. But there's no way I can do all of
that by myself."

"See!" Templar exclaimed in mock horror. "It's not just
me! We do one good deed and now we're being punished.
We never got into this kind of trouble when we were just
playing Nightball!"

"Well . . ." Omen stalled. "I'm pretty certain it's not supposed to be punishment!"

"Did you tell your family you saved the world,
Liethan?" Avarice asked mildly, her know-it-all gaze worri-
some to Omen.

Liethan shook back the blond curls from his face and
made a show of contemplating the matter. "Well . . . I may
have said something along those lines," he admitted cautiously. "But I didn't brag or anything."

Both Avarice and 7 chuckled, and Omen quietly groaned
as he realized where this was heading. *At least no one has*

asked me to do anything — all I have to do is help Templar and Liethan. How hard could that be?

Memories of the dinner in the Summer Lands still fresh in his mind, Omen asked, "Did you mention what Queen Il-lythia said about your grandmother?"

The Corsair gave a sheepish shrug. "No." He sighed. "Grandmama is always so happy and cheerful. I couldn't. And who should I ask — no one has ever mentioned some sort of great tragedy from her past. Just doesn't seem right. Proper." He shot a look at Templar. "Did you ask about your grandfather?"

Templar refilled his empty wine goblet, positioning it out of Liethan's reach. "I was going to," Templar deflected. "But someone had spilled lamp oil in one of the local duck ponds, and when I found my grandfather, he was literally elbow-deep in a soapy tub washing the ducks. How am I supposed to ask someone if they used to be a bloodthirsty warlord when they're busy cleaning baby ducklings?"

"Probably best to leave ancient history where it belongs," 7 told all three of them, though he looked in-trigued despite himself. "There are some secrets you may not want to unravel."

Omen took another bite of apricot crisp, barely tasting the treat as he thought about his father's words. He'd want-ed to ask about King Charaathalar, but he was beginning to wonder if there was any point. His parents both knew about their visit to the king's chamber — Dev would have told them everything. If they didn't bring it up, he doubted they wanted to talk about Charaathalar and his disastrous deal with the Night Lord.

"There you all are!" a cheerful voice greeted them in sweet Melian tones. Shalonie, wearing a pale blue summer dress, curtsied quickly to his parents. His father rose to his feet, and Avarice elbowed Omen sharply in the ribs before he remembered his own manners and rose as well. Templar and Liethan quickly followed suit. *Hard to remember my manners when we've been traveling with her for so long.*

Lilyth sniggered again, obviously finding Omen's bumbling humorous.

"Please join us, Shalonie," Avarice greeted the girl, motioning to the chair across the table from Kyr. Kyr remained focused on his carving, lost in his own world. Neria and Breea hurried over to hold Shalonie's chair and add another setting for the Hold Lord's daughter. Across the room, Omen could see Jarlen wringing his hands in exaggerated nervousness, his gaze moving from the Deldano table to their own as he no doubt worried about the large number of nobles in his midst.

"How is Nikki getting along with everyone?" Shalonie asked lightly, turning to glance over her shoulder at the gathered Deldano crowd. She smiled and waved toward Nikki in greeting. Omen saw the moment the young man spotted her; a familiar sappy smile stole over his features, one noticed by all of his new siblings. The laughter at the Deldano table was raucous but lighthearted. Omen, Liethan, and Templar snickered.

Poor Nikki! Growing up an only child and now he gets to learn all about the relentless teasing of siblings. Nikki, for his part, didn't seem at all upset. His sappy smile never wavered.

"So how did your meeting with the dragons go, Shalonie?" Omen asked, drawing her attention back to their group.

"Oh." The girl gave them all a wry smile. "It was . . . peculiar to be honest with you." She gratefully accepted the goblet of cool peach tea one of Jarlen's daughters set before her. "All twelve of the Hold Dragons were present, and Lord Sylvan himself," Shalonie continued. "I didn't really expect that. They'd also read all my notes — I'd left several of my notebooks with Lord Geryon to review, but I suppose I didn't really expect anyone to read them."

"Did they disapprove of something?" Omen asked perplexed, wondering why the girl seemed disturbed. There was a worried frown between her brows.

"Oh, no." She waved her hand dismissively. "Quite the opposite. They were pleased. By everything!" She sounded baffled. "I told them the whole story of our trip, and I tried to explain, repeatedly, how badly I had miscalculated things. I mean the equation I used against Galseric didn't work at all the way I intended, and certainly I horribly miscalculated the equation I used on the Golden Voyage. I'm lucky I didn't destroy the entire ship. And let's not forget the dozens of failed attempts I made trying to get Templar's sunlight spell to work on the walls of Kadana's keep. I mean, the only spell that really worked as intended was the one I used with the sunstones, and even still you almost fell off the tower."

She shook her head — worry clouding her blue eyes. "But the more I explained, the more pleased they looked. And instead of reprimanding me, they rewarded me. They gave me this long list of things they want me to do — places to go, things to investigate, tasks to accomplish. They even want me to go to the Corsair Isles and set up another portal."

Omen knew he was staring, uncertain what to say. So were Templar and Liethan. Beside him Lilyth giggled uncontrollably. Even his parents were unable to hold back their laughter.

"A list?" Templar asked flatly. "A long list?"

Shalonie looked at once guilty and happy. "Very long," she agreed with a smile. "I'll be busy for ages. Though of course all of you are welcome to come along with me — it wouldn't be fair to keep it all to myself. You're all far more deserving of a reward than I am — you were the ones who took all the risks."

Templar filled his wine goblet again, and poured more for both Omen and Liethan as the three of them let the girl's words sink in.

"Well, that's . . ." Omen began. "Yes . . . well . . . imagine that."

"Ommmmyyyyy!" Tormy's happy voice called out from across the tavern. Omen turned his head to see Tormy wind his way through the crowded room, little Tyrin following closely in his wake. Neria and Jarlen hurried over to help the cats navigate between the crowded tables. More servers appeared from the kitchen. They hoisted large serving plates filled with mounds of braised meats and grilled fish certain to satisfy the cats' enormous appetites. *No wonder Neria was so worried that Tormy wasn't coming. They must have prepared all that food just for him.*

All of them shuffled their chairs around to make room for the cat's large blue pillow at the table's end. Tormy plopped down happily while little Tyrin took a mighty leap and landed on the tabletop next to Kyr. Kyr paused in his carving to pat the little cat on the head.

"We is having excitingnessness news," Tormy exclaimed, ears perked forward and nose twitching as a plate was set before him. Several platters piled high with mouth-watering offerings were placed in the center of their table, and Omen hurried to load Tormy's plate with steaming salmon steaks before the cat could bury his face in one of the main serving dishes.

"The most excitedness!" Tyrin agreed, stealing the last apricot crisp from the plate with one tiny clawed paw. He pulled the crisp onto the table and took a large bite out of it before Lilyth managed to get another plate under it.

"We is telling everyone all our news about our great quest," Tormy explained.

"Everyone!" Tyrin agreed between bites.

"We is talking about the questings and the rescuings and the grand adventurings since we is being great hero cats," Tormy continued.

"You didn't tell everyone you saved the world, did you?" Omen asked uneasily. He shot his parents an exasperated look. *They might have warned me about this!*

"Oh yes," Tormy agreed enthusiastically. He took a large bite of salmon, purring happily at the taste. "We is bragging to everyone! I is being great at the braggings. So is Tyrin — he is being even bestester!"

"I is being the bestest at the braggings," Tyrin agreed sagely. "On account of the fact that I is being so good at the maths! You is having to be able to know your numbers to get the bestest braggings."

"I is not being good with the big numbers, so Tyrin is being much betterness," Tormy explained blithely. "And, Omy! We is getting all sorts of new quests — lots of peoples is asking us for help! And we is telling them that you is helping too — on account of the fact that you is being Omy, and you is helping us save the world." The cat wiggled in excitement and turned his amber eyes on Omen. "Isn't you being happy, Omy? We is getting to go to lots of new places and eat lots of new dinners! We is probably finding fish we is never even heard of before."

"Well . . ." Omen sputtered. He looked from his friends, to his parents, to his sister, and back again to his cat. "How . . . extraordinary . . ." he stated weakly.

"Oh, yes, the most extraordinaryestest," Tormy agreed. "We is being adventuring cats after all."

"We is being &*%#!@ adventuring cats!" Tyrin shrieked loudly.

Kyr paused suddenly in his carving and looked up at his brother, his violet eyes shining with certainty. "You're going to need your own battle horn, Omen," he told him.

Beside him, Templar and Liethan started laughing, and Shalonie reached out to pat the boy on the shoulder.

"Right." Omen nodded decisively. "Battle horn it is."

Want more?

If you've enjoyed AUTUMN KING, please consider telling a friend, or leaving a review. Help us spread the world Of Cats and Dragons. And, as Tormy would say, that is being greatlynessness!

More OF CATS AND DRAGONS tidbits and artwork are waiting for you at OfCatsAndDragons.com.

Join our adventurers by signing up for the OF CATS AND DRAGONS Newsletter.

For Audiobook Lovers! Listen to OF CATS AND DRAGONS on Audible.

Thank you!

Carol

We are hard at work on book 6, but books 1-5 were a strange struggle for us. Writing novels is one thing, but to have to go through such a horrible illness as cancer in the middle of it was something else entirely. This last year would not have been possible without my friends and family and I want to thank them all. My parents, my siblings, and Camilla have been my constant support. But along with them have been a whole host of friends who have done their part to make this year easier on me. Hopefully, the next year will be better!

I also want to thank all our fans. You guys have been amazing! We have received nothing but good will and prayers from all of you and that has done wonders to improve my spirits. I hope you continue to enjoy Tormy and the gang for a long time to come.

❖

Camilla

I am thankful for every day I can pick up the phone (or click the "accept" button on FaceTime) so I can spend time with my best friend. I am thankful we're writing and creating worlds beyond this one. I am thankful for the magic of the page.

Thank you, Carol, for fighting so hard and never giving up.

Thank you, P.J., for encouraging me and giving me the space and time to work. And thank you for continuing to give voice and color to all the adventures. I laugh EVERY time I hear one of your Tyrin imprecations.

Thank you to the friends and fans who continue to take this journey with us. I am so happy that you all want to travel by our side. There are still a lot of stories left to tell.

And, as always, a gigantic thank you to everyone who keeps asking, "What s next?"

About the Authors

Carol E. Leever:

Carol E. Leever, a college professor, has been teaching Computer Science for many years. She programs computers for fun, but turns to writing and painting when she wants to give her brain a good work out.

An avid reader of science fiction and fantasy, she's also been published in the Sword and Sorceress anthologies, and has recently gotten into painting illustrations and book covers. A great lover of cats, she also manages to work her feline overlords into her writing, painting and programming classes often to the dismay of her students.

Camilla Ochlan:

Owner of a precariously untamed imagination and a scuffed set of polyhedral dice (which have gotten her in trouble more than once), Camilla writes fantasy and science fiction. Separate OF CATS AND DRAGONS, Camilla has written the urban fantasy WEREWOLF WHISPERER series (with Bonita Gutierrez), the mythpunk noir THE SEVENTH LANE and, in collaboration with her husband, written and produced a number of short films, including the suburban ghost story DOG BREATH and the recent 20/ 20 HINDSIGHT. An unapologetic dog lover and cat servant, Camilla lives in Los Angeles with her husband actor, audiobook narrator and dialect coach P.J. Ochlan, three sweet rescue dogs and a bright orange Abyssinian cat.

Get in touch

Visit our website at OfCatsAndDragons.com
Like us on Facebook @OfCatsAndDragons and join the
Friends Of Cats And Dragons Facebook group.
Find Carol:

caroleleever.deviantart.com

Find Camilla:

Twitter: @CamillaOchlan
Instagram: instagram.com/camillaochlan/
Blog: The Seething Brain

Or write to us at:
meow@ofcatsanddragons.com

Made in the USA
Las Vegas, NV
10 January 2022